THE SIGHT

Also available by Melanie Golding

The Hidden
Little Darlings

THE SIGHT

A NOVEL

MELANIE GOLDING

NEW YORK

This is a work of fiction. All of the names, characters, organizations, places and events portrayed in this novel are either products of the author's imagination or are used fictitiously. Any resemblance to real or actual events, locales, or persons, living or dead, is entirely coincidental.

Published in the United States by Crooked Lane Books, an imprint of The Quick Brown Fox & Company LLC.

Crooked Lane Books and its logo are trademarks of The Quick Brown Fox & Company LLC.

Library of Congress Catalog-in-Publication data available upon request.

ISBN (paperback): 978-1-63910-461-1
ISBN (ebook): 978-1-63910-462-8

Cover design by Heather VenHuizen

Printed in the United States.

www.crookedlanebooks.com

Crooked Lane Books
34 West 27th St., 10th Floor
New York, NY 10001

First Edition: September 2023

10 9 8 7 6 5 4 3 2 1

For Ada, Eric, and Audrey

You're going to live it better, and more meaningfully, if you understand every day that you're going to die.

—Nell Gifford (1973–2019), speaking in 2019

Then he saw that she had become a black bird upon a branch near to him. "A dangerous woman thou art," said Cú Chulainn. . . . "It is at the guarding of thy death that I am; and I shall be," said she.

—A. H. Leahy, *Heroic Romances of Ireland* (1906)

Hush little baby, don't you cry; you know your mama was born to die. All my trials, Lord, soon be over.

—Traditional spiritual

CHAPTER

1

BEFORE
Faith, age ten

BY THE TIME she left the wagon after breakfast, she had almost forgotten about the dream.

Her mother wrapped her up warm and told her to be back at midday to practice with the horses. She'd been learning to stand on the back of her horse, Macha, as he walked, then trotted, cantered, and finally galloped around the ring. She wanted to do the trick her mother did, balancing on one galloping horse, waiting for exactly the right moment before crouching, springing, flipping backward through the air, and landing on her feet on the horse galloping behind. Faith's legs were not as long as her mother's; she would need to spring harder, to leap farther than her, but she knew she would get there if she practiced every day.

The sun was low through the woods as she walked, flashing in her eyes so that she closed them, trying to see how many steps she could take with them shut, the sunlight strobing like fireworks bursting on her eyelids. She counted out loud as she walked, her hands out in front so she didn't crash into a tree. On the twelfth step there was the sound of a twig breaking close by. She opened her eyes and screamed.

The boy laughed in her face. "Scared you."

"Get lost, Samuel. I don't want to play with you." She pushed past him, walked faster through the trees, ducking under bony branches where ice crystals were melting in the morning sun, dripping into silver puddles on the dead leaves of the forest floor. The branches shuddered where her coat caught on them, a shower of heavy drops landing, chaotic drumbeats.

"Stop following me," she said.

All the way to the lake he trailed her. She could see her brother, Tommy, up ahead, and he was not alone: Samuel's older brother, Peter, was there too. The boys had been hanging around them like flies ever since the show closed for the winter, since her mother and the rest of the Harrington family parked up at Home Farm the way they always did in the off season. Faith's circus friends had flown away to the warmer countries they came from: Amara and her acrobat parents; Romi and Remi, the children of the fire-breathers; everyone. She was envious of that. Each winter they got to go to these exciting places while Faith's family returned here, to what was essentially a field with a fence around it. Her mother said it needed to be simple and calm because the idea was to rest, to regenerate, for the core company members to begin to create a whole new show for next season's carnival. All Faith saw was that for three months she was stuck in one place with only her brother and her cousins to play with, all of them too old and aloof to play now. Macha would play when they weren't training, but Faith longed for Amara, the only girl who knew what life was like for an almost eleven-year-old born into a performing circus family. Faith could tell Macha her secrets, but for all of the love he gave, he couldn't tell his own in return.

Amara did write to her. She'd promised to bring her a surprise, a gift from her country, and the thought of this was enough to brighten Faith's day whenever she thought of it.

Samuel might have been her age, but he was nothing like Amara. There were no secrets she would share with this boy. His constant questions about the carnival were tedious, and he only ever wanted to play games where they took off their clothes or pretended to kiss each other, activities she would rather die than do. She knew for a fact that Tommy didn't like Peter either, but every time she or her brother left the yard, there they were, these house-dwelling boys with nothing better to do. She couldn't wait for February, when the carnival would be on the road again and she wouldn't have to deal with them. At that moment, the wagons where the circus people lived were parked up with the lorries. In a couple of months, they would be lined up end to end, ready to travel. That's when her life would begin again. Home Farm wasn't really home, despite the name. Their home was the road.

At the edge of the lake, she shielded her eyes against the glare. The water was frozen nearly, but not quite thick enough to skate. A light dusting of snow in the night had created a perfect surface, like poured cream. She gasped as a feeling washed over her, the overwhelming certainty that this moment had happened before.

Tommy and Peter were throwing sticks, seeing how far out on the ice they could get them. Peter's face was red with the effort, but he would never throw a stick as far as Tommy. Her brother drew back his arm and sent one flying, spinning through the air, his body perfectly balanced, strong from years of climbing ropes, of juggling, of pulling himself up on the aerial silks.

Faith's hand went to her neck, where her grandmother's necklace should have been, but was not. She cried out, half gasp, half shout, and Tommy yelled, "What is it?"

The words echoed around her mind. *"What is it?"* He had said that in the dream. Her brother dropped the stick he was holding and started toward her along the shoreline.

He had done that in the dream too.

She had lost Grandma Rose's necklace, and the terror and panic of that was overlaid on the fear that she knew, before she even turned around, that Samuel would be dangling it from a finger, a look of triumph on his face. She swiveled and there he was, just as she knew he would be. The world slowed down as she tried to snatch the necklace, but in the struggle it flew into the air, the silver chain and the precious ring that hung on it flicking up, arcing, glinting once, and landing on the frozen lake, too far out to reach from the shore.

"You threw my Grandma's necklace—you lost it!"

Samuel was stricken. His eyes scanned the blinding white surface of the lake. "I didn't. It was you. I found it for you! You dropped it—*you* lost it, not me."

All of this she had seen before. She stared and stared at Samuel, at the words he had spoken, that she'd heard him say before, exactly like that.

When she'd woken that morning, her mother had asked her what was wrong, why she was shaking, why there were tears in her eyes, but she didn't say. She couldn't find the words. *"Just a dream,"* her mother had said, stroking her hair. "*It's not real.*"

And now the nightmare was coming true.

Tommy yelled at Samuel—"You stupid little creep!"—and the world at once had fuzzy edges. She was there, but powerless to do anything except be pulled along by events, the sounds loud but dull, as if her ears were stuffed with cotton wool, her throat tight as if there were hands around it, strangling her, stopping her from speaking, from changing how she knew this would end. Inside, she was screaming at Tommy—*Leave it, it's too dangerous*—but she was silent, unable to speak as the scene played out the way it had in the dream.

Her brother inched out onto the ice. Faith was a statue of horror, frozen in place. As she knew he would, Peter waited on the shore until Tommy's fingers were almost on the necklace before he ran out himself, every reckless step causing a terrible popping sound that reverberated in the valley. Peter stopped dead when he realized, too late, that the sound was the ice giving way. His face changed, from mischievous to horrified. He looked at his feet. It happened so fast that Tommy didn't even have time to warn him. There was a loud creaking noise, a terrible splash, and both boys were gone.

Wake up, she told herself. *This is where the dream ends.*

A beat of silence.

Next to her, Samuel was screaming, flapping his arms. She took one step onto the lake, but her foot went through into the freezing water. She pulled it out, turned to run back to the yard for help, but by the time Granddad and the others got there, she knew it would be too late, because she'd seen all this before.

CHAPTER

2

NOW
Faith, age twenty-two

FROM THE PODIUM I watch Amara fly through the air, head down on the trapeze, nothing to hold her but gravity and the muscles in her neck. Every member of the audience knows it's no illusion, that there was no trickery involved as she flipped over the bar and down, hanging by her hands twenty feet above the ring. A second later her legs divided as she went under and back, and up into a handstand, like an Olympic gymnast on the high bar, only more impressive since she's suspended from a rope slung over a joist in the apex of the tent, rotating in a circle at the same time. Then, as the drums began to build, she lowered herself until her head was in contact with the bar, and carried on spinning.

The benches surrounding the ring are full of transfixed faces tilted up, open-mouthed and silent, eager for what comes next. The danger of it has hit home: there is no safety net. How long can she stay balanced like that; what if she slips? Perhaps they've had dreams of doing what Amara does, but they'll never know what it's like. This is in my world, inside the ring, while they are beyond it, outside of it, looking in. The circus world and that of the rest of society, those who live in houses, will never meet. Except for here, at the edges of the ring, this sacred space.

To the sound of drums and cymbals, pounding and crashing, she spins for the fifth, sixth, seventh time. I clap my hands in time above my head, and the audience takes the cue, starts to clap along.

I won't get tired of watching this act, no matter how many times I see it. My friend's body is all muscle and grace. She's been training for this since before she could walk. Her father, who first placed Amara on a trapeze as a baby, stands directly below, his face relaxed, his arms tense on the rope that anchors her in the air, high enough that the audience also strain their necks upward. Some of them occasionally glance quickly from Amara to the ring floor, hard ground covered by a bit of sawdust and carpet, a bullseye she could hit should she fall. It's like the feeling you get looking over a cliff at the crashing rocks, the thrill of being on the cusp of something life-threatening. She's making shapes with her legs, spinning faster, and there—she lets go with her hands and flings them to the side, so that she's doing a headstand, still spinning. Every person in the tent breaks into applause.

I'm at the back of the ring, by the velvet drape doors, on a podium we painted at the start of the season, in bold stripes, me painting the red, Amara the yellow. I'm dancing in place, pointing my toes, smiling. My role in this act is to balance the visuals, to engage the audience; the choreography is mainly repetitive stepping, with flourishes at certain points and cues to the audience if they don't clap in the right places. My routine is a mirror of the dance by Amara's mother, Stacey, who is at the other side of the doors on the other podium. While in this act we essentially do nothing but smile and step in time, my main skill is horsemanship, and Stacey is a talented aerial silk artist. She and Amara have another act later in the show, a two-hander with hoops and midair juggling. All three of us wear high-cut, kingfisher-blue leotards, and Amara wears ballet shoes for the ropes while we are in knee-high boots and feather headdresses. On the podiums we turn with the music, practiced and smooth, entirely together. Stacey moves like she was bred for it. The choreography is hers; every movement, however small, is deliberate and designed to charm. In the ring nothing goes unnoticed. Uncle Mike's voice is in my head, mixed with the voice of my mother: *"When you're in the ring, don't walk backward: flirt with your eyes; smile at anyone looking at you."*

Something is bothering me, and my eyes move from Amir to the audience. Scanning the shadows at the back of the tent, I feel someone watching me. No one should be paying attention to me when Amara is performing this trick. Then I see the person, intensely staring at my face. I stare back. The lights are angled in my eyes—all I can see is the outline of a closely cropped haircut, but the sensation of eye contact makes my neck itch. He might be wondering about my eye patch. I give a twinkly smile and look elsewhere.

People are going to stare; they always stare, in awe and wonder when I'm performing, for other reasons when I'm not. But this man, staring at me, this feels different from the usual gaze. It has intention, and something else—perhaps *knowing*—in it. The man's looking chills me. I let my eyes wander the back row, and when I glance back, the outline of the man has gone.

Amir, at the anchor end of Amara's rope, rolls his head, and despite the sound of the band right behind me and the applause in front, I hear his neck crack.

There's a shift in the music, the next section beginning. "One, two, three," Amara says, loud enough for Amir, but not for the audience, transfixed as they are on her body, its tautness, the strength of her, her beauty. On three, her father lets the rope slide through his leather gloves to the second knot. She drops, and swings her legs down, grips the pole so that her body goes under the trapeze, flips around and up and suddenly she's standing on it, one arm stretched in a flourish, hip thrust out: *"See this? Be impressed: I survived. I am beautiful, and impossible. I am magical."* The audience gasps, the applause reaches a crescendo. But I freeze in place on my podium.

Stacey hasn't seen yet. My breath has stopped because of what's happening at the anchor end of the rope: Amir is on his knees, face contorted. Something is very wrong. Amara is still ten feet above the ring, and the danger, measured and controlled by the combined skill of these two, the unbroken trust between the father and his daughter, is suddenly very real. The line to stop her falling from the trapeze is held only by Amir; it's not tethered to anything else—that's part of the act. His grip is loosening. I run; a second afterward so does her mother, though I'm closer. I get there first, grab the rope just as Amir lets go, and his body falls in a heap. He's moaning, clutching his arm. Two of the tumbling boys appear from backstage, where they've been watching. They take his arms, one each, and carry him through the ring door to the back of the ground. Stacey glances from me to Amara and then to the sides of the ring, looking for my uncle, Ringmaster Mike, but I nod, reassure her I'm okay to hold it for now, so she follows through the curtains.

The whole episode took probably ten seconds, two rotations of the trapeze, and now it's just Amara and me. I have her full weight in my hands. My body strains to hold the rope. Amara takes in the scene as her circling allows. She sees I've gone from my podium before she sees that I'm on the end of the rope, and not her father. She does a double take. I smile, a circus smile, for her and for the punters. *"Look at me, I can do anything."* But this time the confidence is all false.

I'm not heavy enough to be her anchor, and without gloves the rope burns my palms. I'm digging my heels into the sawdust of the ring, but I can only fight gravity for so long. Amara has hooked her legs over the pole and is swinging in a large circle, upside down, holding a pose I know she usually moves straight through. The circle is getting smaller, momentum lessening. Amir would control it from here, but it's all I can do to hang on. There is a ripple of uncertainty in the audience, growing by the second. Soon all their trust in us will be lost, and with it the show too. There's no question of stopping; I've never heard of a show being abandoned for any reason except fire. Horse kicks a dancer: dance with one down! Rope breaks: pick them up, move along, next act! Aerialist collapses: the show must go on!

My arms strain against the rope and my feet slip. Amara slips too, dropping by a foot, almost losing her grasp of the pole. Some members of the audience inhale audibly; there are one or two stifled shrieks. They're not sure if this is part of the act. I wrap the rope around my back, feel the rough tautness of it dig into my skin where my costume is cut away. Uncertainty builds again; Amara is at the center of it, her own uncertainty on show now, affecting everyone inside the tent. I don't know this act the way Amir does. Watching them practice, seeing it every night for all this time—none of that's going to turn me into an anchorman. Amara's wondering where her father is, what's happening, and I catch her questioning eyes as she flies past.

"I've got her," murmurs a voice by my ear, and the strong arms of Fyodor, the bigger of the two Russian acrobats, encircle me to take the rope.

"Thank God."

"Do not thank Him yet," he says. "Pray first for Amir."

I make sure he's got a good grip before I let go and head for the back of the ground where Amir was taken. I run across the ring with poised spine and dancer's toes, face stretched into a smile, one arm held gracefully behind me, moving as if through water. The curtain is drawn back, and I curtsy to the audience as I leave the stage. They applaud. Amara stands up on the trapeze, focused now, ready for her final few moves, the one-handed spin, the neck balance, the dismount with the triple somersault. She must push away her anxiety to make it work, be in the moment and nowhere else. Like all good circus artists, she does this with ease.

CHAPTER

3

BEFORE

THE TWO BOYS lay on the shore, side by side, clothes soaked, skin glistening in the sun. Perfectly still, perfectly beautiful. Ice cold to the touch.

Many of the adults were soaking too. The whole family was there, everyone who lived at Home Farm: Granddad Harrington and his cousin Billy Ward, the joint heads of the business, widowers both and the only surviving grandchildren of David Harrington, the founder. There was Faith and Tommy's mother, Iris, and her sister, Linda, the children's aunt. Billy's adult children Mike and June and their spouses, Christine and John William, had been the first to arrive, along with Granddad, after Faith had raised the alarm. Off to the side, faces drawn with shock, were June and John William's two grown and two almost-grown kids, Vicky and Sarah, Finlay and Calum.

They all watched, helpless, as Granddad and Mike pressed rhythmically on the boys' chests while counting to ten. When they stopped, John William pinched Tommy's nose and blew in his mouth and Auntie June did the same for Peter. Billy Ward, crippled by arthritis, leaned on his cane, his face grave. He was powerless in this moment, in a way he never was.

Faith knew it was called a "rescue breath," when you blew in someone's mouth like that. The breaths made the boys' chests inflate for a moment, but then they fell flat and the air came out of them. The grown-ups checked for a pulse, found nothing, and the men started again with the chest compressions. Both boy's eyes were closed. Neither made a sound.

Linda had her arm around Iris. The two sisters were shaking with cold and shock, but they were clinging to each other, and to hope. Faith had no such delusions. She knew that Tommy was dead already, that Peter also would not be saved. Not only because they had been underwater for far too long. Not only because of the terrible cold or the fact that she was watching each time as her grandfather checked for Tommy's pulse and couldn't find it. She knew because she'd seen them die already, in her dream last night. She'd felt the freezing water as they sank as if it were on her own skin, the panic as they struggled as if it were her own panic, and the peace that followed, the drift, and then the darkness.

In the dream she'd seen herself sprint back to the yard, screaming for help, exactly as she had done this morning. She'd seen them come running, all of the family, all of the carnival people, arriving at the shore to a deathly silence, a blackening hole where the two boys had dropped through. With spades and pickaxes they got to work to smash a path through the ice, wading knee-deep, hip-deep, neck-deep, and then her uncle Mike took a deep breath, dipped underneath and came up with Tommy. She wanted to stop her mother going in, but she couldn't even do that. Iris waded straight in, first in the dream, and then in reality. Faith couldn't move a muscle; it was Linda who had held Iris back from diving under. Aunt

Linda, not Faith, who helped her mother and her uncle drag Tommy onto the shore. Not Tommy, not anymore: Tommy's body. Faith stood by, unmoving, even though she willed herself to spring into action, to be of some help, to do something, anything at all. Her grandfather, her mother, and her aunt: they pulled Faith's limp and lifeless brother up to the dry ground; water seeped from his clothing, darkening the shore around him where a dusting of snow had settled, while Mike went in again and came up with Peter.

The few minutes waiting for the ambulance stretched out like lifetimes. The sirens were approaching too slowly, frustration building in everyone, especially Billy, who stood with his arthritic fists clenched on his stick, muttering, "What the fuck is taking them so long," but then two ambulances were there, lights flashing, green-uniformed, no-nonsense paramedics taking over the job of trying to save these boys, shouting clear, calm instructions to each other as they worked.

Now they stood, the Harrington's crew, breathing hard, forming a ragged half circle around Tommy and Peter as they were loaded onto stretchers, as plastic ventilators were placed on their faces and squeezed. As paramedics held fingers to necks and stared at wristwatches with stony expressions.

Mike moved across to stand in front of Faith. She could see his trainers dripping lake water onto the ground. He touched her shoulder, but she couldn't look up. "How did it happen?" he asked her. "What were they doing out there on the ice?"

It was my fault, she thought.

Her mother was nearby, listening, waiting for the answer. When she spoke it was mainly to her mother, not to Mike.

"I saw it," said Faith. "I dreamed it last night. I knew it would happen."

Iris sucked in a breath of shock. She said, "That's not true. Say it's not."

"I tried to warn Tommy when he was on the ice, but the words wouldn't come out of my mouth. I knew it would happen. I saw it in my dream. If I'd told you this morning, maybe you could have . . ."

"Faith!" yelled Iris. "Stop!"

But it was too late. Her uncle had taken a step back, as if repelled by her words. The cousins, her grandfather, her great-uncle Billy, they all heard. They all stopped to look at her.

"What did she say?" asked John William, in a tone that meant he heard it, but he couldn't believe it.

The boys were in an ambulance each, engines on. Linda climbed in with Tommy. She called, "Iris, we need to go."

There was the sound of feet crashing through undergrowth, a shrill voice crying. A woman Faith recognized as Samuel and Peter's mother broke through onto the shore and made straight for the ambulance, where Peter was being loaded. She pushed the men aside, tried to push aside the paramedic, who firmly told her, "Ma'am, we're helping him. You need to stand back and let us do our job."

"Peter," cried his mother. "Wake up now! Wake up." She shook him by the shoulders. He did not wake.

Uncle Mike put a hand on Peter's mother's shoulder, and she recoiled as if it burned. She scowled at him and he stepped away. If she had known that his hand on her shoulder had been pushing her son's chest, trying to save him, she likely wouldn't have been so quick to shove it away.

"What happened here?" Her eyes beamed hatred into every one of the carnival people. She pointed with a trembling finger. "You did this. Samuel said it was one of you."

Samuel was cowering near the edge of the woodland. He was staring at his feet.

"It was an accident," said Granddad. "The kids were playing. No one's fault."

"No," wailed Peter's mother. "No. No, no, no no no."

"We need to leave," said the paramedic. "Are you coming with us to the hospital?" Peter's mother climbed in. Faith caught her eye just before the doors were closed, and the sky went from bright to dark in a single second.

Faith fell to the ground as if she'd been struck by an iron bar. Everything was blocked out but the vision. She saw a flash of something that hadn't happened yet, couldn't have happened yet: Peter's mother behind the wheel of a car, hurtling along a road in darkness, the white lines moving like snakes as the car started to swerve left and right. It was summer and the windows were wound down, letting in a rush of warm air. She smelled alcohol in the air, tasted it on her tongue, and heard the tires screaming, the radio blasting out rock music. There was a sharp corner, much sharper than she'd thought. The steering wheel was fighting her as trees loomed closer, closer, too close.

Smash, and the lights went out.

Faith felt the snowy ground under her as the vision faded away. Her face was wet from the tears.

"Mum?" she called, but her mother had gone with Tommy to the hospital. Faces appeared above her: Mike, John William, Granddad. They glanced at each other for a second too long before they helped her to sit up.

"Does she need an ambulance too?" one of her cousins asked.

"I'll be fine," said Faith, though she wasn't sure if that was true at all. Her legs felt absent, then the feeling slowly returned and instead they felt made of jelly.

"She's in shock," said Billy.

Granddad crouched near her, examined her face for a long minute. "Stay sitting there for now, Faith. Tell me if you feel sick, won't you?"

The adults talked among themselves, not wanting to name the thing that had happened, reassuring each other that Tommy and his friend would be fine, that they were in the right place now.

"We should get her inside," they said of Faith, but no one moved to touch her. The cold entered through the thin fabric of her leggings, numbing her backside. As the sirens traveled further away, the wobbly feeling in her legs eased a little.

"Come on," said Granddad to Faith. "Let's get you back to the yard. Nothing we can do now, and you're freezing."

Faith had seen something shining on the shore, near the water. She made her way over and picked it up, her heart pounding, her mind refusing to believe. She brought the object to her face, but there was no mistaking what it was: her Grandma Rose's necklace, the silver chain with the ring still attached. Nothing made sense. Her legs gave way, and she lurched sideways, stumbled toward the lake, fell to her knees at the edge of the water, wracked by sobs that seemed to come up from the earth.

CHAPTER

4

NOW
Faith

THE CURTAINS FALL closed behind me, the music muffled somewhat by the thick velvet fabric. Amir is lying in the prep tent on a couple of straw bales, his face pale. He's breathing, but his eyes are closed. The two tumbling boys are standing there.

"He won't wake up," says one, his voice heavily accented. This pair don't usually speak English to me—only one of the six in the troupe, Hugo, speaks it fluently, but he's not here.

"Did you call an ambulance?" I ask.

The boy looks panicked, and while I try to remember the Spanish for *hospital*, the other one nods.

"I phone," he says, his hand by his ear in the international gesture for telephone. Beyond the stage curtain I hear the audience applaud and cheer, Amara's music having come to an end, signaling the end of the act. Uncle Mike's voice over the microphone: "Show your appreciation for the amazing, the beautiful, the death-defying Amara and the Flying Fantastics!"

There's the sound of hooves nearby and the comforting smell of the animals; the next act to go on is mine. The groom has brought Macha through. He'll be made up ready with his headdress in place, mane braided, tail brushed. Amara appears next to me, chalk on her palms, grief and worry on her face under the greasepaint. I stand aside, let her go close. She puts her head on his chest.

"Daddy?"

I've not changed yet for my act. It's a frantic change but well-rehearsed. I just need to swap the blue for the gold, take off my boots, lose the feathers. But I don't move. I feel a soft nuzzling at my back, and I know I can't stay. Macha, in his unmistakable way, is asking me why we're not lining up, ready for our grand entrance, for the trick-riding act, the *voltige* we've been practicing all season. The routine of the show shouldn't be disrupted, for him, if not for anything else. *"This is what we do,"* he's saying. He recognizes the music, our entrance music, because he hears it every night in the show and every morning in rehearsal. I play it so often to him, it's like some kind of Pavlovian response now. Here's the music; let's start the act.

"It's okay, Macha. I won't be long."

I see Mike's ringmaster shoes in the straw next to Macha's hooves.

"Faith, you have to go on now."

I try to stand but am stopped by Amara's grip on my hand. She hisses a question to me. "Will he die? Tonight, I mean. I have to know."

Before I can really think about it, I slip my eye patch up a little and run my eyes over Amir's unconscious form. Nothing happens. I need to look right in his eyes.

"Faith," says Mike. "They're waiting. He'll be okay. There's nothing more you can do."

I know I need to be gone, up onto Macha's back and away. I can hear the band circling the few bars that build up to my entrance. It's important not to break the spell for the audience. But Amara says, "Please, Faith."

Quickly I lean forward and pull Amir's eyelids open so I can see his irises. I concentrate, the sound of the circus band and the time pressure receding in my mind, the volume turned down to a background hum. I don't think it will work, but then he comes to consciousness for a single second, our eyes lock, and I feel it, like a thump in the chest, like being hit by a heavy thing at speed.

I see his death play out. Not quite in my head, not quite in his, but in the space between us. He's in a hospital bed, and for a horrible moment I think it will be today, that he is about to die in the hospital he will be taken to, that this news will break Amara. But then I look more closely at the image of Amir. He's old in the vision, much older than this, and that's all I need to know.

I let go of Amir and take precisely three seconds to center myself before I stand, grab the horse's mane and swing up onto Macha's bare back. Amara's pleading eyes are on me, wanting and not wanting to hear what I will say. She felt the jolt when I saw his death; she knows I know something.

"Not tonight," I say, and her spine straightens like a huge weight lifts from her back. Next to her, Mike's eyes darken, lips pressing together in a thin line. I don't have time to process this. Macha turns, the curtains are pulled aside, and we step out into the ring together, forgetting everything except the moment we are in.

CHAPTER 5

BEFORE

AS SOON AS the ambulances were gone, Mike and Christine headed back to the yard to get warm, followed by June and John William, and all four of their kids. June hugged the younger two tightly as they went, no doubt thinking of Tommy and how it could easily have been one of her own who had fallen through the ice, so that June rather than Iris would be in the ambulance on the way to the hospital. Her boys, Calum and Fin, were arguably the wrong age at seventeen and eighteen to walk hand in hand with their mother, but today was far from a normal day. They leaned into June and went solemnly into the woods that stood between the lake and the yard, their heads close together. The narrow path forced the family into a kind of procession, slow and steady, as if they were following a coffin.

It seemed that everyone was pretending Faith wasn't there, curled in a ball at the edge of the water. Everyone except Samuel, whose eyes bored into the side of her face until she shifted her back toward him.

She heard her grandfather's voice speaking to him. "Son, you got anyone at home?"

Samuel didn't answer, or if he did, Faith couldn't hear it. Out of anyone's sight, she picked up her grandma's ring, placed it in a small hole in the ground, and covered it with a flat rock. The silver chain seemed to burn her fingers. Even once it was hidden, she could feel the imprint of the ring on her palm.

Her grandfather was still talking to Samuel. "You want to come with us for now, until your mum gets back?"

"Fuck you," said Samuel, and took off the way he and his mother had come, back toward the housing estate where they lived.

Faith heard her grandfather's shuffling steps getting closer. She observed his feet, still in their slippers, the plaid fabric ruined now from the wet and the grit. Anger stirred in her guts, mixed with guilt and fear. She got to her feet, shivering, teeth clanking together uncontrollably. She glared at the place where Samuel had last been seen.

"What happened out there?" he asked. They both looked at the black water where the ice had been broken up.

"Tommy was looking for Grandma Rose's necklace," said Faith, knowing that Rose's name would invoke something primal in Granddad. "Samuel threw it onto the lake."

She heard his breath stop momentarily and then start up again, hard blasts of air through his nostrils.

"An accident, then," he said eventually. "Like we thought. No one's fault."

He took her arm and turned her toward the woods, started walking back to Home Farm. Before they reached the edge of the shore, the old man stopped to cast his eye over the lake once more. "So it's gone, then?" he asked. "Her ring?"

"I'm sorry, Granddad," said Faith. "I promised I'd always keep it safe." The ring was Grandma Rose's engagement ring, passed down from Great-Grandma Daisy. Rose had been wearing it when she'd fallen from the trapeze in the accident that killed her.

"Nothing to be done," he said. "It's only a ring. I probably shouldn't have let you look after it. I've no one but myself to blame."

Faith thought he sounded almost relieved that the ring was gone. "Tommy's all that's important now," he said. "And the other boy. Peter, was it? They're what we need to worry about. Not some silly bit of silver."

"Peter," she said, spitting out the name, then feeling terrible for speaking ill of the dead. She tried to shake the feeling off. No one but her was sure either of the boys was dead, and while that was true, while both possibilities existed, she could cling to hope. And to hate. "He was the one who made the ice crack. He ran out. If it hadn't been for Samuel throwing the ring, Tommy wouldn't have gone at all. But he'd have been fine if it hadn't been for Peter showing off . . ."

"Shh," said Granddad. "No one meant for this to happen. None of those boys knew the danger. Let's get back in the warm."

At the yard, the family were milling about by the door to Mike's wagon. When they saw Faith and Granddad coming, they stared at the ground or passed looks between themselves that Faith couldn't interpret. The only person to look directly at them was her cousin Calum, who openly stared, like when you walk into a room and people have been talking about you.

June nudged Calum and he closed his mouth, took the cup of tea she was holding out. Faith climbed the steps to the wagon and went inside.

It was only an hour or two later when Granddad's phone rang. Faith was in the bathroom, but she could hear it through the thin wall. She opened the door and hovered there, in the narrow gap between the rooms.

"Linda?"

Faith held her breath. A thread of hope unspooled in the few seconds of silence. Was she wrong, was the dream wrong? Is Tommy all right? And then it snapped, that thread, as surely as she knew it would.

"Oh god," said Granddad, and made a high, squeaking snort that sent Faith scurrying into the bedroom so she didn't have to listen to him cry. She had never seen him crying, this strong man, this sober, sensible, sometimes harsh man. He might have been her mother's father, but Granddad was the closest thing she had to a father of her own. He must have cried before, she assumed, but not for years. Maybe when Rose died, his young wife, mother of his two babies, Iris and little Linda. Maybe that was what it sounded like: as if the world had tilted badly, had lost something irreplaceable, that nothing would ever be the same again.

Iris didn't come back that night. At some point Granddad left the wagon, and at some point Faith passed out from exhaustion, but she couldn't say what time either of those things happened or which came first. She knew that he was gone when she woke, that she was alone.

Daylight streamed through the open curtains. She pulled on two pairs of socks and opened her bedroom door to see Tommy's bedroom open, his bed unmade from the day before. She went in and straightened out the covers, folded down the sheet, tucked his shoes under the bed.

Still in her pajamas, she headed out to Macha's stable tent to muck out. Then she opened the stable door and led him out to the yard, where she grabbed a handful of his mane and swung herself up onto his back.

Her mother returned in the middle of the next night. She opened Faith's bedroom door and stood there, looking in, for a long time, not speaking. Then Faith put out her arms, and her mother went to her. Iris never said that Tommy was dead, but Faith knew it, had known it longer than any of them. Together they cried until the tears ran out. In the morning, again Faith woke up to find herself alone.

In the following days the carnival people moved silently around the yard, with lowered voices, and when they saw Faith on her way to tend to Macha, they averted their eyes. When Iris was at home, she may as well not have been; she sat at the little fold-out table and stared out of the window at the yard, her eyes on the gates that Tommy had walked through before he went down to the lake that final morning. It was as if she thought if she waited for long enough, he might come strolling back through like nothing had happened. Maybe he would be in a mood because the kids from the estate had been bothering him again, trying to get him to teach them how to juggle fire or hang from a strap by their teeth. He wasn't coming, though. He would never wear that frown of his again.

Faith didn't like to look out of that window herself. You couldn't see the lake from there, but it loomed large in Faith's mind, just beyond the trees.

When Iris wasn't staring out of the window, she talked on the phone to members of the family Faith didn't remember, to the funeral parlor, and once to Tommy's dad. Faith knew that was who it is for two reasons: after the initial hello, Iris tensed up in a way she didn't unless she was talking to, or about, that man. Second, he was the only person her mother referred to using such bad words. Iris stabbed the phone with a finger to end the call, and dialed again.

"Linda," she breathed, "can you come?"

A couple of minutes later, Linda opened the door to the wagon, and Faith retreated to the bedroom, feeling like a shadow. She sat with her back to the door. Not exactly listening on purpose, but she couldn't help hearing every word.

"He said *what*?"

"I know," said Iris.

"But that's his son. His flesh and blood. You would think he could come back for his son's funeral."

"You would think," said Iris.

"That bastard. That motherfu—"

"He never came back for the birth either. So I don't know why we're surprised."

"Oh, honey," said Linda, "I'm not surprised. Not at all. I'm just angry. To be honest, I never stopped being angry, not since he—"

Faith shifted her weight slightly, and the bedroom door creaked.

"Shh," said Iris. "I think she's listening."

"Faith?" called Linda. "You there?"

Faith stayed as still as she could. After a while the sisters went back to discussing Tommy's dad, but they did it in whispers. Linda sucked her teeth and muttered sharp words beginning with 'c' that Faith knew were the worst curses in the English language. After a while, all was silent, and Faith came out of her room to an empty wagon. She put her boots on and headed out to the stable.

Everyone blamed her and everyone was ignoring her. Only Macha still seemed to know she existed. She rode him in the fields, avoiding the woods and the lake, and especially the estate where Samuel lived. At night, when all was silent, she sat on the floor of her room, drawing elaborate circus set designs by the light of an LED headlamp. She drew Tommy over and over again, one-handed on the ropes, upside down and spinning from the silks, ready to catch hands with her in midair, the way they'd practiced. She drew him in the costumes from last season and in new ones she'd designed for him, jumpsuits of green silk, flashes of silver lightning across his chest like a superhero. Her eyelids drooped, but she was trying not to fall asleep. She had known what would happen at the lake that day, and she hadn't told anyone, not even her mother, not even when she'd asked straight out what the nightmare had been about.

Secrets were killers; she'd heard that before. Secrets were bad, worse than lies. She couldn't go back now and tell her mother what the dream was about, before the accident, but she could resolve to do things differently next time.

The night before the funeral she led her horse back in the early dark, left him in the stable with a bucket of water and some hay. As she walked across the yard past her Granddad's wagon, she could hear voices.

"We need to talk about what Faith said. What she did." It was Uncle Billy.

"Not now," said Granddad.

"Do you think she's got the same . . . problem your mother had?"

"I said not now," said Granddad, through what sounded like clenched teeth.

"Because if she has, you know we can't let her—"

"I know you're my cousin, but by god, shut your fucking mouth before I fill it."

"I've as much right to speak—"

"My grandson is dead, Billy. We're burying him in the morning."

"But if she's like Daisy, then—"

"Get my mother's name out of your mouth," Granddad yelled, and there was a bang as the wagon door flew open and slammed against the wall. Billy came out fast, as if he'd been shoved. At the bottom of the steps, he saw Faith and recoiled. She took a step toward him and he scurried away, leaning on his cane, as if he was frightened of her.

CHAPTER

6

NOW
Faith

I'M WOKEN BY the cold, from a dreamless black, as if someone just switched me back on at the plug. I lie there, feeling mucky. It's too early. The predawn light is gray and weak, but I can't get back to sleep because of the many uncomfortable feelings, which I run through one by one: My body is tired, coated in dried sweat. My limbs ache. The skin on my face is tight, partly stuck to my pillow with the stage makeup I usually take off before bed. There is an unpleasant buzzing in my head. I need to empty my bladder with some urgency.

A year or two back, during the tail end of the season, I might have woken up feeling like this perhaps once a week. That was when the communal showers were my only option, and by the time I got to the front of the queue, the hot water had run out. Those days are over now, or they should be. This new, expensive wagon has hot and cold running water for showers, but it was beyond me last night, after the vision, then the show, to do anything but lie down and pass out.

The moment I open my eyes, I see Amir's death again. There is the vision of his hospital bed, him lying there, shriveled and dark against the sheets, the bed surrounded by vases of flowers. His hair is gray, almost white, his body thicker than it is now, his neck shorter, as if he's been compressed by the gravity of years. I don't fight this image as it hovers superimposed on the present, like a cartoon thought bubble, a muted light-show projection existing only for me.

Over the next few days it will haunt me several times a day, though its power and vividness are already fading. No point fighting it, as resistance only prolongs these things. For now, I sit with it, pondering the details. I'm guessing that when he dies, Amir will have long retired from performing with the circus. I don't see Amara in the vision, and I wonder what will keep her from her father's deathbed, whether she's just outside at the moment of his passing or if she's somewhere else entirely, and why. There is Stacey, also much older, her hair a bright yellow color with an unlikely thickness in the front that could only be a wig, and I wonder about that too. Radiation treatment, perhaps. Or stress. She stares into her lap, twisting a handkerchief, echoing the twisted mouth of her grief.

I think of the Amir of yesterday, lying on the straw bales backstage. I hope Amara is satisfied with what I told her, that *not today* was enough for her, that it will provide enough reassurance in her mind that it's not the end yet, that her father will pull through this crisis and live a while longer. I hope she isn't going to ask me anything else about the vision, anything specific. The answers won't be what she wants to hear—they absolutely never are.

Enough. I fumble under the pillow for my eye patch. Once it's in place, the visions stop.

Last night, Amara and her father went off in an ambulance before the show ended. The paramedic didn't say what he thought was wrong with Amir, but they got him on a stretcher and out of there swiftly. Before she left, Amara asked Mike if it was okay that she missed her second appearance, that her mother would stay behind and do the act alone. It made me ashamed when he took a moment to think it over before nodding. I wonder if he'll dock her pay—and Amir's. I decide he most probably will. I broke a leg in a fall once when rehearsing with Macha, and Mike never paid me a penny until I could get back in the ring. It's the way it is, according to Mike: the business is struggling. He'd love to pay everyone sick pay, but the money simply isn't there.

It's unlikely that anyone in the audience will know what happened unless they were watching Amir as he collapsed, or they glanced down in the few moments it took for me to grab hold of the rope then pass it on to Fyodor. They will have been focusing on Amara, her captivating moves, her beautiful body, and the tight-fitting costume sparkling in the stage lighting. We are the masters of distraction, of directing the gaze of an audience, of manipulating what they see and don't see. If anyone saw the swap, they may have thought it was part of the act.

If they saw the boys from the tumbling act dragging Amir away, they may have been waiting for the punch line, for him to return, for the reveal—but by the time the show was over and they spilled out into the night, they will have forgotten all about it, that small hanging thread. If they do remember and wonder, they'll also remember the tumblers when they came to do their act, standing on each other's shoulders and flipping off the top, flinging the littlest from one human tower to the other. They will remember the clown duo we have this year, the best German double act we could afford, the cleverest visual gags, both of them acrobats, dancers, musicians in their own right, standing on Macha and playing the mandolin, making it look as if they might fall, their balancing act as perfect as any other in its parody of amateurism. They'll remember the beautiful dancing girls, Amara and the Flying Fantastics, the hoop girls who suspend themselves from carabiners that protrude from loops of braided hair, nothing but the combined strength of their own follicles keeping them airborne. The ringmaster himself, standing as tall and unlikely as something from a Victorian sideshow.

They won't remember Amir's collapse because they have been dazzled by our display of talent, both human and animal. Maybe, for some, I will be the highlight, standing on my hands in the saddle as Macha trotted the ring, leading him to the center for his dressage routine. And for sure they will remember the Goose Lady, how the great bird flapped up to the rafters and then back down, sat on her mistress's head, and honked in time with the trombone.

Here's what I remember. That despite having sold only half of the tickets for last night's show, the laughter was just as raucous as when the place is full, the gasps as dramatic, the applause as loud. I heard it from the ringside, from the back of my beloved Macha, and from backstage, vaguely, deadened by the thickness of those drapes. I recall the lights from the ambulance flashing and mingling, through the slivers of gaps in the side doors, with the stage lights. I recall the sound of its engine drowned by the band, this emergency illness of one of our company masked, hidden, swept away behind the scenes. I remember how the vision of Amir's death—though not for several years—drained me of everything I had, and that I had to hide that from the audience, and from Mike. When I entered the ring for the finale, to dance the ensemble routine with the entire cast and mingle with members of the audience, children of all ages who we always invite to join us in the final moments, I could barely hold my head up. I smiled, though; I always manage a smile.

The muscles of my face ache from all the smiling. The bedroom looks odd, and I realize, my thoughts slow and treacly, that I'm in Mum's bed rather than mine. Her room is almost the same, but closer to the door of the wagon, with the bed at the other end. We bought this thing for her, this fancy motor home with the hot and cold water, because she was dying. Is dying. Spent all our savings on it, to try to make life nice in the time she has left. We both hoped it would make everything as easy as possible for her in her increasing decline; that she could go on living with the carnival, on the road with us, all the way to the end. But we were fighting fate. We both knew she wasn't going to die traveling.

But you tell yourself stories, don't you? Convince yourself the truth is different, because it hurts too much to admit it. That's how we all get through the day, every day, constructing our own little illusions of a never-ending life, of a reality that we have the power to control.

Now she's back at Home Farm, being cared for by private nurses, I feel guilty and relieved, and then more guilt about feeling the relief. I don't have to worry about nursing her as well as keeping up my part in the show, but I worry that she's being looked after by people who aren't me, no matter how compassionate and professional they are. On the one hand, I don't have to worry that the wagon is warm enough for her, that she's eating properly, all the personal care stuff; but on the other, I do have to worry about finding the money every week to keep paying the lovely nurses we found, a pair of sisters in their sixties who have been doing end-of-life care for many, many years. I worry she won't last much longer, and I'm afraid that she will last too long for me to afford to keep up the payments. It's quite the headmash.

Lying there in Mum's bed, something tugs at me that I had forgotten: that close-cropped shadow in the back row, an intense stare that was there and then not there. I was wearing my patch, so I know it was real, that it can't have been a vision. Someone there, staring at me, for some reason, like they wanted something. I shiver but then dismiss it. I've had advances from audience members before; we all have. They always want us, but they never get us—that's the rule. I decide if he turns up again, or approaches me after a show, I'll smile coyly and flash the fake ring on my wedding finger.

On the floor is a little heap of my costume, but under the covers I'm still wearing two pairs of tights, one sheer and one fishnet, and I've sweated through both. There is mud trailed through the cabin, and I kick myself for not having left my ground shoes outside. The tip of one of the gray plastic clogs can be seen poking out from under the diamanté cape, and I think, *If it's dirty, I'll just have to wear it dirty.* I don't have time to get to the dry cleaners today. Time is precious when you're on the road. Routine is everything, with two shows a day and the stalls to run. Everything is back-timed to fit into the hours of the day. The routine, as much as the guy in charge, is our mistress. It holds us, protects us, keeps us safe.

There isn't a part of my body that doesn't hurt, but I get up and under the shower anyway. The heat is a balm. I stay in there a little too long, until the water tank is dry and I've given myself another task, to fill it up again. Back in the cabin I strip Mum's bed, bundle the sheets into a bag, and do my best to spot-clean my costume for tonight. There's a mud stain under an armpit that won't go. It does not smell good, but that's just how it is sometimes. It'll have to do until there's time to get it cleaned properly.

When I move back into the kitchenette, I nearly leap out of my skin. Someone's sitting at the table.

"Hey," says Betsy. "You're jumpy."

"Fuck's sake," I murmur. "You scared the shit out of me. Didn't hear you come in."

She laughs. "You should lock up if you don't want people to wander in and sit down."

I usually lock the door with all three locks and the bar. Today I forgot, the state I was in. I'm struck by how vulnerable that makes me, and tell myself to be more careful. Living on the road, being burgled is a regular occurrence.

"I thought I did. Stupid of me."

"Well, good job it's only me."

I lift the kettle to see if there's water in it, then set it on the gas. "You off to work?"

"I worked the night shift, just popped in on my way by. You look awful."

"Thanks."

"No, I mean, really awful. What's been going on? Is it your mum?"

"Oh, shit. Mum."

I scrabble around for my phone, but when I finally locate it, facedown and switched to silent on the floor of the bathroom, there are no messages from Toni or Terri, mum's nurses. I relax a little. They know to ring or message if there's any change or if it looks like there might be. I drilled it into them that nothing is too small to bother me with, and if I don't answer, I'll ring as soon as I can. I have complete trust in them never to overlook something that could turn out to be the start of the end. So I should too, the amount it costs for the constant care she needs.

I return to the living space with my phone. "Mum's fine, as far as I know. I saw her yesterday morning."

"She's fine?"

"As fine as she can be, anyway."

"That's great. They're taking really good care of her. But what about you? Did you get in a fight?"

I catch my reflection in the shiny surface of the cooker. My eyes are ringed in black, stained with makeup. This is a permanent look for me when I'm not stage ready. So many years of makeup, it's ingrained in my skin. I guess Betsy doesn't see me in the morning very often.

"Oh yeah. I do look like a panda, don't I? Couldn't get all the paint off. Doesn't matter, I'll be putting it all back on in a couple of hours."

"Panda, or vampire? You're so pale."

I don't comment on this. Instead, I pile coffee into the French press, set it on the counter, and slide in opposite her. Betsy tries to meet my eye but, like always, I avoid total contact, out of habit more than anything. The eye patch works—it stops the visions, but I don't like to get complacent. I focus on her left eyebrow.

She leans her face on her hand to take me in. "So, come on. What happened?"

Her concern is what cracks me open. I try to say words, but all that comes out is tears and snot. *I'm lonely,* I want to say. *I'm exhausted. I miss Mum and the life we had.*

I can only make incomprehensible noises, and with my eyes I ask her to wait; I can't speak yet. The lump in my throat feels like an apple is stuck in there. Unripe and bitter.

"Nothing happened," I say eventually. "I mean, lots of things happened."

She raises an eyebrow, waits. Soon I start laughing at the absurdity of it, the drama, the relief of letting it all out finally, of allowing myself to cry. "It's everything, I guess. And I'm tired. Amara's dad collapsed . . ."

There is a knock on the wagon door. Betsy's head snaps up. "Who's that?"

I go to the door and open it. Amara is there. She looks as bad as I feel—she's still in her costume from last night, but with an old wax jacket thrown over the top, one of the big ones from the stables. I stand back and let her come inside. When I hug her, I feel her shivering.

"You've been crying," she says.

I laugh a little. "You too."

Betsy's disappeared, so I tell Amara to go ahead and sit. I head back to the bedrooms and find Betsy half undressed.

"Is it okay if I take a shower?" she asks.

I know what she's doing. She avoids Amara whenever she can. I've never really got to the bottom of it, though I have my theories. I roll my eyes. "Sure."

"Won't be long."

Amara is the same age as me, the same age as Betsy. On paper the three of us should be thick as thieves. Amara and I used to walk the rope together as children, before Tommy died. She was like a sister to me, but her parents kept her away after what happened with Tommy. So when this year the family turned up at the beginning of the season, clutching holdalls stuffed with costumes and notes for a new act starring Amara, I could hardly believe it. Twelve years have passed; we are women now, but seeing her I felt like a little girl. The same little girl who had waited for her to come back and after three seasons finally lost hope; who had looked forward to the carefree mischief of the two of us hanging out once more with Remi and Romi, the fire-breather's toddlers. An image of those boys came to me in the moment I locked eyes with Amara. I hadn't thought of them for years. I wondered what they were doing now.

The day she returned, I'd spotted her across the yard; I wanted to run into her arms, but her father held her back, still wary. I don't know why they decided it was safe to return; the reason doesn't matter—only that they did. Even now, after nearly two months of nightly shows, the parents give me a wide berth, but Amara is my friend, no matter what. The years fell away that first day. She doesn't judge me for what happened or for what others think I am, even if her parents do. Betsy took one look at Amara, at the way I was so overjoyed to see her, and I guess she decided she didn't like it. For a long time, Betsy was all I had. Maybe she preferred it that way.

Amara tells me her father is doing much better, though they don't know what's wrong with him yet.

"I wanted to say thank you. For what you did last night."

I stare at my fingernails, the lacquer chipping off in places. "Don't mention it."

She sighs. "I know how they feel about you doing that. I'm sorry I put you in that position."

I want to tell her it's okay, that it doesn't matter, but it wouldn't be true. Seeing Amir's death was a big deal for me. I've avoided that part of myself for so long; I've been so careful. My body aches from it, my mind is emptied. But I would do it again, for Amara. I would take the visions for her, and everything that comes with it.

"He'll get better from this," I say. "I'm glad I could do something to help."

Amara gets up to leave. She has to change and go back to the hospital to be with her mother and Amir. I shut the door and turn back to find Betsy in the kitchenette, a towel bundled over her hair, hands planted on hips.

"What did you do for Amir?" she asks. "No, that's the wrong question. What did she make you do?"

CHAPTER

7

NOW
Faith

"I THOUGHT SHE WAS your friend," says Betsy.

"You don't understand," I say. "She was desperate."

"But she knows what happened last time, when you were kids. She knows how damaging it is for you to do that, especially in the tent, especially during the show. What kind of friend would put a friend at risk in that way? So selfish."

I hadn't thought of it like that, but I don't like the way she's making out that Amara is some kind of bitch. "I was happy to help."

"She was happy to let you, I'm sure. But she isn't the one who has to deal with any consequences."

I'm tired of the conversation now. "I appreciate your concern, but Mike hasn't said anything. He might not even have noticed." I'm not sure about this, but right now I just want her to stop talking, to stop bad-mouthing Amara. I know Amara wasn't trying to hurt me. I know it in my bones.

"She wasn't thinking about you at all. She was just looking out for herself," says Betsy.

"Which is understandable," I say. "Her father might have been about to die. Wouldn't you have wanted to know too? If you knew there was someone there who could tell you one way or another?"

"Who's looking out for you? Because last night it wasn't Amara, was it?"

The kettle whistles. I get up to make the coffee. She's got a point. Granddad's been gone several years, and Linda left to be a house dweller not long after his funeral. Since Mum has needed round-the-clock care, there isn't anyone in the company with me as their first priority. I'm the last little twig on this branch of the Harrington line.

"Tell you what," she says. "If you want, I can move in here for a bit."

"Into the wagon?" My heart lifts a little at the prospect. Living with the circus, I'm never entirely alone, but apart from Amara there's no one in the company who I would call a friend. The other acts see me as separate, part of the management, even though I'm kept away from the business by Mike and Christine, who wouldn't let me help with it even if I wanted to. And then there are the rumors about me, recycled every year, maybe even passed around to other shows when acts who know us travel to other carnivals.

"Might be fun," says Betsy. "Ever since I met you, I always wanted to run away with the circus."

"But what about your job? We'll be moving on at the end of the week, and then . . ."

She puts a finger on my lips. I smell her hand cream and something faintly antiseptic. "Don't worry about that."

"Maybe Mike will let you work in the stables?"

"Rather die," she says.

"Oh yeah, fair enough. Not a horse person—I forgot."

"I wouldn't mind keeping house for us both, just for a while."

"I would love that too. You're not expecting to be a kept woman, though, are you?"

"Okay, not keeping house, but I can help out. I can pay my own way," says Betsy. "I'll work more nights. Might pick up some sleep-ins—they're easy. They just want someone there in case something happens, but you don't have to do anything. Then we can hang out more in the mornings, when we're both free. And you know if it gets too much with the show, you can just quit, come work with me again, like in winter."

"I can't quit halfway through a season. They need me in the show."

"Hey, I'm not saying they don't. I'm just saying you need to look after yourself. That maybe your well-being is more important that a couple of stupid juggling acts and a few horses."

"Don't let Macha hear you say that. Or Mike."

When the season ended last year, I took some shifts in the laundry with Betsy, to pay the loan on the motor home and to help with Mum's nursing fees when there was no money from the circus. Betsy's agency mainly staffs the bigger, more expensive retirement homes and is always happy to have extra workers, especially in the colder months, as the turnover in those places is quite high at that time. I didn't even have to worry about the visions creeping up on me and ruining my day. All the old dears in the homes die the same way—when I do see the visions, which is rare anyway, it's like glimpsing a lot of people peacefully drifting off to sleep.

As for Betsy moving in with me, I'm hesitant, but then I think maybe it could work. Betsy is a good friend, and we get along great, even though—or maybe *because* of the fact—she's not carnival. She can see things differently, give me a bit of perspective. And if she could stay in the van with me, keep me company, it might make things bearable again, bring a bit of life back to the wagon I should have been sharing with Mum. I wonder what Mike would say about it.

Before I can voice this, Betsy says, "You don't have to tell him. I'll keep out of his way. I'm always here anyway—he'll never know the difference."

"He'll know. He knows everything."

"Everything?"

I laugh. Mike hasn't got time to know everything. He holds tight to the reins of Harrington's—the money, the acts, the grounds. But he can't keep his eye on everyone all the time. He missed something huge last night when Amir collapsed during Amara's act, and that happened in a ring he was supposedly the master of. Over the years many things have been kept from Mike, and no doubt from me, though one or two things get back to me, occasionally, especially now Amara is around again. I happen to know that Mike's wife, Christine, sometimes sleeps with one of the juggling twins. Blissi is a good person, and I would never tell a soul, but sometimes I see Christine and him together, and I wonder how Mike hasn't worked that one out for himself.

"We had a pregnant rope act one year," I say. "Mike didn't notice until she went into labor."

"I bet that annoyed him," says Betsy, and I laugh because it did. Not because he didn't know, but because it meant the show would have to be changed, another act rehearsed or bought in to fill in for the new mother until she could once again climb the rope in her stiletto heels and fling open her legs at the top to set it spinning, the way she did every night for almost the entire nine months of the pregnancy.

"So, what do you say? Shall I go get my stuff?"

CHAPTER

8

NOW
Faith

THE WEATHER IS grim—cold and wet, typical English summer. My face feels sticky and tight, the consequence of leaving the greasepaint on overnight and not cleaning it thoroughly enough before starting my morning shift at the box office. We all have more than one job on the road, sharing the duties around according to a big roster drawn up by Christine, and today for me it's ticket sales. It's one of the better duties, especially when the list includes toilet cleaning and kitchen skivvy. I'm sucking bad coffee from a thermos and shivering, thinking I should have brought another sweater, wondering if I can close for a few minutes to go and grab one.

Footsteps squelch up to the back door of the little wagon. "Morning, Faith."

I nod. "Uncle Mike."

He maneuvers himself inside. The box office is a converted horse trailer, designed with two windows for two sellers, but it only really works if each of the sellers possesses the diminutive proportions of your average acrobat. Mike, who a few decades ago might have been hired as a sideshow giant, folds himself gracelessly into the chair next to me. I have to shift over so only half my backside is in contact with the seat. We both stare out at the gray day, the fine rain falling on the ground. One of our Harrington flags droops from its pole, stuck to itself and flapping dejectedly.

"Sold much?"

I shake my head no and show him the books. Today's matinee is less than half sold, the evening show a little more. We'll get walk-ups, but there'll need to be a lot of them to break even. He whistles with disappointment.

I say, "It's still early. If the weather clears up, there'll be good sales."

He looks out over the field toward the tent. "I guess so." His voice is gravelly, different from the booming ringmaster voice he uses in the show. He's like most of us: two different people, one in the tent and another outside of it.

No one else is around. All the acts are shut into their wagons, staying indoors until the moment they need to emerge. Many of them have come from countries with far better weather than this. The team of jugglers from Sierra Leone seem the most baffled by the almost constant drizzle. It has improved slightly since they arrived in November, but not enough. At the airport they all wore flip-flops, with spare pairs in their cases for when they wore out. We had to go to charity shops and buy them proper clothes, and although it's now been half a year since they landed at a fridge-cold Heathrow, I still sometimes catch them glaring at the sky with a mixture of hurt and confusion.

Mike and I face the morning fog, side by side, like a pair of sad clowns. Bad sales compound everything. The future seems more uncertain than ever.

"What do you think it is?" I wonder aloud. "Ticket prices too high?"

Mike snorts, shakes his head. "Screens."

We are better than a screen. We are the wide sky, the smell of the canvas, the spectacle of performing animals. The pure display of humanity, of talent. Anyone will tell you there's nothing like going to a live show. The magic of watching real artists perform acts they've trained for their whole lives: special, extreme, niche skills that were sometimes chosen for them as toddlers or passed down from one generation to the next. The sacrifice it takes to learn to hang upside down from a rope, to spin, to flip and land on your feet, all the while smiling, all the while making every member of the audience feel like you're doing it for them.

I'm not saying screens don't have a place in our lives. They've played a part in making the circus more popular, made it more visible to more people. Sometimes people take videos of the acts, even though it's against the rules, and Mike reminds the audience twice a show not to do so. I would never tell him, but I often go online and watch the forbidden footage, just to marvel at the variety of the acts that have passed through our tent over the years. There are lots of recent ones, but the one I'm really interested in is a little more than twelve years old. It's all I have of the time before, and the last video I'm aware of that features my brother performing in the weeks before he died.

The Family Harrington was the act I was born into, where Mum, Linda, me, and Tommy all joined in. I first appeared in a show as a newborn, strapped to my mother's back as she rode her old horse Twister, a majestic Clydesdale, while standing on his back in a ballerina's pose. There's no video of that one, but I have an image of it in my mind, the audience appalled and amazed at her bravery and daring, her willingness to include her small children in seemingly dangerous acts. The routine ended with her throwing the baby bundle to then-five-year-old Tommy as he followed behind, riding a Shetland pony, both the boy and the pony in matching outfits. He never once dropped it, but Mum would nevertheless have to show the audience that I was safe and sound, still strapped to her back, and that she'd thrown a doll that looked like me. She still laughs when she tells this story, though I'm not sure how funny the audience would have found it at the time.

As for the film of Tommy, I've saved the video link in my phone so I can always return to it. There's a trick where I balance on Mum's and Linda's joined hands, and they flip me through the air, to land on Tommy's shoulders, in a reflection of that baby-throwing bit from our first ever act together. It's a tragic mirroring, this choreography, being the final show before the winter when he was taken from us. Tommy's just turned fifteen in the clip, all muscles and youth, handsome, full of potential. While he moves through the video, I can pretend that this isn't the best he will ever be, that he's got so much more to come, that I will be flung in various ways into the safety of his arms every year until we are both too old to do it anymore.

I can't decide if watching us in that film makes me feel better or worse. Both? I can't stop looking, whatever it is. I need it sometimes, to remind me. My uncle thinks screens are killing the circus, but for me, and maybe for others too, they keep it alive.

Mike sighs heavily, and I wonder what he's thinking. Even though I see him every day, my great-uncle is always older than the version of him that lives in my mind, his eyes droopier, his movements slower. I'm often surprised how haggard he is when I get a good look at him in daylight. It might be because he's been dressed the same forever, in one of two outfits, which means his face ages, but his clothes don't. In the ring he wears a traditional top hat and tails to introduce the acts, like his father, Billy, before him. Offstage, you wouldn't think he was the same man. The costumes, the tent, and the ring itself—together, they transform people. He's a better man in the ring, an admirable one, a funny yet noble one. During the show, the ringmaster is the proud figurehead of something magical, a wonderous event that exists for your delight. The plainclothes Mike Ward isn't as likeable. He's certainly unmistakable, even at a distance, entirely bald and looking very much like a bouncer, with his black bomber jacket and shiny boots; he could be part of the security crew rather than the boss of the entire business. The invisibility of his daywear is deliberate, another circus trick. To outsiders who don't know him, even those who have seen him in the ring, he could be anyone.

My coffee has run out, and I want to get more, but Mike's in the way of the door. I'm sick of listening to his mouth breathing. He's clearly here for a reason, and I'm impatient for him to get it over with.

"Did you hear any news about Amir?" I ask. "Amara said they hadn't got to the bottom of it yet."

He rubs his eyes before he replies. "Not good. They think it's a brain thing."

"Like a stroke?"

"Maybe. Apparently, the doctor said there was a chance it could be a tumor. They're going to operate tonight."

"Poor Amara. Poor Stacey."

When I first heard the news about Mum's cancer, I remember sitting there in my tights and feather headdress, the stage lights glinting off the sequins on my bodice, and suddenly my whole life seemed stupid and pointless. So much effort, so many years of striving, of rehearsal, of days and weeks and months of building up that tent and pulling it down, in the wind and rain, then getting up the next day on no sleep to practice the horses—and for what? So that myself and a ragtag group of obsessives could strut around a ring in search of applause. So that our family and a handful of others could carry on doing the few extremely niche things we were good at, as long as people would pay to watch us do it.

The seriousness of the diagnosis made our whole way of life feel futile, silly, no way to spend a lifetime when you could have been doing anything, something worthwhile, something that helped people. Taking on the laundry in the winter helped me with that, but even as I washed sheets and towels, doing my small part to make people comfortable, I knew I would always come back to the show when the season started. I know in my heart that our life is not silly or irrelevant. We live in the moment, bringing light to dark places. Circus does help people: without it, life would be a little less worth living. Our sacrifice is worth something, to us and to the rest of society.

When Linda told me, I was standing in the prep tent with a bantam under each arm, about to enter the ring as part of the clown routine. Linda said, "I'm so sorry, baby." And then the music kicked in, and I turned, posed in the gap between the doors, skipped out in front of the audience with my head held high and a huge fake smile on my face.

I get that same feeling now, a clash of big and small things, those that matter and those that may not, thinking of Amir, holding the rope while his daughter showed off her skills, then a few minutes later lying unconscious on the straw bales, being taken away in the ambulance into that other world of hospitals, of drugs and cutting tools and bright unyielding lights. Amir isn't in the protective magical ring of circus now; he's in a place where his hard-won skills don't matter at all. He has no power or agency, handing his life to doctors, people he only just met. But we'll be here, whether he is or not, whether

Mum is or not. The circus goes on in spite of illness, in spite of death. That's the entire point of it. It matters, more now perhaps than ever before, to keep it going, for me and for Amara, for the next generation.

"I hope he'll recover quickly," I say. "It's very worrying." I know he won't die of this—not yet—but my vision didn't tell me what suffering he and his family may endure in between now and when the vision comes to pass. It was just an image of the future, and how useful was that, in the face of a possible brain tumor? I couldn't say what kind of life Amir will have from now on. So much is uncertain.

"Yeah. It's a disaster. Someone else will need to learn the act, to be the anchor. We need to keep things consistent."

It shouldn't surprise me that this is Mike's main concern, for the show. Not for Amara or her mother, or even Amir himself, who Mike has known since before I was born. Now he's written him off in a few callous words, as if Amir's entire human worth is measured by his ability to perform.

I can't keep the shock from my voice. "The act? Really, that's the disaster?"

"Without the Fantastics, we barely have enough content in the show to charge the amount we do. And we can't charge less, with ticket sales so slow."

I close my mouth, consider it from his perspective. He's got a lot to think about, with so many people relying on this show making every date through the rest of the season. And it's true there are a few of us, the family members, who are entirely reliant on it continuing beyond that, into next year and the year after. Of course he should have a long-term view: someone needs to. I'm just glad it's not me. I've enough to think about with Mum.

"I don't suppose Fyodor could do it? He was there for me last night."

He nods. "He's stepping in tonight and will do until we need him. But we may need to rethink, maybe hire someone new to fill the gap."

"I guess because Fyodor needs to be fresh for his own act?"

"Yes. But he can cover, for now. We might need another act for that spot."

"Okay, I guess." Though what Amara and Stacey will do if they get replaced entirely is another matter.

"But that's not what I came to talk to you about. Losing one performer halfway through the season is bad. But we got bigger problems than that."

Losing a performer halfway through the season? What about losing your father halfway through your life? I think of Mum then, wasting away in her hospital bed, each day bringing her closer to the inevitable. In Mum's case, from day to day, Mike appears sympathetic, but is Mum's absence no more to him than a casting problem to be solved? I wish I could be as cold as that. Life would be so much easier to cope with.

I don't say any of this to Mike. He, by his own admission, has got bigger problems. "Oh?" I say, trying to keep the anger from my voice. "You mean tickets?"

"Tickets, yeah. That's one. And then there's you."

He turns slightly, because the space in here only allows him to turn slightly. He waits for me to look up, so I don't.

"Me?" I say it breezily, like I couldn't imagine what he's referring to or why.

"You know what I'm talking about. That fortune-telling shit. You did it last night, to Amir. You know not to, but you did it anyway. And the tumbling boys saw you. I saw you."

There's probably no point denying it. "No," I say. "You're wrong. I never did that."

"I wish I was wrong. It happened quick—I'll give you that—but we all know what you did. Right in front of everyone, so not that clever was it?"

"I didn't—"

He cuts me off, "Anyway, whether you did or didn't, faked it or whatever you're going to claim, it doesn't matter. It's too late now. Everyone thinks you did it, and that's all that counts."

My stomach clenches painfully. "The boys told everyone, did they?"

"Word gets around."

"Huh."

I suppose once you hear that a person can see the future, you don't tend to forget it, especially not if you're one of those who risks their life to perform, who believes in luck, both bad and good. *"The girl with the patch—watch her,"* they whisper. *"She is bad mojo. She will kill you with her visions: It's happened before."*

"It was so hard to get acts after what happened with Tommy. I told your mother to take you away, but she wouldn't listen."

"Take me away? But family is—"

"Everything. I know. That's why I gave you both a chance, even though for a long time the best artists wouldn't touch us with a barge pole. Years it took, of negotiating, of reassuring. Of offering better pay than any other outfit. We were getting somewhere. This year we've had the best reviews for a decade. I was about to admit to Iris that she was right, that it was just about possible to keep you in the show despite the bloody curse. And now it's all fucked."

He spits out the word *curse* like he's been dying to call it that for a long time. I don't know what to say, so I say nothing. My mouth hangs open. I close it.

"You know what happens when you do that thing? When you lay someone's future death on their conscience?"

I remain silent.

"Mutiny. That's what happens. That's what I'm dealing with."

Without thinking, I say, "I didn't want to do it. She asked me straight out. She needed to know."

"Nobody needs to know. There's a reason that it's forbidden, that we . . ."

My ears start ringing with a high-pitched sound, which fades near the end of his sentence so that I catch only the words: ". . . the family of that kid isn't going to forget."

"It's been more than ten years since the last time, Mike."

"It's taken that long to convince people it's safe to work for us. All we had were English acts one year, remember that? A few dancing dogs and a man juggling on a stepladder. Custard pies. We nearly went under."

"I was discreet. I just wanted to reassure Amara. She thought he was about to die, and he wasn't—I could see that. The vision wasn't about the show, not like—"

"Don't talk about it to me. I don't even believe in it, Faith."

"If you don't believe in it, why are you so worried?"

"I'm not worried. I'm stressed. They came to me this morning, the lot of them. They all know about it. They're saying you caused it, that you being in the show taints it, and that's why Amir collapsed in the first place."

"Did Amara come too?"

"She was there and she spoke up for you. She said it was her that made you do it. But the reason doesn't matter. You broke the rules. They say you may have set something free, something evil."

There is a sinking feeling in my body that takes me all the way back into my ten-year-old self. The shame I felt at having ruined everything, without meaning to, without even trying.

"It's not evil. They don't understand."

"They are saying that unless you're kept out of the ring, they won't perform. It's too dangerous."

I feel as if someone has punched me in the gut. I can barely get the words out. "That's ridiculous. Why would it be dangerous?"

"Don't try that. You know why. It's not about what's real to you—or me. It's about what they *think* is real. I shouldn't have to tell you that."

I slump down in my seat, defeated. He's right. If you lose confidence in your own ability in the ring, it can be deadly. Tell yourself a story, make it come true. It's like magic, as elusive and powerful as that.

"Who was there? The twins?" I wonder if Blissi knows that I know about him and Christine, if that's got something to do with his betrayal of me, like a preemptive strike.

"No, Faith. I told you. They all did. The tumblers, the goose lady, the ring girls—all of them. And yes, the twins too."

I look out toward the area where all the live-in trailers are parked. I feel eyes on me from every darkened, curtained window. Then, my mind starts to gather the evidence I haven't allowed myself to examine before, like when Tertio, the little clown, and his wife first came to us: she crossed herself when we met. The Russian contortionists, who switch to their mother tongue when I'm around. What about Amara? She's always been friendly, though her parents are not. She convinced me to look at her father's death, and she must have known what it might cost me. Maybe she's not my friend at all. All these little things adding up. I realize that I feel like an outsider in my own circus. I've felt like this forever, but I've gotten used to that feeling. I thought it was normal.

A stubborn part of me rears up. "I have a right to be in that ring. Me and Mum own half of it."

He blows air out of his nose, and I'm reminded of a bull pawing the ground. His anger fills the space between us. "It's conditional—you must know that. You're only here at all because your mother made the case for you. My father wanted to throw you out the day they found out you were like Daisy, and he would have done so had it not been for your grandfather. The year you spent at Home Farm wasn't long enough—I don't care what Iris says. Those rules were put in place by Billy for a reason: to keep Daisy, and everything she stood for, separate from the tent. Because the abilities your great-grandma had were bad luck. Even your granddad agreed with the changes we made to the constitution. The circus is no place for dark forces."

"Hey, it's not—"

"Daisy wasn't allowed to travel with us anymore. It kept the performers safe."

"What are you saying? I shouldn't be here at all?"

He points his finger at me. "Your grandmother died when your great-grandma broke the rules and came into the tent during a performance. She *died*, Faith."

"It's not like that. It wasn't because of her. It's not fair to let them think that when it's not that simple."

"Seems pretty simple to me. I want you to stand by the rules of the business. And you didn't. So that's that. You can't be in the show anymore. At all."

The world tips slightly, blood rushing in my ears. "You can't fire me. Mum's a partner."

"Unfortunately, you're right. But the other acts won't perform unless you don't. So, you know." He raises an eyebrow. "You choose."

What kind of choice is that? If I refuse to leave, the circus will die. My circus, my life. If there is no circus, there will be no chance of making this right, of returning to where I should be, where I belong.

"So what the hell am I supposed to do instead?"

CHAPTER

9

BEFORE

THE THIRD TIME it happened was the morning of the funeral.

"Will Amara be coming?" Faith asked her mother as they got ready in their mourning clothes. For the women in the company, Harrington's funeral attire was a version of the showgirl's outfit: satin, fitted jackets, feathers, knee-high boots. All in black, with black sequins. The men wore black tail suits and top hats. It was a sight to behold, one last show for the dearly departed, a tribute to the life they'd lived. Macha would be part of the procession too, in a black headpiece and harness as he helped to pull the coffin on its cart, alongside the other horses.

"No. Just the family."

"Were they not invited?"

"They were, but . . . they couldn't come. It's a long way for them."

It didn't make sense to Faith. "But Amara loved Tommy. She said he was like a brother. She'd want to say goodbye. Portugal isn't that far away on the plane, is it?"

Iris put her arms around her daughter. "She'll say goodbye in her own way. Don't worry."

Faith could tell that her mother was holding something back. Circus funerals were crowded affairs, usually. Everyone the dead had ever known and every artist they had ever performed with turned up to pay their respects. It was never just the family. The church should be packed to the rafters, with Tommy having been such a popular young man and so talented.

"Is it me?" she asked. "Are they scared of me?"

Iris blinked. "I don't know."

Faith was not convinced. "What's wrong with me, Mum?"

She hadn't told her mother about seeing Peter's mother's death. She hadn't told anyone. As far as the family knew, she'd had only one dream, and that was all they needed to know. She told herself that seeing Peter's mother's death was like a waking dream, a reaction to the shock. She ignored the voice inside her that whispered she was open to it now, that it was just the beginning. The dream had loosened the floodgates, and now she had this ability to see death. She was horrified by it, never wanted it to happen again. She could still be normal, she thought. If she tried hard enough, she could seal those floodgates again, go back to how she had been before.

"There's nothing wrong with you, sweetie. But the dream you had, the fact that you saw it before it happened. It's too . . . they don't understand it."

"They don't? Do they think I do? I couldn't help it. I'd do anything not to have seen it."

Iris hugged her tighter. "I know, baby."

She stroked Faith's cheek and then pulled back to look at her. Faith concentrated on her mother's chin.

"Why can't you look at me, Faith?"

"I'm scared I'll see something I don't want to," she said.

"Don't be scared," said her mother. "I'd never hurt you."

Faith still would not look. She wasn't afraid of her mother, but of herself. She shook her head no, and closed her eyes.

"You can't spend the rest of your life avoiding looking at me," said her mother. "What kind of life would that be?"

So then, despite her fear, and because she desperately wanted to believe it would be safe, she looked.

It was like being plunged into dark water. The room fell away, and Faith was transported to another place.

In the vision, there they were, the two of them, inside a room Faith had never visited, in a place she didn't recognize. It wasn't the wagon where they lived, or in any of the vehicles she knew from the carnival, but a room in a house with a hospital-type bed, white sheets, soft lighting. There was a big window looking out onto farmland, the walls painted yellow, a wooden dresser with stuff on it. And though she could tell that the version of Mum lying in the bed in the vision was the same person with the same eyes, the same mannerisms, she looked radically different from the one in front of her in that moment, whose voice was barely there, who she could feel shaking her gently by the shoulders. She fought the vision, kicking against it as if she were submerged, swimming up to the surface, back to her mother, back to the moment she was in.

"What's up, sweetie? What's happening? Are you okay?"

Faith had been right to be scared. She'd been right to avoid looking. But now it was too late, once again.

"You're going to die, Mum. I saw it."

Faith watched the color drain from Iris's face, and wished straightaway she could take the words back. Auntie Linda was there, then, standing at the end of the kitchenette, staring down at them where they'd landed, on the floor of the wagon. "What is it?" Linda asked. "What now?"

"It's happening again," said Iris, and Linda groaned like she was in pain.

Her mother picked her up from the floor, and she and Linda carried Faith over to the bench, laid her on her back.

"Don't cry, honey," said Iris. "It's going to be fine—you'll see." She glanced at Linda, who looked away.

All Faith could see was her mother's face, close to her own, full of concern; and in her head but just as real, the vision of the unknown room: a smaller Mum, bony, deathly pale. Seated next to her, a fully grown Faith, her hair pulled up into a bun right above her face, the tips dyed pink and curled around like icing on a cupcake. So strange to see herself as an adult, she couldn't tear her attention away from the memory of it. Was that a tattoo on her arm? She couldn't imagine a time when her Mum might let her get a tattoo. Faith's grown-up self was weeping in the vision. Her mother was dying.

"But I don't want you to die, Mum. Not ever."

"Of course you don't," her mother said. "You shouldn't have to think about it."

Linda said, "She's too young for this," and sounded a mixture of angry and bewildered. Mum shushed her.

"Faith. Listen. Can you hear me?" Her mother's voice wasn't getting through. She sounded distant. Faith was crying, wailing, losing control. Iris squeezed her hard on the arm so that she stopped for a second.

"Open your eyes, Faith. It's going to be okay."

Faith would not, because in Mum's eyes was where the vision was found, and if she opened her eyes, she would see it again. Faith curled up, away from her mother, covering her face with her hands.

Macha whinnied then, from outside in the yard, where he was lined up, ready to go, hitched to the gun wagon that held Tommy's coffin. To Faith it sounded like he was calling out to her, reminding her of what was important: *It's Tommy's day, today*. She needed to show up for him if no one else would, whether or not the low turnout was because of her. He was her brother, and she needed to make sure this final show went without a hitch, for his sake. Because in the end, family is everything.

CHAPTER

10

NOW
Faith

THAT EVENING I feed Macha, but I don't dress him in his ribbons for the show. I think he knows something is wrong. He nuzzles me before he sticks his face in the bucket.

Mike has made it quite clear I'm not to go anywhere near the tent. My act is finished, barely halfway through the season. I don't know how he's going to plug the gaps: without me, and without Amara and the Fantastics, he's got much less of a show, but that's his problem to solve. I stroke Macha's soft nose, feeling sad that we can't perform together for the next few months like we'd planned, that the audiences won't get to see this beautiful boy strutting his stuff. He's getting old now; his joints are not as nimble as they once were. This was probably going to be his last show before retirement, though I hadn't said that out loud to anyone but Betsy. Such a shame that it's been cut short. I lace up the stable tent before climbing into one of the little work vans and setting off for Home Farm. If there's one good thing to come from all this, it's that tonight I have the time to see her. I don't have to wait until after the show, or worry that it will tire me out and affect my act tomorrow, because there won't be one. Not tomorrow and not the day after that either.

While it still has the same name, Home Farm is not the same Home Farm we had when Tommy died. Billy and Granddad didn't want our base to be by those woods and that lake anymore, and after what had happened with me at the local school, Mum also thought it would be best if we sold up and moved somewhere a bit more remote. The following year we bought an actual farm, albeit without any animals, and changed the name to the one we were used to. I was excited: the new place had land, not just a yard, and came with a workshop, a four-bed farmhouse, and a set of barns for storage. It had real stables, and plenty of them, and it was possible to ride straight from the stables into open countryside without seeing another person for miles.

The house was the kind that a child might draw, a house-dwelling child at any rate, and although none of us were going to sleep in it, everyone agreed it would be useful with its fully fitted kitchen and luxurious second-floor bathroom. The bedrooms would be for extra accommodation, for when acts arrived from overseas or needed a place to stay during the year.

I loved every part of it for the first few days. Then I walked into this room and recognized the view from the window as the same as the view in Mum's death scene, and everything changed.

As I sit there by her sickbed, I'm all too aware of the fact that the present scene is almost, but not quite, exactly the one in the vision I first had at the age of ten. Things are aligning slowly, as planets do. In the moonlight I can see the farmland out the big window, the river in the distance. I'm staring at the line of items on the dresser, arranged the way they were when I first saw this glimpse of our future, and then each time I've revisited the vision since. There's only one thing out of place. I wonder, if I move that tub of cocoa butter to where it should be, will she die? She's lying there with her eyes closed, but her face is turned away. In the vision, she was staring straight up in that final moment, eyes open even as they dulled. I reach out a hand and place it gently on hers, avoiding the cannula.

For all these years I've known how my mother would die, how it would look, and from that I've had a good idea of when. I've held this image in my mind, drawing strength from the fact that until now our lives didn't match the vision, we hadn't arrived at the place I would have to say goodbye. Part of me hoped we never would. But it was inevitable, this event, this quiet ending. *Is* inevitable. There was nothing either of us could have done to stop it. There still isn't.

She shifts her head in my direction and opens her eyes.

"Faith," she says with warmth in her voice. She looks at the time. "Is everything okay? I wasn't expecting you tonight."

"It's fine, Mum. I'm having a night off."

She doesn't say anything, but we both know that you don't get a night off when the show's on the road. I think she might ask me what's going on, but then she says, "My special girl. You know how special you are?"

"I'm not special, Mum."

"You are." She glances around to make sure no one else is in the room, that neither of the nurses are here, measuring drugs into dispensers, noting down stats. When I arrived, I told Toni, the older of the two sisters, that she could have a break, get some rest. I can hear her downstairs, making tea, settling into the bed we've got made up for them to use. Terri will be on duty in the morning. The nurses are both in their sixties and have been caring for end-of-life patients privately for many years. I joked to Mum that they only needed one bed in their house because they are never asleep at the same time.

They get breaks together when the family is here, when Linda or I can stay for a night or a day. Mum loves both of them—we all do—but some things they just wouldn't understand.

Satisfied it's only the two of us, she pulls me in to whisper a question. "Can you see it yet?"

"See what?"

"The light, coming for me. My grandma always said there was a light, just before. Like a tunnel calling you toward it."

She's talking about the Sight that Daisy had. I've worked out over the years that while Great-Grandma Daisy and I have been put in the same box, perhaps understandably, our skills are totally different. Hers, indeed, from what I've heard, were a lot more useful. In terms of special abilities, it seems that I'm a one-trick pony. Visions of death I can do, but I don't know anything about tarot, seance, crystal balls, or anything else Daisy could do; things like talking to the dead or moving things with her mind. From the stories Mum and Auntie Linda used to tell, Great-Grandma was a powerful woman, and people came from miles around to see her, to have a reading. Sometimes they stayed for the show itself, sometimes not. In my mind it was a golden time, smashed to pieces by the accidental death of her daughter-in-law, my Grandma Rose. I wonder why she decided she had to be in the tent that night, when she'd promised never to go inside during the show. I wonder why she sneaked past the ring girls to the place on the back row, where there will now forever be a gap in the benches.

One time, not long before she died, Calum had gone missing, and all the men went out looking for him. He was probably eleven or twelve. Mum joined the search party, leaving Tommy and me with Daisy, and with instructions not to move or do anything while she was gone. I was crying, I remember, and Daisy had me sit at her feet so she could pat me on the head.

"Don't worry, Faith. Calum's fine. A little drunk, but fine."

"How do you know that?" asked Tommy, who would have been nine or ten. Her answer was lost in the sounds of the adults shouting to each other outside, and Tommy ran to the door to see what was happening. No one heard her answer but me.

"Because I can see him," she said, her gaze unfocused. "I can see you all, wherever you are."

I had many, many questions about this, but I went to the door to see if Calum was back, and saw him there, in his father's arms, a half bottle of vodka tucked in his pocket. When I turned back, she was asleep and snoring. I never did get to ask her: at that time she was ninety-something, and she died soon afterward.

I wonder what she'd say to me if I had the power to summon her, through the veil, from the Other Side. The idea makes me smile. For that to work I'd probably have to start believing in the afterlife. Then I stop smiling, overcome by a kind of longing. It would be nice to be surrounded by spirits. Comforting. You'd never be alone. And when the time comes, Mum will never really be gone.

Mum's hand loses its grip on mine and drops down next to her. I think she's asleep. When I look more closely, I can see she's gazing out the window.

"Will I see the light when it comes?"

Not for the first time, I wish it were easier for me to lie to her. "I don't know, Mum."

She sighs, a little disappointed. She can tell I feel bad. "It's okay if you don't know," she says. "Some things we're not supposed to know. Right?"

I nod. "If you knew everything that would happen, nothing would be a surprise."

"Nothing would be an adventure." She sounds wistful.

Linda used to say that as a child growing up, Mum was conservative, cautious by nature. Of the two siblings, Mum was always the sensible one, unwilling to take risks in case something bad happened. I don't remember her being like that, but memory is a funny thing. When I was a little kid, for ten months of the year I didn't actually see Mum all that much. She was always working, rehearsing, or performing the show, grooming the horses, doing her housekeeping duties. I was always with the other kids, not exactly looked after but certainly in sight of Tommy, who was five years older and therefore tasked with keeping an eye out. We were a gang of carnival kids, running together, eating together, learning and earning as we grew. We were often found sleeping in the overhead storage or curled up in corners, and apparently, according to Mum, sometimes even under the big water barrels the jugglers stood on top of. Harrington's kids belonged to the circus, not to any individual parent. Raised by the village, as they say.

After our year of purgatory, Mum was wild, no longer the sensible one. The very first thing she did when we were allowed back in the show was learn how to trapeze, because the bad luck that had killed her mum had been neutralized in her mind by the knowledge that she would definitely die in bed, and not in the ring. She would go to the tent in the very early mornings to practice, persuading the women from the acrobat troupe to spot her, to teach her new tricks. She was a natural, flying through the air without fear, her body made for it, her balance perfect. She would never get to perform it, though. When Granddad found out what she was doing, he begged her to stop, and she did. Trapeze was the only thing he forbade us to do. The Family Harrington were primarily a horse-based act, with a little bit of tumbling, nothing too risky in his eyes. Mum could have argued that she would always be wearing a safety line, that trapeze was no riskier than silks or high balancing, but Granddad used to say that Harringtons were not born to fly. The sadness in his eyes when he said it was enough.

Mum still seems a little disappointed by my vague answer. I want to fix it, to make it all okay, so I say, "Hey, if Great-Grandma said there'll be a light, I reckon there will be."

"You do? You believe that?" I can hear the smile in her voice. It was the right thing to say.

"Yes, Mum. I do."

We both stare at the low sun through the clouds, bright silver edges where the beams are breaking through, the dense gray of coming rain. Still a little time left for us, but I can't tell exactly how much. My power, if you like, is pretty useless in that respect. I get a vision, but no matter how accurate the details, there's no countdown timer, no date or anything, just that one image, and that's all I have. I've studied Mum's death scene more than any other, but I still don't have absolute certainty about when. She thinks I do, and I've let her think that. For better or worse, that I don't know.

* * *

I first saw Mum's death on the day we buried Tommy, before we left for the crematorium. I was crying, really wailing, I remember, when suddenly I heard Macha whinnying, and I remembered that the day wasn't about me. I sucked it up and told Mum I would be fine. I stepped out of the wagon in my funeral black and kept my head up all day, through the service and the tiny family wake that followed. Only ten years old, and I didn't feel like a child anymore. I was protecting Mum and Linda. I didn't look in anyone's eyes because I was protecting them too.

Later that day, when things had calmed down a bit, Mum said, "I know it was scary, seeing what you saw, but you shouldn't be afraid."

I didn't understand. What I'd seen was the most frightening thing I could imagine: Mum dying. Of course I was afraid. Those few weeks before, I'd dreamed about Tommy dying, and now Tommy was gone. Now I'd seen Mum dying, and I'd told her, but the telling hadn't made things better. Eventually I would see how it could be a positive if you chose to see it that way, but in that moment everything seemed bleak.

I'd seen how great-uncle Billy looked at me at Tommy's funeral, like all his love for me was gone. Mike was kind, but June and the cousins kept their distance. They'd all thought I was a bad seed then, and I felt like it, like the devil had laid his hand on my shoulder, and I couldn't shake him off. It took a lot to turn it around, for them to look at me without suspicion. June left the circus and sold her share to Mike, taking her family with her. When Billy died and Mike took over, the first thing he did was offer to buy our half of the show. He said it was business, but I knew it was about me, and the rumors, and somehow about my great-grandma Daisy too. The old stories had life. They were always going to start seeping through eventually.

I said to her, "Am I a bad person, Mum?"

"No, love, of course not."

"Why do people have to die?"

She left a long silence. Then she said, "Look at Grandma, in the picture there."

"My Grandma?"

"Yes. My mum."

I stood up and went to the place where the silver frame was kept when we were parked. My mum's dad, in shirt and suspenders, sitting on the front of one of the old wagons, smoking a pipe. He looked cheeky, a twinkle in his eye. Next to him was her mum, my Grandma Rose, her hair curled and pretty, laughing, her head thrown back. She was wearing her costume, a close-fitting jumpsuit, low cut in the front, covered in sequins. She had feathers in her hair, ready to fly.

"We loved her," said Mum. "We loved her with the strength of ten elephants."

"Elephants? Ones as big as Rumbelow?" There was a picture of our beloved Rumbelow there too. She'd been bought in 1900 by David Harrington and lived with the show until she died in the 1960s. Mike remembered her being buried at Home Farm in a grave the size of an omnibus. In the photo she's standing on her back legs, blowing water in a silvered arc from her trunk, into the sky above.

"Yep. Ten Rumbelows and three great big trucks worth of love. With everything we had."

On the shelf Granddad smiled his cheeky smile at Grandma Rose. I loved her too, even though I'd never met her. I loved her from the stories I'd heard.

"But she died, sweetie. Even though. Nobody's fault."

My lip started to wobble, looking at the photo, thinking about how much she was loved, how much Granddad must miss her, the way we missed Tommy. Next to it was a picture of Great-Grandma holding Granddad on her lap when he was a little boy, that same cheeky look on his face. I touched the edge of the frame. Mum loved these people, and they had been wonderful; I knew that much from what she told me. I'd never really thought of them as dead people before.

She sat me on her lap, sideways. She rocked me until I stopped crying.

"Death comes to us all, my love. It's very sad, and that's okay—you are supposed to be sad. The saddest ever. But it's just a part of life, like being born." She stroked my cheek, pushed a clump of unbrushed hair behind my ear. "And after that, the people that love you keep you alive with their stories. Do you see?" We both looked at the big funeral picture of

Tommy, its frame wreathed in flower garlands. It was a color print of him standing proud in front of the tent, balancing on a ladder, grinning ear to ear. There would be stories about Tommy, many funny stories, told with a smile. But it was too soon for that. I still have that picture somewhere, but I haven't hung it up for a while. His carefree smile started making me feel sad again.

* * *

Sitting by her bed, something occurs to me then, that Linda had said all those years ago about me being too young. "How old was Great-Grandma when she got the Sight?" I ask.

"Oh, she always had it," says Mum. Her eyes land near mine, and she takes a breath. It's getting more difficult for her to speak for long. She says, "Don't you have to get back?"

"They can manage without me."

She considers. Then she says, "You're sad, baby. Tell me why."

So, I do. "I broke the rule, Mum. Mike saw me do it."

"What rule?"

"You know the one. *That* rule." I drop my head in my hands.

"You saw a vision? In the tent?"

"Yes."

"Who? Why did you do that? Was it a mistake?"

"No, I did it on purpose. One of the acts collapsed. Then Amara asked me . . . It was her father—I had to. She had to know. I didn't mean any harm. It didn't cause any harm."

"Oh, honey," says Mum, "that's hard."

"Mike says I can't go back in the ring." I feel like I might cry.

"He might be right. Not this season. Superstitions. And your grandmother. Goes too deep."

Her broken sentences pull at me. She's wheezing, trying to keep talking, and I think, *Why did I tell her this?* I don't want to hear that Mike is right. I want to hear that he's wrong, that Macha and me deserve to keep on performing, that we've worked as hard as anyone. That we belong, and that she believes in me. I feel like I'm ten years old again, with a child's righteous anger.

"I can't help what I am, Mum." *Just like you said,* I think, *all that time ago.*

She gazes at me, takes two shallow, difficult breaths, and tries to smile. "You're perfect," she says.

And it's suddenly okay. I know she means it's not me; it's the situation. It's not me; it's everyone else. She's on my side. That's all I need.

"Mike says I can carry on traveling with them, though." I stroke her hand. The truth is I told him I wasn't leaving, there was no way I was going to abandon my entire life because of some superstitious crap. I'm not a kid anymore, or an old lady like Daisy was. He can't banish me. While she's alive, my mother is his equal partner in the business, so I said if he wanted to stop me performing, then he needed to come up with something for me to do instead, and quickly because I can't afford not to be earning.

"As long as I agree not to go in the tent, I can stay with the company. We've actually got a plan. Might even work out better for business, in terms of revenue."

She raises an eyebrow in a question, asking, *"What plan?"*

"Food vans?" she suggests.

I shake my head. "We're going to buy a fairground ride."

Her face creases up, as if she's in pain.

"Are you okay? Mum? You need a spray?" I glance behind me to make double sure the nurse isn't about to come in, hasn't heard me say that. The opioid solution is a secret between

Mum and me. If the nurses knew about our little stash, they wouldn't let her have so much morphine, and as far as I'm concerned, she ought to be allowed to drink that stuff like soda if she wants to.

She shakes her head no. Then, unexpectedly and to my delight, I realize she's laughing.

CHAPTER

11

NOW
Betsy

THE LIFT DOOR opens into the silence of the laundry. All the overnight cycles have finished. Betsy flicks on the lights and pushes the cart, overflowing with dirty linen, out of the elevator, across the room, to the washers. The washer door creaks as it opens, clangs as she pushes it back out of the way.

A smell of detergent emanates from the machine, a fake-flowery scent that she really likes, associating it as she does with sunny days and line-dried sheets, even though these sheets have never seen the sun, are dried in the huge industrial driers. She knows it's because her mother used a detergent that smelled the same, and she would help hang out the sheets every Sunday. It was her job, then, to watch the sky for rain, to run out and grab them if it was about to pour. Betsy still thinks that sheets drying in the sun is the most calming sight, and hopes that one day she might live somewhere with a garden herself, where she can string up a washing line and peg it with linen. Not yet, when she's just agreed to stay with Faith through the rest of the season, but it's lovely to dream.

When she's unloaded the clean washing and got it in the dryer, her blue-gloved hands haul the dirty load from the cart to the machine. The sheets are supposed to be white—they started off white—but when they're in the dirty cart, they're a rainbow of effluent. The residents here are leaky in all the ways there are. Abundantly leaky, all the valves that used to work just flapping open whenever. Exuberantly, generously spilling their fluids, day after day, causing stains in every shade of yellow, brown, and red. It's Betsy's job to keep the linen white, to keep it smelling pleasant, to provide the residents with something clean and fresh to exist upon, to spend their remaining time on. To die on. Because that's why they're here, all of them. Families choose care homes for their loved ones because of the high standards, the lovely staff, the excellent food. But it's a sad fact that no one gets out of here alive. Each person who has laid on these sheets is a human being, someone she might get to know, and likely grow fond of, in the time they spend together, but she does it knowing she will soon need to say goodbye. When she's on a sleep-in at a care home, most of her job is to be there, to be the person who will make sure that the resident is comfortable, that all their needs are met. While she is the guardian of her charge's slumber, there's not much sleeping on Betsy's part: after the regular staff head home, she will lie on the fold-out cot and doze between alarms set every two hours, when she will carry out her routine checks. If there's an emergency, it's her job to be awake and to summon the nurses. If her charge stops breathing, even if there's no machine to beep and tell her, she always wakes up, alerted by the lack of sound.

Many of the residents have legal documents signed by the family, stating that they are not to be resuscitated. So when that breath stops in the night, no nurses are required. It's down to Betsy to make the calls to the next of kin, to wait for the doctor to come and sign the death certificate. In the meantime, Betsy is right there, to gently roll them over, to gather up the sodden cotton and place a fresh, white, flowery-smelling sheet under them, to carry them onward in dignity.

The dirty load is objectively repugnant, but Betsy is not fazed or disgusted. More importantly, she doesn't let it affect her view of the residents. It's just a part of life. The human body starts to break down at the end, and she knows it is important to separate the grim fact of that from the people themselves, who have as much right to proper care and privacy as anyone else as they approach their death.

Thoughts of death are everyday here. Betsy, though she knows she ought to be far too young to worry about it really—when her time comes, it would be her preference to die quickly. A heart attack would be her number-one option, but anything that takes you quickly here one minute and the next, gone. A fall from a high building, she thinks, might be a good second choice, though there is a danger that she might hit someone else on the way down, and that would be awful. She plans to die in the prime of life, while she can still take care of herself, but if that isn't the case, if she's not brave or lucky enough for that, she'll happily die in one of these homes. A close second would be to be cared for at home by private nurses, like Faith's mum, as long as the nurses were like Terri and Toni: solid, kind, dependable. Either way, she hopes the person doing her job, the sleep-ins and the laundry, will be someone like her, who will wash the sheets without prejudice, who will not judge, and who will wake at the first sign of trouble and take some pride in some small way.

As she leans down and pulls at the last of the sheets, she can smell that it's a bad load, a shitty one, and she spots the yellow of vomit, the red-brown of dried blood. She cranes her neck away from the fabric, bunches it all up, and shoves it in as one big wad. There's a trick to it that she's learned over the years. She makes good use of disposable aprons, always, and masks if they're available. She hardly ever gets any of it on her skin, and when she does, there's a washroom right there, with a stack of fresh overalls for exactly this reason. It's been a while since she's needed a full shower after putting a wash on. In the first few months of the job, she always felt unclean, but now, like everything about the role, she's used to it.

Betsy works very hard, but those sheets, she thinks, work harder. They have a truly thankless task, to soak up the tragic stainings of the residents. And you have to hand it to the industrial washers. Time and time again they take this stuff and process it, and an hour later out it comes, clean and white. A small miracle.

When the cart is empty and the machine is full, she adds stain remover and a hefty scoop of washing powder. There is a satisfying click as she shuts the washer door and pushes the button for a boil wash. There are other settings, irrelevant ones—it's always a boil wash. The noise soothes her as she works, moving to the second dryer, dragging the clean sheets out and folding them, ready to be put back on the beds.

There is a noise, footsteps in the stairwell, which makes her jump. She's been alone all night, but it must be six AM now, with the daytime staff coming on shift. She's glad she managed to clean up the man she'd been looking after last night, that she'd folded his hands over his stomach and combed his hair. In death he seemed much younger than he had when he was alive, all of the tension and confusion gone from his face.

"Hey, honey." The woman leans in the door, wearing her purple carer's tunic and gray trousers.

"Hey, Celeste." Celeste is being nicer than usual, which makes Betsy suspicious. She usually only calls other people "honey." People she likes. "You need something?"

"Were you on duty last night with Mr. Grossman?"

Betsy carries on folding sheets. "Poor old guy. He was ready to go. I called his daughter—she's on the way. Did you see him? He looked peaceful."

She nods. "It was a slow one, though, bless his heart. He'd been ready for weeks. Sometimes I can't bear it when they fade away like that."

"Yeah. He was such a lovely man."

"His little jokes."

They both smile fondly. Then Celeste comes into the room, goes over to the washer, and peers inside. The sheets revolve slowly, water filling up the window, bubbles forming.

Betsy says, "You looking for something? Need some bedding?" Celeste is being sneaky; Betsy knows this. The woman's not good at hiding her sly eyes.

"Sorry, but I just been asked to check for misuse of machines. I know you wouldn't use the washers for personal stuff. But I got asked to check."

Betsy laughs. "I wouldn't try that. Not since I saw what happened to Rebecca when she did her duvet. I need this job."

"That the only reason you wouldn't sneak a load of your own? You need the job? Otherwise, that washer be full of your underpants?"

Betsy doesn't take the bait. She does what think thinks of as a tinkly laugh and carries on folding sheets.

Celeste and Fiona, the boss, are old friends. It was Celeste who got Rebecca in trouble in the first place, and that's why she's the self-appointed washer monitor now. Fiona never comes down here herself. She would never have known about it if someone hadn't told her, and the only other person who saw Rebecca's blue bed sheet and duvet set as she bundled it into her backpack from the dryer was Celeste. Since then, Betsy has known to be careful. She'd seen the look on Celeste's face when she'd clocked what was happening, seen Rebecca gather her bag and coat half an hour later after being summoned to the office. Betsy's and Faith's washing had stayed in her locker that night, made its way to the launderette instead.

"Oh, and the small matter that it would be wrong to use company equipment for my own personal ends, of course."

"Good. I wouldn't want the boss finding out and having to sack you too."

Betsy is losing patience. "Right, Celeste, and she won't find out anything, because I don't do that. And I can't imagine why anyone would think I do, or think of telling anyone else that I did."

"They don't. And they won't if they don't need to."

Betsy ignores the threat. "Well, good."

Celeste leans on one of the empty washers.

Betsy nods at the pile of unfolded sheets. "You can help me out if you've nothing on." Celeste stays right where she is.

"I'm going to miss old Grossman."

Betsy stops folding. Something in Celeste's voice is more sinister than usual.

She waits while Celeste clears her throat. There's obviously something she wants to get off her chest.

"What about you? You going to miss him?"

"Of course. That's what I said."

"He was on some pretty strong stuff at the end—phew-eee. Those drugs would be making a lot of money on the streets. Right?"

"Would they? I don't know. I'm not into that sort of thing."

Celeste says, "Sure."

Betsy stacks the folded sheets. She loads them into a clean cart.

"Doctor says he filled the prescription yesterday. Another twenty doses."

Betsy shakes out a sheet. "I can't say how much was in there. I gave him a dose at bedtime. One at two AM. Like the schedule says."

"The thing is, when I went up there, those drugs were not there. Just an empty box."

"That's weird."

Celeste fixes Betsy with a beady eye.

Betsy says, "I need to get by."

Celeste doesn't move out of the way. "You don't usually work on a Wednesday, do you?"

"Depends. I don't have regular days. Someone rang me from the agency. To cover the night shift."

Celeste steps closer. "Oh, they rang you, did they?"

Betsy looks at the ground. Meeting this woman's gaze is like poking your finger into a wasp's nest. "Yup. That's how an employment agency works, I believe."

"I won't judge. I know you mean well. And he was in pain. It was hard to see him suffer. But you didn't . . ."

"What?" Betsy stares right at Celeste—she can't help herself. After a moment, the other woman breaks it off. Betsy's got a good stink eye, when she wants to.

"Nothing."

Celeste turns away, but Betsy won't let her go. "No, say it. What were you going to say?"

"Well, maybe you're the charitable type. It's been a long road for old Grossman. He's been begging to go, ready to go. Did he ask you to help him along?"

Betsy is open-mouthed. She draws herself up to her full height, which isn't as tall as Celeste but makes a point, nonetheless. "I'm going to pretend you didn't say that."

"I'm not scared to say what I see. I've seen your type before, honey," says Celeste. "Night shift, is it? There's a reason people like you prefer working at night. No one around to stop you doing what you do. It's all quiet and dark. Think you're an angel, don't you?"

Betsy is too shocked to speak.

Celeste backs away toward the stairwell, where she pushes the door open with an elbow.

Betsy says, *"How dare you?"*

"I'm watching you," says Celeste, and she goes through, letting the door swing shut as she climbs the stairs.

"I'm watching you too," says Betsy quietly to herself.

Once she's completely sure that Celeste has gone, she can't help herself. Her hand goes straight to the back pocket of the jeans she wears under her care assistant tabard, to check that the pills are still there. She feels the crinkle of the blister pack against her fingers and lets out a slow, controlled breath. Then she turns and places both hands on the cart with the stack of newly folded sheets, ready to push it into the elevator. The fresh scent of fake flowers wafts into her nostrils as the lift doors slowly close.

CHAPTER

12

BEFORE

IN THE SPRING after Tommy died, Harrington's Traveling Carnival was almost ready to set off for the new season. There was a new show, with a new artistic director. There was a band who had never traveled with them before, seven musicians from France who'd arrived in a burst of color and sound, their music a mad fusion of mariachi and funk. New costumes had been sewn, a fresh set built and painted. Acts had joined the company from far and wide: this year the theme was "flight," and among the offerings was a dove woman who spent all day covered in flurries of white feathers, training her flock to swoop in synch and land in time to the music. There was a pair of brothers who performed a version of the shot-from-a-cannon trick; a clown act that, like all the best clown acts, was as technically difficult and as dangerous as what the acrobats did, except the clowns had to make it look like a string of accidents. The tent, where rehearsals had been taking place since December, had been packed down and loaded up, and the kiddie rides used to entertain the crowds in between shows had been taken out and tested before being packed away in the lorries, ready for transportation.

Faith watched the preparations from behind the window in the wagon. She saw them training when she made her way across to tend her boy, Macha, but she wasn't allowed to be part of it, and the pain of that was almost physical. Growing up, there had been six children belonging to the two strands of the family descended from the founder: June and John William's four, and Faith and Tommy, slightly younger, with Faith the baby of the group. When acts joined the company, they brought their own families, so that for preseason rehearsals there could sometimes be a gang of up to twenty children of various ages. The spring had always been the best time of year for Faith, when her old friends returned and new ones came, when they started to bond as a company, as a group with a common goal. Faith hadn't realized that she belonged. It was just the way things were, right up until the bad visions started, when suddenly she didn't. Things were confusing for a while, but now she thought she knew what was going on. Amara and her family didn't come back for that season, even though they said they would, even though Amara promised. Faith wrote, but weeks went by and she didn't hear back. This was the first clue that things were never going to be the same again.

Those children who were part of that year's company ran away from Faith if she got too close. At first she thought it was because Tommy had died, and they didn't know what to say to her, but it wasn't that. It was about what she saw, what they thought she was, which she eventually deduced was some kind of witch. There were a pair of twins, children of this year's dancers, who hid their eyes, like Faith was Medusa and they risked turning to stone if they looked. They didn't need to worry. Since her last vision, of her mother's death, she'd stopped looking at people's faces entirely. What she didn't understand was how everyone knew about it, this bad secret of hers. Billy had made every family member swear secrecy when talking with other circus people. But someone must have talked.

Uncle Billy, head of the Ward side of the family, always oversaw the pull-down, the packing of the lorries, and that year was no different. He leaned on his cane, his limp more pronounced than ever. He snapped instructions to the young men, guiding them as they lowered heavy stacks of seating into the trucks, using the winch. Old Billy was the circus man, the older of the two cousins. Everyone knew he saw himself as the "real" boss, but legally he and Granddad were equal partners.

Granddad was responsible for the sideshows, the food vans, the vehicles, and the rides: everything that happened outside of the show that kept the show on the road, kept the punters spending. Billy could strut all he liked, demanding that the circus was always made the priority, that it was the heart of Harrington's, but it was no secret that Granddad's side of the business often made more profit than the show itself. They were symbiotic, the two sides, as without the circus to draw them, the punters wouldn't be there, but without the other stuff there wouldn't be enough money to run the operation. So Granddad let him peacock, didn't seem threatened by his cousin's ego or bothered by his inflated claims. Billy was a Ward, after all. His mother's maiden name had been Harrington, but his was not. It was Granddad whose actual name was on the trucks. Faith felt doubly wronged, then, because it was her mother's name and hers too, yet that year she was outside, looking in. She wasn't practicing with Macha for her own act, perfecting the backflip she'd been working on since last year. She and her mother had been told they couldn't come. They were not welcome in their own family's business.

Just after Christmas there'd been a big company meeting in the tent. An intervention, Linda called it. Granddad was there, his face grim. Mike and Christine, June and John William, Fin and Calum and Vicky and Sarah—everyone who had been there at the lake that horrible day, plus the new director and a few of the more senior members of the various troupes. Uncle Billy did the talking, and Faith kept glancing at Granddad, waiting for him to say it was all a joke, that it wasn't true what Billy was saying. But throughout it all, Granddad didn't say a word until afterward, and then all he said was "Sorry."

"Family is everything" was Billy's classic opener. He'd ignored the flat, mirthless laugh from his cousin and steamrollered on. "But business is what feeds us, keeps us alive. And this year we've got problems with the business. Problems, unfortunately, caused by members of the family."

"What kind of problems?" asked Linda, a little aggressively. Iris was silent, green-looking. She held Faith's hand in hers, squeezing it a little too tightly.

"I don't take this kind of thing lightly—not at all. I wouldn't do this if I didn't have to, but my hand's been forced."

He left a long pause.

"Spit it out," said Linda.

Billy cleared his throat. "Some of the acts won't travel with us if our Faith is part of the company. It's too risky for them. We have to respect that. Without the acts we don't have a show. So."

"It's just superstition, Billy—you know that," said Linda.

Faith's cheeks were burning hot with all the eyes on her. She looked at Granddad, who stared at his feet.

"They don't see it like that. They see it as . . . history repeating itself." The silence that fell after the statement had a thick, suffocating quality. Some of the members of the company's eyes were drawn upward to the apex of the tent, from the place where Grandma Rose had fallen, the place so many of them hung their equipment, their safety lines. Some glanced fretfully at the gap in the seating where Great-Grandma Daisy had been sitting when it happened, where no one had been permitted to sit since. The missing seat was like a lost tooth in a familiar face, always there but never discussed. In the meeting, jaws were clenched. Granddad rubbed his eyes. Mum jumped up and fled through the tent doors, unable to listen anymore. Faith followed shortly after.

For the first few years of Faith's life, Faith's great-grandma Daisy had been a fixture of Home Farm, the only member of the family who didn't travel. While they were away during the carnival season, she wasn't really mentioned apart from in whispers, in stories that Faith didn't fully believe were true. Then, when the family returned for the winter, there she was, like part of the furniture, an almost entirely mute old lady in a rocker. *"Witch,"* muttered Calum whenever he wanted to get a rise out of Tommy or Faith. "Your great-grandma is a witch." He would sing it, *"Na-na na na-na."*

"She's related to you too, you know," Tommy would say, giving him a shove.

"Only by marriage" was the retort.

Faith wasn't convinced there was anything dark about her great-grandma. She'd liked Daisy. As far as she could recall, the old lady had never done anything more threatening than drink tea and dutifully observe the grandchildren in training when required. Witches weren't smiley like Daisy was, and they didn't smell faintly of lavender. It was true that all of the old lady's clothes were black, and she had several large witchy warts on her face, evidenced in old photos, but that didn't prove anything. She'd died when Faith was only five, so her memories were sketchy and perhaps embellished by those family rumors. Sometimes Faith imagined that Daisy used to wear a pointy hat when out around the yard, but this was pure invention. When Faith looked at photos of Daisy, her hair was always immaculately coiled into a beehive. No pointy hat in sight.

As for history repeating itself, Billy was saying that because Faith had predicted Tommy's death in a dream, she must be the same as her great-grandma Daisy. She must have the same powers, the same badness in her, that needed to be contained and kept away from the show, lest something terrible happen.

For many years, her great-grandma had run a very successful sideshow conducting seances and reading tarot, but she wasn't allowed inside the tent because of superstition. The night Rose fell, for some reason she had been there, watching, from the back row. It was obvious to all where the blame for that accident lay: the dark, unknown forces that Daisy carried around inside her, that allowed her to see things that weren't there, and to delve into the hearts of men in a way that seemed unnatural. Since Rose's death, all forms of fortune-telling were banned at the carnival, for being bad luck. It followed that those who performed such tricks ought to be banned as well.

No one said at the time that Daisy had predicted the death, though over the years the story took on a life of its own, as stories will. Each of Faith's cousins had a different take, each account containing wildly alternative theories about what Daisy had done in the days before and after Rose fell. Faith had heard it all, from the notion that Daisy had seen it in her crystal ball and tried to warn Granddad, to the idea that Daisy had hated her daughter-in-law Rose and killed her on purpose, using her powers of telepathy to ensure she lost her footing during the act. Granddad was silent on the subject, turning to stone if Rose's name was so much as mentioned. Iris and Linda, little girls at the time, hadn't liked to talk about it.

They'd lost their mum, and their dad was alone after that, with two young children to care for and a business to run. Rose had been a talented performer, a star at Harrington's. She'd been a mother and a wife. There was never a time that talking about Rose wouldn't be painful for them.

Despite the only person who knew the truth offering no information from her rocker in the corner, everyone else in the family seemed to take great pleasure in passing around the details they had gleaned, embellishing them as they saw fit. With so much speculation, so much secrecy, the stories got mixed up with early childhood memories so that Faith couldn't help but see Daisy as a witchlike figure casting spells on people. Sometimes good, sometimes evil. She'd found pleasure in having such a controversial figure as a great-grandma, and never really considered how Daisy might have felt, being left out of everything, blamed for such a terrible accident. Faith had listened to the rumors, tried to decide what she thought was the truth.

She'd never imagined that one day the rumors would be about her.

And words had power, especially whispered ones. Now that the various stories about Faith had flown into the ears of everyone in the world of circus, Billy had decided that Faith and Mum, like Daisy before them, were to stay behind in the yard. They would be there alone with the old machines, the empty storage containers, the workshop full of half-painted signs and colorful wooden creatures destined for the carousel.

After they left the meeting, Billy came to the wagon to see them.

"I can't believe you had me bring her to that," said Iris. "She's a little girl. You as much as told the world you would disown her for business reasons."

"I needed to show them. I have to have their trust. But I'm sorry. I know I should have thought of another way."

He looked at Faith. "I'm sorry, Faith. I wish it didn't have to be this way."

"What are we supposed to do?" Iris had asked.

"Stay put," Uncle Billy said. "For the season. Then when next year comes, we can think of something."

As if Faith and her mother could simply decide to become house-dwelling people when all their lives they had been with the carnival. Billy shook his head, gave a big sigh. "It's no one's fault," he said. "But we have to do this. For the family. For the business. We're not abandoning you . . ."

"You are."

"I'm sorry."

"You keep saying that."

"Your father agrees," said Billy. "The decision's been made."

For weeks Iris was angry all the time, and why wouldn't she be? She'd had to cope with loss upon loss: her mother, then her son, then her livelihood, her profession, her art. Her purpose in life.

During development for the new season, the two of them kept out of the way of the company for the most part, but Faith felt uneasy, like she was waiting for something to fall, itchy inside out and unable to do a single thing about it. She rode Macha every day; otherwise, she hid in the wagon, making drawings of shows that existed only in her mind.

"It's only for one year," Linda said, the few consoling words she could manage to scrape from the situation. "After that, things will go back to normal." Linda had pulled up alongside the wagon, all packed up and ready to go with the carnival. She was part of the knife-throwing act that year, an extra body for the husband-and-wife team, to make it more spectacular. Faith glimpsed her training once or twice, learning how to rotate at exactly the right speed for Alan, the thrower, to fling sharpened blades into the gaps between her limbs and those of his wife, Elaine. He'd practiced for hours with an outline of Linda to throw at, and only after three days of no mistakes did she allow herself to be placed on the target. It was a truly terrifying act in the old style, relying on skill and trust, and rather too much luck.

"Do you think people will forget?" asked Iris.

"Yes. Eventually. Or they'll move on."

"I don't want them to forget Tommy," Faith said.

"Me neither, kiddo," said Iris. "I just want them to stop thinking of us like we've got some kind of disease."

Faith likes that she said "us" when they both knew it was only Faith with the disease. "Is that what they think, Mum?"

Iris sighed. "I don't know, darling. Not for certain. All I know is that some of the acts won't work with us if we travel with them. They need a little time."

"Because of what I saw?"

Iris nodded sadly. "Like your great-grandma. Or that's what they think."

"Calum told me that Great-Grandma Daisy could cast spells on people. She could speak to ghosts. She knew what you were thinking as if you were speaking it out loud. Is that true? Because I definitely don't have that."

"Calum told you that?" said Linda, her brow creasing. "That boy's got a wild imagination." She laughed but it sounded false.

One of the big lorries growled across the yard and pulled up to the gate. Mike was driving. He leaned on the horn, the signal to buckle up.

"I'll be back," said Linda. "Every weekend."

"You don't need to do that. You'll be too busy with the show."

Linda dropped her gaze. "I'll try to come back. Some of the grounds aren't too far away. But if I can't . . . I'll miss you."

"You too."

"Stay strong, Iris." Linda gave her sister a hug, planted a kiss on Faith's cheek, then straightened up. "You look after your mum, won't you?"

Faith nodded and glanced at Linda's face, skirting the edges, avoiding the eyes.

Linda left the wagon and climbed up into her own. After she'd pulled away, John William drove past, eyes straight ahead, with his two youngest in the back of the car. Calum showed Faith his middle finger, and she reached up to snap the curtains closed.

CHAPTER

13

NOW
Faith

REGRET BEGINS TO swirl in my belly. For twelve years I've followed the rules about not using the Sight. I kept the patch on all day. Acts came back to work with us; Amara was back in my life. Perhaps I should have said no to Amara when she asked me to look at Amir's death, but it's easy to say that in retrospect. It's ironic because if I could see the future the way Daisy could, I would have predicted Mike would stop me from performing, and I wouldn't have let Amara persuade me to do it. But if I hadn't seen the vision of Amir, or if Mike hadn't known about it, then he wouldn't have stopped me, and therefore I couldn't have seen it, because it wouldn't have been the future that played out. My brain hurts sometimes when I start down this road, so I make a conscious effort to think of something else, something less confusing.

In one of the Harrington's work vans, Mike is driving while I'm in the passenger seat. He doesn't say a lot as we travel, bites his thumbnail as if he's thinking. Eventually, we are in open countryside, but no sooner do I start wondering how far away this place is, than he pulls off the road into a large, mostly empty yard.

I recognize the logo on the trucks parked opposite us. "Is this Biggie's place?"

"Yes, but it's not him we're here to see. It's his old man."

Every traveling show has a wintering yard. Harrington's yard happens to be a working farm, all rolling fields and barns. The John Biggins Funfair yard is a bit like the old Home Farm, where we lived when Tommy died, a great expanse of mud, surrounded on four sides by high hedges and corrugated iron sheets. I hear a dog bark before I see it, a huge brown creature streaking out from between two cars, heading right for us. Mike slows down as it cuts in front of the van, baring its teeth, a low, insistent growling sound punctuated by barks. I watch it, from the side mirror, trying to bite our tires as we drive up toward the far end, where several big lorries stand side by side. We go slowly. Nothing is going to destroy a business deal quicker than a flattened pet.

Eventually we reach the far end of the yard, where we park next to a mobile home that has grass growing through its steps. The door is open, but I can't see anyone inside. Someone must be there, as I hear a whistle and the dog stops barking, stands very still with its ears pricked, and then charges up the steps inside the wagon. A woman appears for a second before the door is shut. She was as bent as a shepherd's crook and didn't look too pleased to see us.

"That Biggie's mum?"

Mike says, "I guess it must be."

There are tire tracks all over the yard, where funfair wagons and vans have been parked in the winter. It must have been full to bursting, as no part of the ground is not scarred with vehicle tracks.

The grass growing around the steps speaks of a stationary life. Like Daisy was forced to do, it looks to me like these Showman grandparents stay year-round in the winter yard, enjoying a nice retirement, occasionally taking care of business, like today. For Daisy, and for us during the year we were banished, it was more like being in prison or a kind of purgatory.

"I thought you and Biggie didn't get along?"

"We don't."

There were rumors that John Biggins had poached some of our chaps, the men we employ to help with physical tasks like building up the tent and taking it down. There were further rumors that we'd poached them right back, offering more money again, and better conditions. One of them had brought along one of Biggie's younger daughters, who stayed with us for a season, working the cotton candy stall. I can't confirm or deny, but our chap and Miss Biggins are not together anymore, and the story goes that Zoe went back to her dad with her tail between her legs and a baby on the way. None of this was Mike's fault, but in John Biggins's world there is no doubt about where the blame lies. Not with his daughter, who ran off, or with the chap she ran off with. It was Mike, who shouldn't have allowed it to happen on his show, under his nose.

"Is this a good idea?" I ask. "You really think his dad's going to give us a good deal?"

Mike shrugs. "Business is business. Everyone knows that, even Biggins."

I don't know what he thinks that's supposed to mean. Biggie's dad isn't going to be unaware of what went on. He's got a five-year-old great-grandson to show for it, and a granddaughter who, as far as we know, remains unmarried. Why would he be inclined to do anything but try to screw us over?

We kill the engine and wait there, listening to the ticking of the metal as it cools. After a few minutes the trailer door opens, and a man comes out—beige cardigan, jeans covered in engine oil. He makes his way slowly down the steps and over to us, his face in a fixed grimace as ugly as the dog's. Not even making an attempt to smile.

I chuckle. "Oh yeah, he looks friendly. Ready to do a completely unbiased business deal."

Mike tuts at me, gets out of the van, and strides over, meeting him halfway They clasp hands. I watch the body language. Mike laughs, the old guy relaxes a little, shakes his head, seems to think about something. After a few minutes they both turn toward where I'm sitting in the van, and Mike gestures to me to join them.

When I climb out of the van and straighten up, I swear the old man's jaw drops open for a second before he collects himself and makes his face go blank. I touch my eye patch. I'm thinking I should have stayed out of sight.

Mike says, "This is Faith. She's going to run the ride for us."

The old guy takes a deep breath, blows out through his nose. "Faith, is it?"

Mike starts to tense up, and I wonder what is going through his mind, if he is thinking the same as me.

"Faith, yes, that's right," says Mike. "She's my niece," and he leans on the word *niece* so that old guy gets the message not to say anything more disrespectful than what he seems to be saying right now with his tone, with the air forced out of his flappy old nostrils.

Biggins Senior doesn't seem to be particularly good at taking hints. He eyeballs me. "Think you're a fairground girl now, do you? Aren't you a Harrington?"

I don't say anything. If he knows who I am, why's he asking? He looks from me to Mike. Mike to me. Back to Mike.

"She's *that* girl, isn't she?"

Mike stares hard at the old guy. "What are you talking about?"

Old Biggins turns away from me, as if I'm something he doesn't want to look at. "You know. I've heard about it. The stories. Everyone knows."

I say, "I've got ears, you know."

"What have you heard? From who?" Mike's voice has hardened to a sharp point. He bares his teeth. The old man hasn't noticed; he's too busy viewing me out of the corner of his eye while trying not to stare or even acknowledge that he's looking. When he does glance up at Mike, the old guy's body language changes. He was all puffed up till he saw Mike's clenched fists, his reddening cheeks. He might be the head of the Biggins clan, consisting of four meaty brothers and their various young, aggressive sons, but they're not here now. None of them are. In this moment he's just an old man winding up a younger, more volatile one. His shoulders drop, he looks at the ground. It's as if he's been deflated.

"Oh, it's nothing," he says. "I just heard some stuff. Couple of your lads know a couple of ours, as you know. Some old story. Probably not true."

"Whatever you've heard," says Mike, "best keep it to yourself. We're not in the business of gossiping over at Harrington's. Dunno about you."

"Lips are sealed, you can trust me."

I've never met a man I trust less. Old guy flashes a vulpine grin, then raises an eyebrow, which seems to dispel the atmosphere. I remember why we're here.

"So, to business." He claps his hands together. "You looking for something in particular? It's a ride, isn't it? One of the big machines?"

Mike says, "We're not sure."

"You're not sure? Not a great start, that." He laughs, but it's at us, not with us. The dog barks again, from inside the wagon, and a female voice screeches at it to stop.

"Something classic. I'll know it when I see it."

"Why are you starting a funfair anyway? Circus not working out for you?"

Mike doesn't miss a beat. "The circus is fine, thank you. We just want a little side hustle. We're not looking to change what we do. We just need to maximize revenue for a few months."

"Yeah, I suppose no one really goes to the circus anymore, do they? Very much old fashioned as a business. Hard to draw a crowd. We don't have that trouble on the funfairs. Never been better. Flocking, they come. Crowds of them. Have to turn them away."

From here I can see three branded trucks, each with gaudy painted sides, each containing a different fairground machine. I wonder why, if what he says is true, they are selling these machines and not running them themselves.

"Are these machines all working okay?" I ask.

"These are the old models," he says. "We've upgraded recently."

"Old models?" I say.

"They are in perfect working order." He's a little irritated by my implication that they might be anything else. "Nothing wrong with any of them. My John, he loves to have the latest thing. Always the same, from when he was a little boy. Could hardly keep up at Christmas. Remember Tamagotchis?" I do not. "He had eight of them. Then it was Nintendo. Couldn't keep up." He pauses to smile indulgently at the memories of his eldest.

While I've only ever bought horses, the rules of trading don't change, whether you're buying a horse or a truck, a mouse or a machine. We were on rocky ground for a while, but I think Mike has got himself under control. Not good to start a fight with the vendor if what you want is a good deal.

The old guy turns to Mike, despite the fact it was me who asked the question. "If you're concerned, I've got all the paperwork. Safety checks, you name it."

Mike nods. "I appreciate that."

We take a stroll around the yard, which in the winter will be once more packed full of fairground folk in wagons similar to ours. There are key differences between the families, of course, between the businesses. Harrington's has an aesthetic that runs across the whole of our fleet of vehicles. We've a color scheme of vintage burgundy, sky blue, and cream. It's recognizable, classy. The Biggins's vibe is more stripes of primary colors, flashing lights, banks of speakers blasting out pop songs.

The old guy leads us toward the big trucks, parked in a neat line, the name of the funfair emblazoned on the side of each. He talks us through what's on offer.

"This here is the Kamikaze. Kids love it. Great ride."

It's one of those pendulum rides that takes you up slowly and drops you down, screaming, hair and stomach flying into your mouth. Mike looks at me. I shake my head slightly. Too raucous for us. Too much screaming.

"Maybe something more traditional?"

The guy smirks. "Sure. You want traditional? I got hook a duck, prize every time, and a couple of hoop throw stalls. Big tombola? All big money spinners, cash no problem, but you need the staff to run them."

Mike shakes his head. "We need a showy ride, but something that just one person can run. Something that will turn heads, bring in the revenue. A machine ride, sure. But not that one. Not too gaudy. Got any gallopers? Anything hand painted?"

"Gallopers we got, but you'll need crew for the buildup. These old machines take muscle to put together."

"Not a problem for us."

The old guy raises an eyebrow.

One of the trucks has the words "Waltz and Spin." I point to it. "How about that?"

"Oh? Your little troupe of fairy dancers going to build up a Waltzer? Don't think so." He smiles like a snake might. Waltzers are the centerpiece of any British funfair worth its salt. The circular design of the machine, the up-and-down of it, the way they start slow and speed up to teeth-clenchingly fast speeds, Waltzers are the definition of a classic ride. These machines are traditional but exciting, made and painted by hand, but still dangerous and thrilling. Part of the attraction is the fact that the cars are spun manually by the operator who exists among all that chaos and noise. It's called "walking the boards." Whoever runs the Waltzer needs a sense of fearlessness combined with a rare grace and skill. The kind of skill usually only seen in the circus.

"Fairy dancers?" Despite himself, Mike bristles visibly. "I'd like to see your Biggie ride two horses at the same time or hang from a pole by his chin."

"Why would he want to do that when he can take it easy and earn more money while he's doing it?"

Mike steps closer. He's smiling with his mouth, but the tension is growing. "Why would he want to take it easy when he could do something that takes talent and practice?"

"Old skills, those. Old and outdated. Not much use to anyone really, are they? Bit of a waste of time. I'd rather sit and watch telly after a hard day of earning three times what you do. We do need strong arms in our trade—I'll give you that."

"Oh?"

"Yeah. To carry all the money home."

Mike says, "Look, mate, we're not here to discuss our livelihood with you. You said you had rides to sell. So sell us one."

Then, the old guy turns away from me slightly, lowers his voice, but not so much that I can't hear. "Does she have to be here?"

"What's it to you?"

He mumbles something then that I can't hear. Mike makes a huffing noise and starts walking toward the van. "Come on, Faith, we're going."

Biggins senior says, "Hey, wait."

Mike doesn't turn but calls, "I don't think so. We don't want it that badly."

"I just thought you should know what people are saying."

He stops, tips his head to the side. He's getting really angry now. "You think I don't know what people are saying? They say it right to my face."

"She's not right for the circus. Or any traveling show. Brings bad luck, and you know it."

"I don't believe in luck."

"You should. Your family hasn't had a brilliant run with luck, or fate, over the years. You got to cut out the bad bits. Take it from me."

I feel something bubbling up in me, white hot and ice cold all at the same time. Mike is at the van, opening the door. I haven't moved from my spot.

"Faith. We're going."

I walk in the other direction, over to the old guy, and when I get close, he starts to back away. My vision is blurring slightly, and I think I might be about to black out, the way it happens sometimes. I'm itching to lift my eye patch, to see this man die. I don't even care that it will wipe me out for the rest of the day.

"You look pretty old," I say, my teeth clenched. "Do you want to know exactly how long you've got left?" I touch my eye patch again, as if I might be about to tear it off. "Wanna see? I can just have a little look for you. Won't hurt."

He stumbles backward away from me, nearly trips and falls on the furrowed ground. "Oh, fuck no, you little freak show."

I step a little closer, pretend to scrutinize him closely, but I leave the patch in place. "Oh dear, looks like it might be bad. You might be heading for a little accident, from what I can see."

"Get away from me!" He falls to his arse on the steps of his wagon.

"Tell you what," I say. "I won't look if you just sell us the bloody ride and get it over with. Not for stupid money either. What's your best deal? Fair price."

And despite all that chat about being rolling in cash, he must be desperate for the sale, because he looks over at Mike and says, "I can give it to you for what I said on the phone."

"I'll pay half."

"Two-thirds."

Mike pauses. "I don't even know if I want it."

Poker faces all around, but I can tell we're going to shake on it.

And that is how we end up driving out of there owning two massive trucks containing a Waltzer.

CHAPTER

14

NOW
Faith

WHEN WE MOVE on to the next town, we have more than just the tent to build up. One of the security guys takes me and Calum over to the Biggins's yard, and we pick up the two trucks containing the Waltzer, Mike having transferred the money. I feel trepidatious about the venture. It belongs to me, this machine—all of it. Mike made it clear that he could stand me the capital if I agreed that the Waltzer would represent the majority of my stake in Harrington's. I feel proud that it's my ride, and the money I make will be mine too. I can pay for Mum's care, and the rest will go to Mike for costs and fees, but it feels good to finally be responsible for something all by myself. It'll be hard to make it work, but I'm used to that.

Calum has been pretty much fine with me since he came back to work with us a couple of years ago. He never wanted to leave in the first place, when his parents did, but his mother told him he had to. Since then he's been working different jobs, everything from builder to pastry chef, but he hasn't been happy. He knew he wanted to be with the carnival, but he also knew that because June gave up her part of the business, he would never inherit. I think he's lining himself up for Mike's share. Must be, the amount of brownnosing he does. Sickening to watch. Mike put Calum in charge of the build crew, and I have to say, he's not bad at it. Not too long ago the build crew was also the company, with all the acts mucking in. These days it's still us, but we hire enough young muscle to help us that the pressure is off a little.

It's handy that some of Calum's crew work the funfairs as well as the circus, so they already know how to build up one of these old-style machines. When we start unloading it, I'm overwhelmed by the sheer amount of labor needed to get it up and running. Every board is winched across and lowered in place. Then a great steel rod is hammered in to join it to the rest of the boards. Only when there's a full circumference of wedge-shaped boards encircling the central booth, like a huge, ruffled collar, are the cars winched over, and finally the roof. By the time we're done, it's pitch-black in the field. The rest of the carnival workers are asleep. We let the crew go off, and I head to the control booth for a test drive.

"You know how to work it?" asks Calum. There's a big green button marked "Go" and a big red one marked "Stop."

"I think I can work it out," I say. He fires up the generator, and the whole thing comes alive, the lights and the music all together. I whack my hand on the "Go" button, and there's a rumbling sound before it creaks into life, spinning slowly at first, then faster and faster. I stand at the center booth, looking down, the painted wood blurring into a smooth wave just beyond the static control platform. Then I step out onto the moving section, and it takes me with it, spinning, sailing through the air. I feel right at home. It's almost like standing on the back of Macha as he gallops around the ring.

The machine's sound system is programmed to crank up louder with the mechanism. Dance music blares out. I can't hear what Calum is yelling at me, so I bang on the "Stop" button and wait while the thing powers down.

"It's two AM, Faith," he says. "You're going to wake up the whole bloody town." He pulls the plug on the generator, and darkness covers us like a blanket.

The next day, I can't wait to get started. Betsy comes early, straight from work, ready to take up residence in Mum's bedroom. I've been keeping my costumes in there, and I take them all out, fold them, and pack them into the storage under the seating in the main living space. Not forever, I think, but for now, I won't be needing them. I pull on a Harrington's branded polo shirt, one of the stock we keep for the build crew and the food-van workers. No need for sequins and feathers if all I'm doing is taking money and monitoring a line of kids.

We have a great start to the week. Word has spread fast in the town that Harrington's have brought something a little different this year. From the first ride, it goes smoother than I could have hoped for. After I've done two nights, I'm enjoying myself so much that I think maybe it will be forever, that maybe I was born into the wrong kind of business, and I should have been a fairground showman. It suits me, working alone and sometimes with Betsy. I don't have to deal with the circus people at all if I don't want to, except for at the buildup and the pull-down.

It's not all perfect. Macha is on my mind when I stop to think. My boy is stabled much of the time at the edge of the pitch, behind the wagons, and I wonder if I should take him back to Home Farm, if Linda would take care of him for a while when she's there with Mum. He's always been fine with the noise of the carnival, but the Waltzer is brighter and louder and more intense than any of the kiddie rides or the live band, even when it's amplified during the show. He's an old man now, in horse terms. He needs to rest.

The only other problem is that I miss seeing Amara. I miss performing with her. Amir is still in the hospital, but he'll be out soon; he's getting better every day. I wanted to visit, but she said I'd better not. Her parents have told her to stay away from me for now, and I understand that. The superstition regarding the Sight is deeply ingrained. The last time I spoke to her, she rang me from the hospital. "My father says thank you," she said. "He understands what you did and why I asked you to. But he's not ready yet to . . ."

"It's fine," I replied. "I get it. I'm just glad he's okay." She's promised to drop by for a catch up when she can, and I believe her. I feel hopeful about it. If Amir and Stacey can see I'm no threat, that my abilities are not malignant, then it's a good start to getting the rest of the circus to accept me. In the meantime, I'm having a ball.

The main show finished an hour ago, but there's no sign that anyone's planning to go home. Every day this week has been the same, more people coming each time. The new ride and the food stalls keep the punters spending after the tent closes, but it's a slightly different crowd once the canvas doors fall shut: families with young kids come early, for the clowns, the fire breathers, the acrobats, and the famous Goose Lady. Teenagers skip the show and just come for the after-party, the cotton candy, and the new Waltzer, an escape for them from the humdrum small-town thing. In the dark, lights from the machine throw shadows where they can conceal themselves in twos and threes, doing I-don't-want-to-know-what. As long as they have money in their pockets, it's all good. Well, they have to be willing to empty those pockets, and so far they have been.

"Hey, look at her."

I don't turn around. I can hear the mockery in this voice, coming from the other side of the barrier. No louder than any other, but somehow it cuts through the music; my brain is attuned to this kind of crap. I carry on with what I'm doing, circling the machine, rotating the cars, flipping all the hand rails outward for the next crop of riders.

"Oi, Popeye," yells the voice, "I'm talking to you." A group of teenagers fall about laughing, their shrieks hysterical; high on something, drunk maybe. Or they might just have had too much excitement, too much cotton candy. I ignore them, hard. What, they think that's the first time someone has thrown Popeye at me because of the eye patch? Come on. I've heard them all, every pirate joke, every One-eyed Willy quip. Mad-eyed Moody, Bazooka Joe, Danger Mouse. Popeye doesn't even wear an eye patch, dumbass—he squints.

By the time I've done a full circuit, come back around to pull the chain aside and let the waiting queue climb on, I'm primed for a fight, but thankfully, the group of little shits has gone. I glance to where I know Ricky is watching, his impressive bulk standing guard in the shadows between me and the popcorn van, ready to step in if things get hairy. He waggles his eyebrows at me. We don't really need security on nights like this, despite the occasional mouthy youngster. Everyone's in too much of a good mood. Nice that he's there, though. Gives me a little lift—mess with me; deal with Ricky.

The sun went down a few hours ago, but the crowds are still swirling, more bodies arriving nearly every second. Party atmosphere is building, with a palpable, collective release of pressure, for us as well as for the house dwellers. Tonight's the first night of the school holidays, and it's the last night before we move on, a final bit of freedom before the quasi-military decampment that Mike and the build crews are gearing up for in the morning.

I see two of the boys from the acrobat troupe wander past, beers in hand, limbs loose and easy; they'll be hungover in the morning, but there's nothing cures that faster than physical work with an early start. They can work, these lads, even after a big night, and it's all hands on deck for the pull-down. Benito, one of the taller of the troupe, catches the eye of a pretty girl, who whispers behind her hand to her friend because she recognizes him from the show. He winks, then runs up the upright side of the Waltzer, pushes off, and lands on his feet like a cat. Everyone applauds. He eyes the girl. "I could show you how to do that, if you like? Is easy."

His buddy shoves him playfully, and they disappear into the crowd, followed by the girls.

There are couples everywhere, as well as groups of girls, giggling, and gangs of boys strutting, chomping on lollipops, larking about. I've had to empty my money belt twice already, and after I've collected everyone's admission, I can feel it's getting heavy again with coins. I check the total on my card reader, do a quick calculation. We've done well.

It's a different feeling from being in the ring, but just as powerful. The ride is darkened under the canopy, lit only by the colored bulbs that line the roof on the outside and the lasers that flash when the machine is in motion. I'm hidden, but I can see everything. From my lookout I can scan the crowds as I work, walking the boards, spinning the cars, slowing them a little if people aren't enjoying it, sometimes stopping them if someone shouts that they're going to throw up. I'm surfing the up-and-down of the ride as easily as if it's not even moving. Riding the horses bareback since I was a baby means that this machine is a doddle. My legs bend and straighten, and my head swivels automatically to stop me getting dizzy. I grab the edge of a car and pull, setting it spinning so that the people inside scream, their long hair drawn straight up and out with the G-force. The music surrounds me, the lights envelop me, the sweet smell of the popcorn and the mint of mushy peas. I'm warm inside, glowing. The queue for the hotdogs has been full all night too, and I can see my aunt Christine has been on duty and hasn't stopped yet. I wonder if I should get one of the door crew to cover for her so she can take a break. For me, I don't need to stop. As the night goes on, I get less tired, more energized, the best of everything Harrington's can be soaking into me, lighting me up. When I'm working, I don't have to think about any of the bad stuff. I can pretend none of it happened.

"Hey."

It's Betsy. She's in her uniform, her bag slung over a shoulder. Only a few days in and she walks the machine the same way I do, a natural, as if she was born to it.

"You going to work?" I grab a car as I pass it, give a heave. The faces inside are a blur. We retreat to the booth at the center of the vortex, where the music is a little quieter.

She leans against the desk where the controls are. "Yep. Night shift, a sleep-in for one of the old dears. Just thought I'd stick my head in. It's busy."

The timer on the ride is about to go off, the red digital numbers counting down, ten, nine, eight . . . I glance at it. "Did you want something?"

"No, just to see your little face before my shift starts. I took our stuff to the launderette earlier, so it'll need picking up at some point."

"You'd think they'd let you use the machines at work," I say. She's always in the laundry at the various care homes, boiling sheets.

"You'd think," she says. "Boss is a bitch at this one, so hey."

A few months ago there was a place where she could use the washers, where no one seemed bothered, and half the staff did it on a regular basis, making free with the detergent, sometimes filling the dryers with nothing but sheets and towels from the wagon and running them through the night. Saved us a fortune.

I suck my teeth. "Pity."

"You seen Macha?"

"We went for a long ride this morning. Can you swing by and give him a bit of attention for me?"

"Of course. He doesn't like the ride, does he?"

I shake my head no. "We moved the stables a bit further away, so it's better."

"Poor boy."

"He'll get used to it."

"How's your mum?" asks Betsy. "Did you visit today?"

"Not yet," I say, quickly checking my phone for missed calls. My auntie Linda's with Mum now. "I might go when I close for the night, just for an hour or two."

"Do you know that man?" asks Betsy. She's pointing in the direction of the hedge where Ricky was standing, but when I look up, Ricky's not there.

"What man?"

"Him, there. Wearing camo. Shaved head."

I see someone moving through the crowd, faster than everyone else, pushing people a little too hard to get by. The back of his head moves away. I can't see his face but I recognize the shape of that head. It's the same man who was watching me in that strange way the night Amir collapsed.

"No," I say. "I don't think I do."

"He was looking at you funny. Staring. Like he knew you."

I try to find the man in the crowd again, but he's disappeared.

CHAPTER

15

NOW
Faith

THE TIMER GOES off and I push the big red "Stop" button. The ride slows and the music fades out to almost nothing. The undulating boards spin around slower, slower, until they stop, suddenly quiet, the oval-shaped cars gently rotating under the strobing laser lights. After I unlock the safety bars, the punters stagger up, dizzy, or they jump out laughing. One younger boy looks as if he might be sick, and I help him get straight off the side of the machine, safely to the grass, where he dry-heaves as his friends gather around, looking worried.

When I turn back to the booth, I see that Betsy's gone. She never said where she dropped off our laundry. I hope there's not more than one launderette in this town, or I'll be in trouble.

I let the queue on, wait for them to settle in the cars before I go around checking the numbers and locking the bars again. I find one car with nine kids in it, sitting on each other's laps. Most of them, even now it's late and the sky has long since darkened, still wear their school uniforms as they clutch the safety bar, huddling together, twitchy with anticipation.

"Five, max." I say, and they groan.

"Oh, pleeeeease," one of the girls says, in her best begging voice, lip stuck out, eyelashes batting.

I shake my head, no way. "I'm not going to start it until there's five of you." I shrug.

Four of them climb out and disappear. I click the safety bar into place and move on. Don't even know how they all wedged themselves in there to start with.

When the ride stops, I release all the bars again. You can lose track of time like this, the easy, repetitive nature of it. Sometimes it takes a minute for them to get out, especially if they're not used to it. I keep a mop and bucket in the control booth for the times it gets really messy, but so far tonight—touch wood—everyone's hotdogs and Coke have stayed down. One of the cars contains kids I recognize from previous nights, who've been getting extra spins this time around. They grin at me, nod and say thank you, and for a second I feel part of something bigger than me, bigger than the carnival, bigger than the town. There's a transaction there: me and them, we need each other.

All the cars should be empty, but there's a couple who haven't shifted. I go over and stand with one leg up on the side of the car.

"Out, please," I say. "I need to let the next lot on."

I think perhaps they didn't hear me. I try again. "I said out, please."

The guy smiles in a strange way and says, "Can't we go again?"

I look at the woman next to him, who must be younger than him by ten years at least. She has a high ponytail, a gray designer sweat suit, lots of makeup. She is cringing, embarrassed. "Sorry," she says to me before leaning in and whispering something to him.

The man, leather jacket and jeans, turns to her and says, "Let me handle it." I think he's got a lot of money, this guy. He has that kind of vibe. His beard is weirdly neat, and the jeans are expensive. I notice that other people are paying attention to our exchange, and I wonder if he's some kind of local celebrity. He looks at me with too much confidence, teeth sparkling white where they peep through his lips. It's as if I should know who he is, as if he's a big deal. Football manager, maybe? He looks fit, but too old to be a player; maybe he used to be one. There's a premier league club nearby, but I don't follow it. I probably wouldn't know Ronaldo if he climbed into a bumper car and waved to me as he went by. Ronaldo is a footballer, right? Betsy would know.

"You want special treatment?" I say in as playful a voice as I can muster. I make sure there's an edge to my tone, but he pretends he can't detect that.

"Yes, please, darling. Just let us stay on for the next one. I don't want to have to queue. Don't make me. We won't tell anyone."

"I don't mind queueing again," says the girlfriend. "We should probably get off, Joey. Come on."

She tries to get up, but he holds on to her arm.

"No," he says. "This nice lady is going to let us stay on for one more. I can tell she likes us. We're getting special treatment, like she said. Because we're special." He pulls the girlfriend close and kisses her on the side of the head. "You're beautiful." He turns to me. "She's gorgeous, isn't she? Isn't she worth treating?"

I'm about to have them thrown off. I straighten up, see Ricky come out of the shadows, his skin gleaming in the dark, fists curling in anticipation as he reads the situation, taking his cue from the way I've stood up, hands on hips. He takes a few paces forward, getting ready to step in, hops up onto the side of the machine. But then this slick punter moves his hand toward mine and folds something in my palm. Feels like a twenty. I hold up a hand for Ricky—"It's okay."

"You're a lucky guy." I smile, slip the cash into my pocket, reach up and push the bar down for them so they can ride again. Ricky hops back down and takes his place, a bit disappointed that it came to nothing. He was up for the action after a quiet few nights. I've known most of the security guys for years, but Ricky's my favorite. I don't know if he's heard the rumors, but he treats me the same as always, with the respect my name deserves: I'm a Harrington. Just like Granddad and Mum, my name's on all the trucks.

"Thanks, sugar," the man says. "I knew you'd be good to me." And then it happens. His girlfriend is looking the other way. Ricky has his back to me. I'm turning, pushing off from the side of the car, and this man's hand slides up my inner thigh, back and around, sending a bolt of shock through me as he cups and squeezes my pubic bone, quick and assured, straight in like a bull's-eye and out, his hand casually landing in his lap. My jaw drops open. I stare at him.

"What's up?" asks the girl when she sees my face. My circus poise kicks in, and I arrange my features in a smile, erasing all trace of the horror I feel.

I weigh up my options, the hard ball of my anger growing, intensifying. I could have Ricky deal with it, but then I'd have to explain. He didn't see what happened. I'm not sure I have the words. Or I could deal with it myself.

Without saying anything else, I move to unchain the gate to the queue, my legs numb, my body operating by itself, without need for thought. A flood of kids run on, crowding into the cars, giggling, chattering. On autopilot I take the money. When every car is full, I go into the control booth and press the button to start the ride.

I spin everyone fast, but leather-jacket man and his girlfriend get special treatment, just like he wanted. Again and again I pull the back of their car around, hard as I can, letting gravity do its worst. I pull it until my arms ache, until I'm grunting with the effort, until Ricky sends me a questioning head tilt, watching me with curiosity from his station at the side of the Waltzer. I laugh, a little bit madly, because they are stuck in the seats at odd angles, the flesh on the man's face pushed back, revealing his too-white teeth in a skull-like grimace. Four minutes later, the ride comes to a stop. I'm sweating, spent, victorious. Everyone gets off before I attend to them. Eventually, I release the bar and raise my eyebrows. "How was that?"

The girlfriend is laughing, her cheeks red, her hair mussed up a little. "So good," she says, then looks at him. "Are you okay, Joey?"

He tries to say something but fails. I've already got the bucket in my hand so that when he leans forward and convulses into it, there isn't any mess left behind. I'm not giving myself a cleaning job for his benefit. People around and about start laughing and jostling each other. Someone is filming it on a mobile phone.

"Another go-round?" I offer, raising an eyebrow.

The man is green. He hauls himself upright, and I realize too late that he's bursting with rage, that he's coming for me. Ricky's too far away to stop it.

Stepping out of the car, he stumbles, throws out his hands and side-swipes me, connecting just before I can duck away. Pain explodes in my cheekbone, and my eye patch comes off. After that, I'm gone. Without my eye covered, there's no way to stop the visions. I see this man's death play out in my head, as vivid as a film clip, as real to me as the carnival is. I'm transported to a place I've never been; the air is warm, bright sunlight, beside a wide, deep river. It's in the near future—the man's beard and haircut are the same as they are now. He takes a running jump and lands in water, but it's colder than he thought, too cold. The shock of it makes him gasp, and his lungs fill with water. His arms fly out, and he's grasping at weeds, but they tangle around him, strong like ropes—he can't get away. He chokes, legs kicking like flippers, but he's weak, he's sinking. After a while he stops struggling, his arms twitch a couple of times. A few bubbles of air escape from his nose. His body drifts, pulled by the zigzag of currents, and I can feel it all, the mud, the water, the scrape of twisted trees with roots growing into the river, the worn rock through which the water cuts. As for Joey, there's no more oxygen for him. His eyes are half open, but he'll not see anything more.

The vision fades. Rock and mud become grass under my body. The gentle lapping of the water is replaced by the booming of a sound system. I can hear Ricky's voice. "Faith, you're okay," he says. "You just had an attack."

The horror of the vision is that it happens in water, just like Tommy's.

"Faith? Can you sit?" Amara is right there, wearing an old tracksuit and looking worried.

"How are you here?" I ask. It's been a few days since we spoke. I didn't know she was on site.

She says, "I came back to get some things and to sleep. I saw what happened. Shall I call an ambulance?"

"No," I say as forcefully as I can. Besides the scratch on my cheek, I'm not injured, but my face feels naked. I clamp a hand over my eye and squeeze Ricky's hand. "Did you find my patch?" I won't be safe until I have it. I don't want to see Ricky's ending or Amara's or anyone else's. That patch is all I have to protect me. I'd almost forgotten how draining it is to see death when I wasn't expecting to, when I didn't consent to it. I know I'll be wiped out for the next few hours. That stupid, leather-jacket bastard. He doesn't know what he's done.

Ricky presses the eye patch into my hand. "You really gave that guy what for. He was totally freaked out. You can be a scary motherfucker, can't you?"

I have no memory of what I said, only of what I saw. I went somewhere else, to a river, to his death. What did I say while I was gone? I try to recall it, but my head starts pounding with a throbbing pain.

I choke out the important words. "Did you get him?"

Amara nods. "Calum and Finlay escorted him off the premises. He won't be back."

"Good," I say. Then I feel very, very slightly bad for the leather-jacket man because for him there are only so many short days left on this earth in which to be an asshole.

CHAPTER

16

NOW
Faith

Mum's been asleep for a couple of hours when her eyes slowly open. The sun has risen fully into the sky, lighting the dust motes in beams through the window, so they shine like glitter. She turns to me and smiles, her voice cracked with fatigue. "Will it be today, love?"

I don't speak for what seems like a very long time. This is our thing, our little script, as familiar as "I love you." The answer I always give has evaporated. I can't say it.

"Will it be today, love?"

"No, Mum, not here, not yet."

"Then today's an adventure, isn't it? Anything could happen."

And what adventures we have had.

Mum flew on that trapeze as if she had wings. Even outside the ring she was fearless, driving everywhere as fast as possible, standing on the edges of cliffs without fear of falling. Seeing myself in that future vision affected me too. There I was, alive and well. A younger, more reckless me concluded that I'd make it to that time and place, no matter what I did. When I was seventeen, I got a motorbike, a proper one, and rode it in shorts in the summer, unafraid of being taken out by a bad corner or a drunk driver. Other parents might have refused to allow it, wrung their hands or worried all night when their child was out and about on such a machine. Mum waved me off happily. I wasn't going to die in a motorcycle accident, because that future version of me was there to prove it.

If either of us was going to do something that carried a risk, she'd ask, "Is it today?" And I'd laugh. We both knew she'd be a different version of herself by then, that illness would have set in some time before. We both knew that there was a room in the farmhouse at Home Farm, waiting for her, but between then and now we had to live, to grab every moment with both hands.

"No, Mum, not here, not yet." You can imagine how that sounded when I was a teenager, rolling my eyes.

Then, the carefree part of my life came to a muted end.

At the time she was happy and healthy, we both were. The storm was coming, something was going to change. The version of me from the vision was almost a match. I twirled a strand of my mousy-brown hair around a finger and wondered when it would occur to me to have the tips dyed pink.

For Mum there would be a slow onset of symptoms, a lump found, a diagnosis given. She would deteriorate slowly, over a period of months, until the day the doctor told us she'd be more comfortable in a nursing home and I thought, No, she needs to stay at the farm. I knew which room it would be. We had a hospital bed installed, and interviewed nurses to care for her while we were traveling. We found Terri and Toni, who were perfect, but she still resisted the day, put it off as long as she could, by buying the new wagon, by pretending she wasn't in pain, by soldiering on. Betsy started gathering meds for her then, but she only took a little, and only when it was really bad. Then one day, in the middle of last season, it was time. She had me drive her back to Home Farm, gritting her teeth with the pain, even with two of the pills under her tongue. I called Toni, who met us at the yard, who helped her up to the room and gave her some different pain meds, the proper dose, which I can see now may have been the start of a slippery slope, with meds on top of meds, official ones and those not so official.

When Mum was settled, I went up. Walking in and seeing her in that bed for the first time, the pieces of the vision sliding into place—it was all I could do not to run straight out again.

"Will it be today, love?" She's been asking every day for a while. Today is the first time I can't say it won't be, with any certainty. I stare at that tub of cocoa butter again. Still not in quite the right position. If I leave it, perhaps I'm keeping her alive. But for how long? She's become the woman in the vision, the shadow of herself, slipping away. Then I remember another important detail: in the vision, the weather was different, raining hard. The sky outside now is patchy blue, the clouds still gathering.

I rub Mum's hand and start to sing, *"Hush little baby, don't you cry."* It's what she used to sing to me. It comforts us both.

Mum frowns a little. I haven't replied to her question. It hangs between us.

"So, is it today? You never said."

I try to smile, keep her hand between my two. She puts the other one on top, in a fist. One potato, two potato.

"Faith? Did you hear me?"

"Not today, Mum. But soon. Maybe tomorrow."

"Good," she says, her voice soft. "I'm ready now. Enough adventures."

I make a strangled noise in the back of my throat, because there will never have been enough adventures with Mum.

"Hey," she says. "Don't cry. We had fun, didn't we?"

I nod.

"Nothing lasts forever, sweetie."

And I know it. But it hurts.

She asks for more medicine, and I give it to her, one unofficial pill to dissolve under her tongue, then a pump on the button for more morphine. I watch her eyes glazing, her pupils slowly spreading. She reaches up and moves my eye patch aside so she can see my face properly.

"I don't regret anything," she says. "Not a single second of my life. It's been wonderful. But I do worry about you."

I shake my head. "Don't. I'm strong. I'll be okay, Mum. I promise."

"You know what I think your gift is, really? It's not seeing the future or predicting things."

"No?"

"You make people brave. You made me brave." She touches my damaged eyelid. "Beautiful girl," she says, and her voice is dreamy as the drugs carry her away toward sleep.

I'm crying, I can't help it. Big, ugly sobs that shake my body from its center, that make my stomach hurt. There's a knock on the door.

My aunt Linda opens it and peeps inside. From the corner of my eye, I watch as she takes in the scene, Mum asleep, my red eyes. I sniff, my breath uneven, and fumble for a tissue to blow my nose.

"You're here?" She's whispering so as not to wake her sister. "We weren't expecting you to stay all night."

I keep my eyes on Mum. I smooth a strand of silky black hair against the pink of her skull. They stopped the chemotherapy because it wasn't going to work, but not soon enough to save her hair.

"I'll be gone soon," I mutter. "Need to get back for the move."

Linda's eyes are wide and worried when she approaches the bed where Mum lies motionless, eyes closed.

"She looks peaceful."

We wait in silence for the soft sound of her breathing. When it comes, Linda lets out the breath she's been holding. She sweeps her eyes over me, and her brow furrows.

"You slept?" She indicates my money belt, my Harrington's branded shirt. It's very early for me to be dressed and ready for the evening's trade.

Because she's whispering, I whisper too. "No." My eyes feel heavy in their sockets.

"What's that on your face?"

She touches my cheek where there is a scratch. I touch it too. It doesn't hurt but I can feel the ridge of it, the heat where the skin has broken, started mending itself. "There was some trouble after the show. A punter."

She's angry then, her breath drawn in. "What happened?"

"He . . . touched me. So, I taught him a lesson. Then I guess he tried to teach me one back."

She clicks her tongue. "Were you on your own? What about Mike and Christine? Weren't they looking out for you?"

"It was busy. But I wasn't on my own. Amara helped. Ricky was there. He dropped me off here afterward." I'd said I was happy to drive, but Ricky said I was being dumb, the state I was in. He had a point. The town the carnival is at now isn't too far away from the Farm. I told him I'd get the bus back.

"He should have taken you to the police station."

I sigh. That's what he'd tried to do, but I didn't want to go. "I wanted to come here, to see Mum."

What's the point of telling the police anyway? No one else saw what happened, only what happened afterward, that I was winding him up. Even if they took me seriously, especially if they did, it would have taken too long to get all the details processed, and then what would they do? Might even be me they arrested. I needed to be here tonight, to not think about what happened. I gaze at Mum. Linda, I think, understands. Because she'd left the carnival by that time, she cared for Granddad when dementia took him from us, but we all sat with him when we could. We drove back here from wherever the carnival was pitched, taking it in turns, subbing for each other in the ring. He died surrounded by love, and Mum will too. Family is everything.

Mum's so close to the end now, I need all the time with her I can get. At the same time, I need to keep the ride going now that we've bought the damn thing. No one's going to do it for me—that much is clear. If Linda really wanted to help, she'd help properly by coming on the road. She knows how things are done. But she left for a reason, and that reason still exists: family might be everything, but she can't work with Mike. She said if she had to spend any more time being told what to do by him, she couldn't be held responsible. Her coming back has never been on the table. She made herself quite clear.

"If not the police, you should go to Mike. Tell him what happened. He needs to put more security in place to protect you. It was his stupid idea to get this ride; he can't just stand aside and let you do it all on your own."

"I can handle it," I say. "Worse things have happened."

Linda doesn't reply, but the face she makes betrays her skepticism, her disapproval. We've been over this old ground before: I know she thinks I should leave, sell my share to Mike like she did, find something more stable to do with my time. She knows I would never do that. Harrington's needs to continue, though every year it's getting harder and harder to make it work financially. And if I leave, who gets Mum's share in the business? Something stubborn in me doesn't want it all to belong to Mike. Granddad wouldn't have wanted there to be no Harringtons on the carnival at all.

Linda sits down next to me, follows my gaze to Mum's face. "Terri and Toni have been talking recently about moving her to a hospice. There's one in town with a room on the ground floor, so she can go outside more easily."

I stare at the cocoa butter for a long moment. This scene is so similar to my vision, so almost it exactly. I look over at my aunt, focusing just below her chin, which for me is just the right side of too intense. "I don't think there's time."

Linda says, "Ah," and it comes out like a small sigh. She nods slowly.

Sometimes Mum used to make me check that the vision hadn't changed. I hated doing it, but I would slide my eye patch off and concentrate on her two eyes, let the vision come. Always the same white room in the farmhouse, the same window, the same version of her, lying in that hospital bed. It wiped me out somewhat, to conjure it, to see it again, but it was worth it to reassure her. The woman in the vision was never her, not quite. Not until now.

Linda tilts her head at Mum and finally speaks at a normal volume. "Hello, Iris. It's Linda." Mum doesn't stir. She turns to me again. Whispers again.

"How's she been, since you got here?"

"Toni said that yesterday was better," I say. "But she was awake a few minutes ago. She only just dropped off."

Mum starts to cough, and Linda fusses around, wiping her sister's mouth with tissues, plumping her pillows, cooing in a calming voice.

"When does the carnival start the pull-down?" she asks me.

I start, look at the clock. The crew will be up and at it already, wielding spanners, operating winches. "I have to go."

"Why? You think they'll go without you?" She laughs, as if.

"I wouldn't put it past them."

Linda looks at me with kind eyes. "The casuals still giving you a hard time?"

I wave a hand dismissively. "It's not so bad. Calum's crew don't really talk to me, but everyone else seems okay. Mostly. They just need a bit more time."

"You don't have to use them. Get some other lads in. It's not all up to Mike."

"I wish. Calum's in charge of the build crew now."

"Yes," she says grimly. "You want to watch him. He's always been sly."

Mum's hands, folded together on her stomach, are lily-white against the sheets, but I can picture them in the old days when they used to be the same as mine, black in the creases and under the nails, from the greasepaint, from the everyday grime and dust of the circus that never quite rubs off no matter how hard you scrub.

"Really, Faith, you should make sure to get some sleep tonight. You look absolutely terrible."

I laugh. "Still famous for your tact, then?"

Her smile is crooked. "Always."

"Are you staying?" I ask. I don't want Mum to be alone now, or ever again.

"I'll stay as long as she needs me to. Terri is due at midday, but I might stay until tonight anyway."

"Will you call me? If . . ."

Linda nods.

I don't want to leave, but I need to be back at the ground to organize the pull-down for the Waltzer. I glance outside to check the weather. No rain. I check the position of the cocoa butter, though I know it's still sideways. I've got time, to go and come back again. I heave myself up, stiff from sitting still for so long, from not sleeping; bruised from falling down the night before.

"Thanks, Auntie Linda. I'll come back when we've done, later. The next town we're moving to is only ten miles on."

I'm nearly at the door when she says, "I still miss him, you know."

"Granddad? Me too."

"Yes, Granddad, but I meant your brother. I think that was the beginning of the end of us."

My throat closes up, as if it would prevent me from speaking even if I wanted to. Opening the door and stepping into the corridor, I push thoughts of Tommy away, as I always do.

"Hey," says Linda, without raising her head. "Sorry. I didn't mean anything by that. I didn't want to . . ."

"It's fine."

"No, but I can't ever say the right thing. I wanted to say . . ."

"You don't have to say anything."

"I've missed you too, you know, these past years, since I stopped. It was always me and Iris and your granddad. We were a tight unit, as close as sisters could be. Even after she had Tommy, and then you. Especially then." She doesn't mention my dad. No one ever does.

There's a photo on Mum's bedside cabinet, of Granddad standing in the entrance to the old tent we owned in the sixties. On either side of him are Mum and Linda, about ages five and six. They're all three grinning madly. It's an idyllic scene, the summer before the accident where Grandma Rose died, the photo presumably taken by her, which is why she isn't in it. You can even see the back end of Daisy's wagon in the background. I imagine her in there, dealing cards, swirling tea leaves.

I say, "You're happy, though, aren't you—settled? Living in one place all the time?" I've been to Linda's on plenty of occasions, but the way she lives is fascinating to me. I can't imagine being happy in a house. My home needs to have wheels.

"Never been happier," she says, and although I don't understand it, I believe her.

"Me too," I say, though even to me the words sound hollow. Last night I might have said I was happy, making the best of a difficult situation and enjoying my new machine. This morning, there is a deep sense that nothing is right with the world. I kiss Mum on the cheek, hug Linda, and set off for the ground.

CHAPTER

17

NOW
Faith

Once I'm outside, I put one foot in front of the other, not really paying much attention to where I'm headed, trusting my legs to take me on the walk into town to the bus stop, and from there back to the ground. Soon the fields are replaced with houses, and I'm pounding pavements instead of grass verges. I'm cold and my stomach rumbles, reminding me I haven't eaten since yesterday. As I walk past a café, the bakery aroma is inviting, but there's a queue of people waiting to grab breakfast before work, so I keep on. I'm already late. The pull-down will already be in progress, all the crew getting to work. I imagine they'll be wondering where I am. I look for a taxi but there aren't any. There's no one I can call to pick me up. Betsy doesn't drive. Ricky was good to drop me off, but I can't bother him again. Everyone else will be all hands on deck.

I decide I need something in my stomach if I'm going to get through the day, so I dive into a mini-supermarket and pick up a tired-looking sandwich. The bus stop isn't far now.

I wrap my arms around myself and keep my head down, cutting through the botanical gardens, hurrying along, trying to get a little blood pumping. Being hungry is making me even colder, but I can't eat while walking, and I can't stop yet.

I'm looking down at the yellowish paving that weaves between the lawns, so I don't see the man before we collide, my shoulder smashing painfully into his chest. I get a face full of sweaty warmth and something else, a very male perfume, maybe a designer scent. Smells have always affected me strongly, but not the usual: I can handle sewage, sickness, death, and decay. I can't bear lilacs. The smell of snow is the worst. The smell of this man is a jolt through the center of my body; my mind recoils from it, horrified at how basic it is, how raw and visceral.

I splutter out an apology and keep walking. My shoulder is more painful than it should be, and moving my arm is difficult. Feels like something is wrong.

"Hey," the man says, following.

I pretend I don't hear him. My body is reacting now, adrenaline pumping, getting ready to escape. He's scaring me.

"Hey, stop," he says, louder. There are other people in the park. I can sense their heads popping up, swiveling like meerkats, seeking out the drama. I don't want to cause a scene, so I slow a little and half turn in his direction. As he gets closer, I can see white trainers with a silver design on the side, and neat white socks pulled up under dark blue joggers, slightly too short for him in the way that could either be fashionable or a mistake. I let my eyes rise as high as his chest, where I read the words "British Army" in small, embroidered letters on his T-shirt.

"Sorry about that," I say, trying to force my voice to be friendly. "I wasn't looking where I was going. You okay?"

"Me?" he asks, like it's the stupidest question he's ever heard. "I'm fine. I was worried about you. I hit you pretty hard there. Are you okay?"

He's searching out my eyes. I look anywhere but at his face, touch my patch to make sure it's there. There's no way I want to see how this man, this soldier, will die. If he's going to some war-torn place with the army, full of mines and snipers with guns, then his death might be sudden or drawn-out and painful. Either way it will be violent. I don't want to see it, to have the trauma of it in my mind.

He asks, "Is your arm hurt?"

I realize I'm holding my left arm with the right, cradling it, and at this comment I let it hang down. The pain is immediate, shooting from my shoulder to my wrist. I draw breath in sharply, and he moves, lunges for me, tries to get hold of the arm, for what reason I don't know, but I'm not going to let him touch me. The memory of what Leather-Jacket did is fresh in my mind. I step backward away from him, nearly falling over as my feet tangle themselves together.

He catches me in his arms.

"Whoa, there," he says, but the way he's caught me has shifted my eye patch. I try not to look him in the eyes—I don't think I do, and yet it comes, the vision, rolling over me like a wave with the unstoppable force of an ocean behind it.

There's a road. It's nighttime, not too cold, perhaps in summer. In the dimness the soldier is propped up on his elbows on the ground, trying to get up, looking up at me. I see a knife, dripping with blood. I see his shocked face, draining white. My hand opens and I drop the knife, step away, the sound of it clanging on the tarmac. The soldier falls back onto the ground, his elbows splaying sideways. I smell alcohol, and blood. His eyes glaze over as he dies. Then there are headlights, speeding toward us. In the vision I turn and run, not knowing where I'm going. I keep running until I can feel my lungs burning, until my legs won't go any further. I fall to my knees, try to catch my breath. I can hear sirens, police cars, getting closer. I try to get up and away, but there are people surrounding me, crowding in, concern turning to something more serious when they see my bloody clothes and realize it's not my blood. Someone gets hold of my arms and I scream. The vision fades, the sound of the scream and the siren the last thing to go.

I killed him. No, that's not right: *I will kill him.*

This is absurd, sick, wrong. I'm not a murderer.

"Are you okay?" It's a woman's voice. Just like in the vision, people surround me, looking down with concern. I'm upright, sitting cross-legged on the pavement. I haven't blacked out, only zoned out for a while. My shoulder hurts terribly. I hold my good hand up to my face and am surprised that it's clean. In the vision both hands were drenched in blood. The smell of it is still inside my head, thick and coppery. But it hasn't happened yet. That scene is yet to come, and no matter how unbelievable it is to me, there must be a chain of events already in motion that leads to this man's death, to me stabbing him.

The soldier helps me to my feet, and when I'm standing up I double-check my eye patch, now back in place, then try to smile in a reassuring manner at the strangers who have stopped.

"I'm completely fine," I say. "I just get a bit dizzy sometimes."

A young person walks past holding a smartphone and staring at me, and I think, *I need to get out of here.*

"I'll take you home," says the soldier, but I want to get away from him more than anything else. My brain is working overtime—why would I want to kill this man? *What will he do?*

"No," I say, walking away, trying to put some space in between us. "No, thanks."

Panic rushes through me, and I see my chance, a cut-through, a gap in the hedgerow at the edge of the park, leading to the high street. I make a sharp turn and start to run away.

He follows me for a while, saying, "Stop!," that he wants to help, that I need help.

I don't stop. Heavy, rhythmic footsteps keep pace with mine, get closer, nearly catch me up, so I dart left, causing a woman with a buggy to shout, "Watch it!" and then I'm out of the park and sprinting across three lanes of traffic. Cars slam on their brakes, horns blast at me, but I dodge side to side and keep going. I head for a large pharmacy and hurry to the far end of an aisle, where I can hide. I edge out to see through the big window to the park beyond. He's coming across the road but looking left and right. He didn't see where I went, doesn't know where I am. I pray he won't guess which shop I'm in.

The gum-chewing assistant doesn't like the look of me. "You gonna buy anything?"

I'm sweating, and breathing heavily, wide-eyed with fear. I gather a few items without checking what they are and stand by the till, watching the soldier retreat to the park, start walking away. When he turns his back, I shove the things I've picked up onto the nearest shelf and run out of the store without stopping to apologize.

In the street, all I can hear is my own panicked breath, my heart pounding, my feet hitting the pavement in a chaotic pattern. It's not until I reach the bus stop, panting and overheating, that I think properly about the man, the soldier, how physically fit he was compared to me, and how he could have done anything to me if he'd caught me. As the bus pulls up and the doors open, I sense that safety is close. There was something about that man's voice that sounded a warning in me, that spoke of danger.

I don't look at the driver when I get on the bus, just tap my card and keep moving. Eyes down, I sink into the nearest seat and turn my face to the window. And that's when I see the soldier again, standing on the pavement across the street, framed by the trees behind him in the park. He has his hands on his hips, and he's scanning the passengers on the bus, looking for me. His face makes me afraid the way his voice did, and as my eyes take him in properly, I feel like I might know him, that I should know his name, but I can't place him. I just have this feeling I've seen him somewhere. Then I know: he's the man in the tent the night Amir collapsed. I never saw his face then, but his head shape, the way his ears stick out slightly, it's definitely him.

And I think he's been in the crowd too, and other places, other nights, different grounds. Betsy saw him when I was running the ride. More than once, he's been there. My mind starts placing him everywhere, in crowd scenes, at the periphery, in the audiences we've had all summer. I feel like he's been watching me for months. And for some reason I don't yet understand, I'm going to kill him. The horror of that knowledge, I can't assimilate it. Perhaps there's nothing I can do to stop it happening, but I don't have to accept it. I will not. If I stay away from him, it can't happen. There must be a chance to change the outcome.

I duck my head, but it's too late. He's seen me on the bus. He's weaving through traffic in my direction, horns are blaring, and the bus doors are still open as another passenger is getting on. Just a few seconds more and we'll be gone. He's only steps away, a car's width.

I can see he's tried to dash across the road but is having to wait for a line of impatient cars who won't let him cross, and he's getting more and more angry, starting to shout. The bus door shuts, and I hear the clunk of the auto-locking system and the engine's swell as we move off from the curb. I'm so grateful I want to kiss the driver as she edges us into traffic and away, leaving the man still stranded between lanes, waving his open hand in the air in a gesture of frustration.

CHAPTER

18

NOW
Faith

It's mid-morning when I arrive at the ground. I've never been late to a pull-down, and the feeling isn't good. Most of the wagons are lined up, ready to go, the matching colors of the Harrington's branding like the contents of a child's toy box made life-size.

On the field there are shapes in the grass, brown patches trodden at the edges by hundreds of eager feet. The circus tent has left one huge circle bordered by rectangles, ghosts of the entranceways and the backstage area, a physical reminder of the circus that will fade in the days to come. All the food stands have been dismantled, packed away into their transport, ready to be built up again at the next town. Everything, in fact, has been dealt with except for my ride. The Waltzer sits to one side of the green like a big jellyfish on a deserted beach, no longer surrounded by the rest of the carnival. Most of the perimeter fencing is gone, with the last few sections being loaded on as I walk up.

"Hey, lads," I call. "Can you make a start here soon?"

Calum stops what he's doing for a moment, clocking that I've come back, but they're busy with the fence. I wait for a while before I walk over.

"Did you hear what I said? I need you to pull the Waltzer down." I'm annoyed they haven't already begun. Maybe they didn't know I was with Mum, but they could have worked it out. Why should it matter where I was? They could have called, they could have started without me.

Calum eyes me with barely disguised contempt. "Sorry," he says. "We're done for the day. You should have gotten here earlier."

I look around. Just me, my ride, my wagon, and the two big trucks that carry the Waltzer are left.

"What are you talking about? How can you be done for the day? Do you not see all of this?" I wave an arm at all the equipment and vehicles.

Calum helps one of the chaps to put the final section of fencing on the back of the van and taps the passenger window so that the driver pulls away. At the entrance to the field, the bigger trucks are firing up engines, ready to roll. He looks at me, his eyebrows raised in a challenge.

I'm confused. "What?"

"If you don't know, I'm not going to tell you."

He shrugs and starts to walk away. The rest of the crew still on the ground don't even glance in my direction. One of our transits, driven by a chap called Phil, is coming our way across the field, and Calum's crew jump inside without looking back. My cousin gets in the passenger side.

The doors on the van shut. Calum turns his head away as it accelerates toward the road.

"Hey," I yell, but they are already too far away to hear me.

I stand there for a second, wondering what just happened, still holding my arm where it aches from colliding with the man in the park. Mike's not here, probably went hours ago with the first wagon. He'll be directing the pull-on in the next town; Christine too. I find my phone and dial his number. No answer. Engines growl across the field. They're going to leave without me. How could they do that? I can't think of a time anyone has been left behind. I've never heard of it.

Amara will help, or she'll get Mike. I dial her number and wait, listening to the phone ringing out. Who else? Christine doesn't answer either, and I know then that they are doing it on purpose. All the live-in wagons used for the acts are long gone, but I can't imagine any of the circus artists would have helped. There's no one left.

I don't want to cry. I absolutely won't.

"Hey, babe." It's Betsy, half-jogging across the field to me. I wonder if she's slept since her shift ended. "Are you okay? I've been waiting for you. I saw the video."

"The what?"

"The video. You haven't have seen it?"

"I don't know what you're talking about. I've been at Home Farm with Mum."

She takes my phone and clicks onto a video-sharing site, then holds it so I can see. The video is captioned: "Carnival girl tells Joey Standish his future—TOTALLY WILD."

I immediately know, without even seeing the footage, why Calum and possibly the entire Harrington's community is pissed off with me today. I don't want to see it, but at the same time I can't tear my eyes away. Someone uploaded it seconds after it happened, and it's got more than five thousand views. Leather-jacket man, who is apparently Joey Standish, is more than a little famous, as I suspected. A contestant on a reality show, he's a presenter on various TV programs I don't have time to watch. He'll be even more famous now, if that's possible, for what happens in the video.

I watch the whole thing in disbelief. I know it's me in the footage, but I don't remember any of it, any of what I said to him or any of the people who were standing around, bearing witness to it. I'm so shaken that when it ends, I accidentally drop the phone in the grass, and Betsy bends to pick it up. I feel winded, like I've taken a sucker punch to the gut. For a moment I can't speak.

"Did I . . .?"

She nods. "You told him how he would die."

"In front of . . ."

"All those people." Betsy's eyes are full of compassion. She knows what this will mean for me.

I'm panicking. I don't want it to be true. What have I done? I need to see it again.

On screen, Joey Standish is retching into a bucket while other people snigger. He finishes throwing up, and I can be heard saying, "Another go-round?"

I don't come across well—I'm smug and annoying. He stands up and puts a foot outside the car, loses his footing, and his arm flies out so that he hits me in the face. The crowd takes a collective gasp, but on the screen it looks like it genuinely wasn't deliberate, even though I know it was, I am certain he meant to do it. My patch has flown off, and he's apologizing profusely, over and over, checking my face, asking if I'm all right. Then I look directly into his eyes and say something to him that makes his face turn white.

The camera is turned around. A grinning face fills the screen and starts to give a commentary.

"Hey, fans! Can you believe what you just saw? It's Joey Standish, yes, *the* Joey Standish, and he got spun so fast on the Waltzer that he . . . what is it?"

Whoever he's with is nudging him, alerting him that the drama isn't over, that something else is happening.

The camera pans back to me. I've got Standish's face in my hands, and I'm still gazing into his eyes.

Someone off-camera hisses, "The eye patch girl—she just said she could *see his death*."

I remember the moment he hit me, the moment my eye patch fell, but nothing after that. Nothing of this. I was inside the vision, completely gone. On the screen I look like a different person, eyes wide, scars on show. What I say to him is only just audible over the music, over the sound of his girlfriend yelling at me.

"Hey, get off him, you freak!" She tries to move my hands, but I'm holding on tight to his face.

"It's okay, babe," Joey says. "She's going to predict my future. I want to hear it." He's laughing.

I'm stiff and straight, my own face and hands vibrating with tension.

"I can see exactly how you'll die," I say. I'm half whispering, half hissing the words. "I can see it in your eyes—it's your destiny."

Joey glances at the camera. He knows he's being filmed, has known it since before he swiped at me. He is all smiles and charm, but now he's becoming uncomfortable; it's not going the way he thought it would. He puts his hands on mine, either side of his face. The pose looks quite intimate. "Sorry," he says. "I'm sorry, darling—I never meant to hurt you. I feel terrible. Let's start over, shall we?"

In the dancing lights, my face is demonic. "You don't have very long."

The person holding the camera says, "What did she say?"

My voice, hissing. "There's a river, some rocks. It's sunny. There's no one there to help you. You drown."

Ricky's great bulk appears in silhouette against the lights behind us. "Okay, kids, that's enough." He takes my hands off Joey's face, puts himself between us, turns me around, and walks me away so that I disappear off camera. I'm docile, like a zombie—just after that must have been when I collapsed.

Joey walks right up to the screen, running his fingers through his hair repeatedly, as if he's agitated or in need of a comb. "Did you hear what she said? That was insane." He's laughing. "I was not expecting to have my death foretold tonight, but there we are." He grins and holds up a hand in farewell, then ducks sideways, out of shot.

The screen is filled with the first man's face. "You heard it here first, folks. What a night! Like and subscribe for more exclusive content."

The video ends abruptly.

The fact that I don't remember any of this won't be good enough for the Harrington's cast and crew. The fact that my patch came off by accident won't matter either. Not even what he did to me, before I gave him the spinning that started it all off. None of it will matter to them—only that I broke the rules again. Only that I read that man's fortune, predicted his death, and by so doing tainted the carnival or whatever superstitious notion they've got.

How stupid of me to have thought that because only Amara and Ricky were there, only they would know. This video changes everything, changes my life, starting now. Of course everyone in the company would have found out eventually. I just never thought *everyone* would include, you know, the world. And I never thought it would happen as quickly as it has.

At eleven years old, before Billy let us travel again I had signed the constitution, promising never to engage in "inappropriate activities" when working on the carnival. At the top of that list is fortune-telling. When I signed it, I effectively swore I would never talk about anyone's future death while I was working. With Amir it was different: I broke the rules for a good reason. But with Leather-Jacket I wasn't in control. It was reflex, a response to something he did to me. And now everything is ruined. Calum has judged me. I imagine Mike and Christine have too, and that's why they're not here, why they won't pick up the phone. I barely recognize myself in the footage, I was so intense. I'm frightened by the fact that I lost time. I thought that had stopped happening. I feel weak with the dizzying sense that I'm losing control of my mind, and with it, control of everything.

I turn to Betsy. "I don't remember any of that. He touched me up, Betsy, and he hit me. Look— I have bruises, a scratch, but none of it is on the video, I—"

"I know," she says.

"Is this why they're being like this? Mike and Christine and Calum? Because of that?"

She looks over at the wagons rolling off the green, the rest lined up and ready at the back end of the retreating van, all of the company ignoring me.

"Those bastards," she says. We both turn to the ride, all eleven tons of it, all its moving parts, its heavy iron up-stands, the roof, the lighting and sound rigs. The twelve heavy cars needing a winch to load them onto the carrier. The wooden boards that took three young lads to sledgehammer in place. Two lorry loads in all, plus the trailer we live in.

Betsy says, "Let's not make it easy for them."

"What do you mean?"

"We can do it. Come on." She throws her handbag down on the grass and marches up to the ride. "Tell me where to start. You know what to do, right?"

I know exactly how the ride goes down and away, but it took a crew of five to set it up.

"I don't know, Betsy."

"How hard can it be?" she says.

We don't have a choice but to try. I climb up and engage the winch that's attached to the car truck. As I do so, a flash of pain zigzags down my arm.

"What's up with you?" asks Betsy.

I grit my teeth. My shoulder feels wrong. It must be sprained, possibly broken. I tell myself I can cope. I'll have to. "Nothing."

She presses two pills into my hand. "Take these."

"But aren't they for emergencies?" I say.

"I have more. You need it today—don't think about it."

I swallow the pills and we get to work.

Three hours later, the van comes back. Calum climbs out of the vehicle and watches me for a few minutes. I'm covered in sweat and oil, my injured arm tucked into my jeans to stop me jarring it. I'm determined not to show how upset I am with him for abandoning us.

"Oh," I say. "It's you." I push the section of board into its place on the second truck, unclip the wire on the crane, and turn for the next one.

"You need a hand?" Calum says, and I hear that his voice is cold and flat.

Inside the van are several of the chaps, I can see them watching me from behind glass. I'm more disappointed in them for leaving me than I am in Calum. The boys in the van, local lads, have been taking my money for years, every time we pull on and build up, every time we pull down. They don't get involved in family stuff—or they never have before.

"Where've you been?" I ask, clipping the wire to the next section. The drugs have taken the edge off, and I feel like I'm floating up here, but my shoulder is throbbing, my left arm useless. I must look ridiculous.

"What's wrong with your arm?"

"What do you care?"

Betsy shouts, "Who are you talking to?" from the other side of the booth, where she's been using an electric wrench to loosen bolts.

"Just my cousin," I say. "He's come to . . ." I turn to Calum, narrow my eyes. "What have to come to do? Apologize? Help?" I turn and shout over my shoulder to Betsy. "He's running very fucking late for either, if you ask me."

She makes a barely audible sound that translates as deeply unimpressed.

"You do want us to help, don't you?" says Calum. He's folded his arms. One of the chaps still lounging in the van rolls down the window, sparks up a cigarette.

I want to yell at him, *"Of course we bloody well do—look at us. We'll be here all day."* There's another part of me that wants to yell at him to go away, to shove his help up his arse.

"I dunno if I do."

"Fine, we'll go." Calum takes three quick strides around to the driver's door.

"No! Stop. I mean, yeah, I do want help."

"Yes, what?" Calum smiles, a mean smile I've not seen on him before.

It takes me almost all my strength to respond. "Yes, please."

"The rates have gone up, that's all."

"Don't be stupid," I say. "We set the rates. Good rates. No one has ever complained."

"If you're not willing to pay the new rates, then I don't reckon we'll help you." He turns again and starts to walk off. If nothing else, I need two of the chaps to drive my trucks to the next site. Three, maybe, as I'm not sure I can drive the motor home with this arm. I'll be nice, play nice, for now, but as soon as I can get hold of Mike, this crew is gone. He'll agree with me that they are totally out of order—I'm pretty sure of that. But in this moment, I can't risk losing them.

"Wait," I say. "How much do you want?"

He tells me. It's nearly all the takings from this week. Triple what I paid them for the buildup on Monday. I don't say anything, my mouth hanging open. Then I nod once and hand him the winch controller. He calls to the chaps, and they all pile out of the van. None of them look at me.

When we arrive at the next town and pull onto the football pitch, it's getting dark. I want to find Mike and shout at him, but no one will tell me where he is. Calum and one of the chaps park up the two Waltzer trucks, and I park up behind them in the wagon. Usually we would set up near the rest of the company, but I can't face any of them right now. I imagine they can't face me either, if they've seen that video. Night is falling and the field is almost silent, just a couple of radios competing with each other from somewhere in the living area.

I go to find Macha and see that he's been stabled with the rest of the circus horses, as if he isn't mine anymore. I reach a hand into his stall and rub his nose, promise to ride him as soon as I can. He nuzzles into me, and it's comforting to know that at least someone is on my side. It goes without saying that whatever the members of the company think about me, they will take excellent care of my boy. At Harrington's the animals are treated with the utmost respect, regardless of who officially owns them. They get better care and attention than the children in some cases, and the adults in most.

Back at the wagon, I take a walk around my vehicles, to check all is well and secure. Calum climbs from the cab of my truck and holds out his hand, flat. He states the amount he's expecting.

"That's even more than you said earlier!"

"What can I say? Inflation."

"You can't do this to me. You're not in charge. Mike can fire you."

"He could, yes. Go ask him if he's planning to do that, why don't you?"

But I'm too tired to argue, too spent, in too much pain. I just want to sleep. Calum thinks he's got the power. Maybe I should let him think that, for the moment.

"Why are you being like this?" I ask. "What happened to the family code?"

He sets his lips in a line. "You're the one who broke it, not me. Twice in as many weeks. Once could be a mistake, but twice seems deliberate. Like you plan to keep doing it."

"Last night wasn't on purpose. Not that I should have to explain myself to you, but what you saw in that video isn't the whole truth."

He shrugs. "Just don't like it, that's all. All that mumbo jumbo."

"You don't even care what the truth is, do you?"

"Reminds me too much of what happened to your brother. I think I deserve danger money, being close to that. It's just business, the way I see it. Insurance."

He thrusts his hand toward me again. Without speaking, I reach into my money belt and count out a figure that might break me.

"What about the buildup tomorrow?" I ask. "Is that included?"

He laughs. "No. It'll be the same again."

"But . . ."

"You can get someone else, if you want."

This is stupid, and we both know it. *There isn't anyone else.*

The first drops fall as I reach the trailer, and I go inside quickly to avoid a soaking. Betsy is gone and I feel desperately lonely without her. I'm hungry and exhausted, so I eat half of the mushy, hours-old sandwich I bought that morning, and drink a glass of milk at the counter before heading for bed. In moments, I'm asleep.

The violence of the dream wakes me with a jolt. I lie there shaking, the images raw and visceral, still running through my mind. I was in the lake at the old Home Farm, inside the dream of Tommy, only it was the leather-jacket man drowning. The water was dark under the snow-covered ice, but I could see his bare chest, his shorts I saw earlier. The struggle against the weeds and the cold, so like what happened with Tommy and Peter. In the man's eyes I saw it from outside of him, but in the dream it was as if I was him, the way it was with Tommy. I felt his hopelessness, his anger at losing his life in that lonely way. So quick, submerged in the hostile environment, but not quick enough that he didn't feel it, every second, that he didn't have enough time to think about the things he would never do, the places he would never visit. In the dream I felt the fear that coursed through him as he tried to get back to the surface. I heard him choking on the water as he cried out for his mother. I tasted the muddy water as it filled his lungs. The worst moment was when he realized he could do nothing to save himself. He had struggled as hard as he could. But then he gave up. The last few seconds were eerily calm before the darkness came.

And there was something I never saw in the dream of Tommy, that I know didn't happen, that my brain has conjured to punish me: As he let go and started to drift, his eyes rested on something caught on the lakebed. An old silver chain, tangled around a ring with a green stone.

The clock tells me it's almost four. I swing my legs out of bed and feel around on the floor for my slippers. The curtains squeak when they open onto the dark sky, tinted orange by the streetlights surrounding the ground.

CHAPTER

19

BEFORE

FAITH AND HER mother had been alone at Home Farm for a few weeks since the carnival left them behind, and both of them were going more than a little stir-crazy.

The days were long and dull, rolling out endlessly in front of them as they tried to learn, in their own individual way, how to endure the long wait for the circus to return. On the wall of her room, Faith had a calendar where she crossed off each day as it passed, but it didn't help. Her mother told her when she put it up that it wasn't a good idea, that she ought to try and forget about the time rather than focus on it, so the act of crossing the days off had become something she did simply to avoid telling her mother she was right. It was as if they had been locked up together in a cell, unable to escape, so that every tiny thing that annoyed them about the other was magnified into something infuriating.

As a result, Faith began to spend most of her time away from Home Farm, just her and her horse, riding in the fields and along the riverside. It wasn't only to get away from her mother: she needed the movement, the feeling of travel, even if every night she returned to the same place to sleep, like a house-dwelling person. Riding every day was better than nothing. She knew that without it her mind started to spin out in a way that felt dangerous.

Everything in her life reminded her of Tommy, from his empty bedroom to the landscape, the woods, and the lake. After a few weeks she saw that it was pointless to try to avoid the places that hurt her heart the most, because she'd worked out pretty quickly where the pain was located. It wasn't out there, in the landscape—not even in the water that took her brother's life. It was inside her. She visited those places in her mind and in her dreams, whether she wanted to or not. So she visited them in the daytime now, and each time she found it easier not to dwell on what had happened there.

She hadn't seen Samuel since that day. One morning Macha started off in the direction of the housing estate where he lived, and she let him lead the way. They crossed the common toward the houses. She'd never seen it in the spring, the grass high and pale with new growth, and she thought she might not recognize the place where he lived, but she soon found herself staring at the entrance where Samuel had occasionally tried to get her to go through into his house. The long wall with the faded blue gate ran along the back of the terrace. Each house had originally had a gate leading straight onto the marshy grassland, though many of the owners had long since bricked up the gaps. It was too easy for strangers to sneak around behind the houses, especially at night.

At the end of the season, when the circus had only been back for a few days, she and Tommy hadn't quite got the measure of Samuel and Peter, of exactly how demanding they could be. It had seemed exciting at first to have new house-dwelling friends who were so keen to hang out. It hadn't become claustrophobic immediately for Tommy, or creepy for Faith, so when invited, they had both gone through this gate. But only that one time.

Inside they had found it to be a very clean, neat little place, Samuel and Peter's mother overly attentive to the point of nervousness, fluttering here and there, offering drinks and wringing her hands. They'd each had a can of cold orange fizz and sat politely chatting, but Faith had panicked when Samuel stood up and announced he was taking his friends up to his room. Her gut had told her not to go. Tommy saved her, saying it was time for them both to leave, and thank you very much for the drink. They'd practically run out the door into the fresh air. She'd thought at the time it was the "houseness" of it, the smell, the hard floors and great glass windows. Looking back, she thinks it might have been a growing feeling of unease, that she just wanted to get away from Samuel. He had been angry at her, his face turning red as he yelled from the gate that she wasn't welcome anyway, but the next day he'd been waiting at the yard, full of apologies. It would turn out that neither Samuel nor his brother were very good at taking no for an answer.

When she reached the gate, she slid from Macha's back and left him chewing on some grass while she crept closer. There was a knothole just below eye level, and she stooped to look through. She expected to see his mother at the kitchen window, or maybe Samuel himself, busy killing insects in the garden. But the house was dark, nothing moving. She scanned to the left and saw something shocking: the words "KILLER KID" sprayed in yellow on the glass double doors. She saw that the glass was cracked, that rocks lay on the patio where they must have bounced off the surface of the doors. Taking a step back, she noticed one of the upstairs windows open, curtains blowing in the wind.

Faith shivered despite her warm layers. The sun went behind a cloud, turning the day dreary. She turned to swing up onto Macha's back and rode straight back to the yard.

When she got there, she found a car she hadn't seen before, parked up near to the wagon. Inside, there was her mother, seated with a woman in a suit jacket with a lanyard around her neck, an ID like a police officer might wear, or a social worker. They were sitting at the little fold-out table, an untouched cup of tea in front of each of them.

"Here she is," said Mum. "We were just talking about you."

Faith looked at the strange woman from the corner of her eye. She wondered if it was something to do with Samuel. "Why?"

"I'm Joan, from the county council. Education Department."

"I'm homeschooled," said Faith. She knew what to say; she'd had this conversation before. On the road, the education people sometimes dropped by. They were usually fairly friendly, and they usually went away without asking too many questions. The carnival kids could read, and they could count and do basic math. Science and engineering were learned on the job. What else would they need? They were being trained for something elite, something specialized. As adults they would have rare skills, and the education people usually got it. This one, however, seemed concerned.

"I'm in charge of alternative provision in the local area, so I know that you're here in the winter."

"Being homeschooled," said Mum.

"Indeed. I haven't noticed you here before, in the spring. You and your mum usually work the carnival, don't you?"

"Not this year," said Iris. "We're having a break."

Joan, the county council lady, gave Iris sympathetic eyes. "I heard about your son, Tommy. Tragic. I'm so sorry for your loss."

Faith walked past them, took a couple of steps toward her bedroom. "Can I go?"

"Wait," said Iris. "I need to talk to you about something first."

"What?" From the way her mother shifted in her seat, she suspected she wasn't going to like it, whatever it was.

"Joan here thinks you should go to school."

"School?" Faith is more surprised than anything else. She's never even thought about going to school. It simply hasn't entered her mind. "What for?"

Joan laughed. "To learn things you can't learn at home."

"Like what?"

Joan said, "Well, lots of things. Actually, that's not the only reason. Like your mum says, you're going to be here for a year, perhaps more."

Iris cut in. "No, I said a year at the most. After that things will be normal again."

Joan nodded sympathetically. "But it's going to be hard for both of you, socially, isn't it? Maybe school would be an opportunity to make some new friends."

Faith thought of Samuel and Peter, and how well that had turned out. "No, thank you."

Mum said, "I'm really sorry, Faith, but you don't get to choose."

"What?"

"I'll be away working in the daytime. I can't leave you on your own."

"Why can't you?"

Apparently there was some rule or law or something that meant she couldn't allow it, not now that the education people had her in their sights. The next week, Iris took Faith into town to shop for a school uniform. Faith tried on the gray polyester skirt, with extremely bad grace.

On her first day, Faith was shown into a room full of children around her own age. She could feel some of them eyeing her with interest, some of them with contempt. She sat next to a girl who looked friendly at first, but when the teacher turned her back, the girl moved away a few inches, wrinkling her nose and waving a hand in front of her face as if Faith might smell bad. Three other girls were watching this. They all pinched their noses and wafted hands in front of their faces while the teacher wrote on the board. Several other kids stifled giggles, and Faith knew that school was not going to be fun. At all. She'd been there less than half an hour.

At break time the girls danced around her, chanting songs they'd made up about what kind of person they thought Faith was, and why that kind of person was inferior to the kind of people they were. Mostly it was pretty basic, having to do with the fact that she lived in a wagon in a yard and hadn't ever been to school, but there were personal insinuations too, about her body, her hair, her hygiene. Baseless but hurtful, nonetheless. Faith had a fairly thick skin from being a performer, but could stomach this treatment for only so long. They laughed and danced around her as if she were a maypole. The ribbons of their taunts pulled tighter and tighter. She stuck her fingers in her ears, but she could still hear it. She tried to warn them in language anyone could understand.

"I wouldn't do that," she said, her eyes on the graveled playground. "I really wouldn't. Please stop now."

"Ha ha ha ha," they laughed horribly. "She's telling us what to do. Smelly yard girl thinks she can boss us around. She's so funny."

Without warning, Faith rammed her way out of the circle of skipping girls, headfirst. She wanted to get away, far away, but the school had a high wall that even she couldn't climb, and locked gates. They chased her, these children, like a pack of devils, possessed. Faith backed into the fence, covered her eyes with one hand, wrapped her arm over her head to block out the noise of the laughter, the taunts. They got closer, too close.

"Don't touch me," she muttered. "Don't you dare."

A dinner lady eventually approached at the moment when Faith thought she could take no more, that she would have to fight back if it went on a second longer. The woman was just in time; she was going to save Faith, to give these bitches what they deserved, make them stop, punish them. She felt like throwing her arms around this grown-up and kissing her. Then the dinner lady asked, "Are you all okay?" and one of the meanest girls linked arms with Faith, smiled sweetly, and said, "We're just playing a game. Aren't we?"

It was too much. Faith looked at her then. Properly, right in the eyes. "I know how you're going to die," she said, the cruelty of revenge swelling within her, twisting her mouth into a smile.

"What?"

"You won't be that old. No one will be there with you. Very lonely. You've got some kind of disease."

"What did she say?" asked another of the mean girls, her voice full of uncertainty. Faith stepped up and looked her in the eye too.

"Uh-oh," she said. "Yours is a car crash. You won't even be twenty. Bleeding out on the side of a road. No more of you, all gone, goodnight." Faith laughed coldly.

"Oh my god," said the girl. "She's a freak!"

They all backed away from her, even the grown-up. "I know how you'll all die," Faith yelled. "I can see it." She rushed up to each of the mean girls in turn, staring in their eyes, calling out their fate, one after the other: "You'll die in hospital; you'll choke to death at a restaurant; you'll die at home."

She ran at one of the bigger girls, grabbed her, and the two of them tumbled to the ground in a heap. "Lung cancer," she whispered, and the girl burst into tears.

Faith was only half aware of being pulled away from the playground, and back inside the building, by strong adult hands. The dinner lady was behind her, a hand on her back, guiding her fiercely toward the headteacher's office, where she was pushed unceremoniously into a chair and told to stay put. She was spent, all her anger gone. She sank gratefully into the chair and smiled to herself. There was no way the school would keep her after this.

She learned that her mother had been called, which wiped the smile from her face as she knew that would cause trouble for Iris. It was only the second week in her new job. The shop she was running would need to close because her mother was the only employee. Faith hoped her mother's boss was understanding.

In the meantime, the headteacher wanted a word, so Faith stood up and went through into the wood-paneled office.

"Look at me, Faith Harrington."

The headteacher used a tone Faith had only heard people use when training dogs. Pack animals needed a firm hand, but Faith did not. She stared at the buttons on the teacher's cardigan.

"I don't think that's a good idea, Miss."

"I said, 'Look. At. Me.'"

Faith wondered if this woman was as angry as she sounded. She hoped not. Faith couldn't be that angry all day long; it would be exhausting. As a performer herself, she suspected it was an act, an illusion designed to control the children, because she had seen the headteacher do it before, to great effect, for a much lesser crime than telling all the girls in year six exactly how they were going to die. This was the first time she'd had the woman's full attention since she arrived at the school. She knew she was supposed to be frightened, to give in, to apologize for what she'd done. But it was no different, what this adult was doing to her now, towering over her, shouting at her to comply, from what those girls were doing. The feeling was the same as when she had been in the playground. Bullying, plain and simple.

"I am looking at you," Faith said, continuing to stare at the buttons. Something shifted in Miss Berwick's composure and Faith thought, *Well, if she wasn't genuinely angry before, she is now.*

The teacher grabbed Faith by the chin and forced her face upward. Their eyes met, and the room fell away.

CHAPTER

20

NOW
Betsy

DAWN HAS BURST into early morning, and the buildup has begun, everywhere but in Faith's corner of the ground.

Faith, who looks as if she's hardly slept, goes out to find Calum. She returns after a few minutes, slams the wagon door, and paces up and down, cradling her injured arm. Every step reverberates loudly in the small space.

"He wants paying before he gets the chaps to start work."

"Do you have the money?" asks Betsy.

"No. I gave him everything yesterday, from the takings. I had to pay Mum's nurses too, so now I have nothing. I emptied my account."

"What about Mike? Does he know what's going on?"

"I couldn't find him."

Betsy says, "Let's look a bit harder, then. He needs to know what's happening in his own carnival. He needs to do something about it."

Outside, the ground is alive with activity. Faith and Betsy walk past members of the build crew as they work, and the chaps move out of the way, their eyes sliding past Faith. It's like she's got a force field around her. They are repelled by it. Faith slips easily into the feeling, donning it like an old jacket she is being coerced into wearing again. It covers her completely, that tainted feeling, and her ten-year-old self is so close to the surface she feels like bursting into tears, like a child.

Calum spots them coming. Leaning on one of the sledgehammers they use to knock the metal poles into place, he points his chin at Faith. "Ready to pay, are you?"

She shakes her head. "I'll pay you after. Like usual."

"No can do, I'm afraid."

"There isn't time for this, Calum."

"You know it. Need to get started soon or you won't be up and ready for the opening tonight. Imagine losing out on all the takings."

"Fuck you, Calum. I'm putting a stop to this right now." She walks past him, in the direction of Mike's wagon.

He swings the sledgehammer up to his shoulder, catches up with them, falls into step, lowers his voice. "I'm being generous here, Faith. No one wants to go anywhere near you at the moment. You're lucky it's me in charge of the build, or I reckon they would refuse to do it at all, even with the extra money."

"You don't get paid first. You get paid after."

"If you're finding it difficult, maybe it's a great idea to talk to Uncle Mike. Maybe he'll lend you the money."

People scatter as they travel across the ground at speed, a straight line like an arrow, making no allowances for those sauntering to and fro with bits of tent in their arms. Faith says, "This is stupid, and you know it. It's always work first, pay after. That's if you do a good job. The crew are only doing this because you're letting them. Do they even know about it?"

"Nothing to do with me. My hands are tied," he says, shrugging.

She marches across the last section of showground, to the door of Mike's wagon, where she knocks three times, hard. "Mike. Open up."

The door cracks open, showing a portion of his old, bald face. "Oh," he says. "It's you."

"Are you aware of what's going on?" she yells at him. "It's fucking extortion, that's what."

"Faith, calm down."

She gestures at Calum, who is still smirking. "Yesterday, he was going to leave the ride on the old ground. He blackmailed me into paying three times the going rate. Now he's saying he wants that much again, or he won't build up. Tell him he can't do this to me."

Still looking through the crack in the door, Mike says, "I can't."

"What?"

"I tried already. The lads are saying they won't work for the old rates if they have to work with you."

"That's not true. It can't be. Which one of them said it? Why are they still working for us at all? Why haven't you fired the lot of them?"

"Calum's just charging the rate they agreed. After that video, they . . . well. They want the money up front. I was going to chat to you about it, but I—"

"Oh, you were?"

"Don't get shirty with me. You're the one in the wrong here. I was busy all night with the pull-down and everything, and then we had a big thing with the drainage that I had to sort out. I just left it to Calum to explain." He gave Calum a sharp look. "I was hoping he would be tactful."

"Of course I was."

"No, he fucking well wasn't." Faith puts both hands to the sides of her head. "Are you telling me that this is going ahead? That I have to find this stupid amount of money, and you think it's just fine?"

"I didn't think about it much, to be honest. I had other things to think about. Like handling the fallout of what you did to Joey Standish."

"What I . . ." She shakes her head, like there's no point trying to explain again.

Mike says, "Look, if you can't pay, I could help you out. Lend you—"

She snaps, "I don't need more credit. I can manage."

Faith turns on her heel and starts marching back to the wagon. Calum follows like a yappy little dog that Betsy wishes she could kick.

"How about this," he says. "I can probably get the lads to build you up today if you promise the money will be with me really soon."

Faith reaches the wagon door and yanks it open. "You're taking the piss, Calum. I know this is you, not the lads."

He doesn't miss a beat. "Market forces, mate, what can I tell you?"

"Tell me you don't need all that money, and you don't need anything right now, for a start."

"Oh, wait, here's a thought. I've got an idea that might solve all our problems."

"What?"

"Sell the ride to me, along with the traveling rights."

"Sell it? You're joking," says Faith. "I only just bought it."

"I'll let you run it—how about that? I'd even pay you. Minimum wage, obviously. And there would be conditions: no entering the tent, no fortune-telling, no witchcraft . . ."

"Fuck you."

Calum smiles horribly. He's still holding the sledgehammer. He shifts it off his shoulder so he's holding it across his chest. "If you won't sell it, and you can't afford to pay us, I guess it'll just sit there in the truck. Quite an expensive thing to leave lying around all packed up and ready to be transported. A thief might find it quite a draw in the dead of night, don't you think?"

Faith says, "Are you threatening us?"

Calum snorts. "I'm not threatening you. I just meant, you know, you can't always prevent those kinds of crimes. I'm assuming you've got insurance for that beast? Because if not, you know—risky. Much safer if it were built up. Much harder to steal."

Betsy can tell Faith doesn't want to speak, but as Calum turns away, she says, "Wait. We'll pay. But I have to make some money first. You cleaned me out."

Calum sighs and rolls his eyes. "When, then?"

"I can get it to you by Friday."

Betsy's thinking that they could, just about, make that much in a week from takings, if things go well. What happens after that, who knows? Faith might not be able to pay for the nurses either, at those rates, so she needs to be careful what she promises. Mum is her priority.

"Tomorrow," says Calum. "Pay the full amount tomorrow if you want us to be available for the pull-down at the end of the week."

"I can't do tomorrow. No way."

He starts to walk away, the sledgehammer over his shoulder.

"Two days."

He stops, turns. Then he nods. "Done."

Fuck, thinks Betsy. Two days isn't long enough. *Why did Faith say two days?*

"And you do realize that by the end of the week we are going to need that amount again to pay for the pull-down?"

"Again? The same amount?"

"If it hasn't gone up by then. Inflation, you know."

And then Calum is walking away, swinging the sledge-hammer as he goes, whistling.

"Two days?"

Faith closes the door and turns to Betsy. "I know. I'm sorry. What else could we have done? He wanted it today. At least I got us a bit of wiggle room."

"Not enough."

Faith is suddenly angry. "Thanks for your support. What can I say? I did my best. But yeah, you're right, it's probably pointless, isn't it? Impossible."

"Hey, it's not pointless, just difficult. Not impossible. Hopefully."

"Why didn't you say anything?"

"You know why. They don't hear me when I speak. You might be the black sheep, but to your family, I don't even exist. Not even a sheep at all, I guess."

Faith sinks down onto the bench. "I'm so tired."

"I know, baby."

"I wish Mum was here. She would sort them out."

Betsy can still hear Calum's voice outside, calling instructions to the lads over the sound of the radio.

Faith moves over and sits next to Betsy. She whispers, "What are we going to do? We don't have the money. Not that amount."

Betsy says, "Don't take this the wrong way, but it was probably slightly dumb to say we would pay up. You should have . . ."

"Should have what, Betsy?" Faith puts her head in her hands, flinches when her shoulder jars.

Betsy can hear Calum and the lads getting closer, starting to open up the back of the Waltzer truck to get the parts of the machine out. "Let's get out of here and leave them to it," she says. "You can come to work with me today."

"I don't know, Betsy. I was going to go and see Mum. And my arm still hurts. I'm no use to anyone."

"You can do laundry with one arm. Take your mind off things for a while. And you can't deny we could use the money. But if you need to head back to Home Farm, then . . ."

"No, you're right. We need all the money we can get."

CHAPTER

21

BEFORE

WORSE THAN ANGER, much worse, was the disappointment.

"I'm sorry, Mum. I couldn't help it. Those girls were being really mean."

Iris was sitting by the wagon window, gazing out. It was as if she couldn't hear her.

"Mum?"

No response. Faith sat opposite her mother and took her hands. "You forgive me, right? For getting kicked out of school?"

A tear fell from Iris's chin and landed on the tabletop with a soft tap. After a while she said, "You can't help what you see. What you are."

Faith's pulse increased. It wasn't the answer she was looking for. Her mother's mouth opened slightly and she shook her head, dislodging another tear. Faith was about to ask again, *But you forgive me, don't you?*

Then Iris said, "I just wish you'd told me about the dream that day. I keep thinking that maybe I could have done something."

She dropped her mother's hands and slammed out of the wagon, rushed across the yard to Macha's side, and buried her face in his mane. She bridled him and opened the stable doors, unable to stop crying as she did. Bareback, she used her heels to urge the horse out of the yard so that they were at a trot when they passed through the gates, and broke into a gallop as they reached the path through the woods to the lake.

As she rode through the trees, green with new growth, she saw flashes of that morning, the ice on the branches. It had been too cold for Macha, but if she'd been riding him it would have been different—she knows it—because whether Macha was there was something she could have changed from the dream, and therefore changed everything. She hadn't needed to walk out, to meet Samuel, to stand there at the side of the frozen lake. She could have turned left instead of right, gone the other way. So many chances when she could have done something to change it.

They broke out of the woods onto the shore, and she pulled up on Macha's reins to get him to slow. There was a branch nearby where Faith tethered him loosely, left the horse to graze on the lush grasses that grew at the land's edges, and walked over the stony ground to the place where she'd last seen her brother alive. The ice was long gone; the water was calm and clear, a huge mirror reflecting the sky.

The hurtful words those mean girls used echoed in her head, their twisted faces looming near to hers.

Freak. Stinker. Loner. Dumbo.

All of these and worse. She ought to have felt bad about what she'd said to them—she knew it *was* bad—but she didn't. They deserved it.

The headteacher deserved it too. She'd forced Faith to look in her eyes. No one should force anyone to do things they didn't want to do. No one. Faith couldn't be held responsible for what she'd done in response to that, partly because she'd blacked out. When she woke up in the medical bay, it became apparent that she'd said some terrible things to the headteacher in the time she'd lost. She'd woken with an image of how the headteacher would die, a death in a hospital corridor from something extremely painful. In the vision the headteacher was clutching her stomach, waiting with the paramedics to be seen, the queue of trolleys and patients snaking around, dozens of emergencies and not enough doctors or nurses to deal with them. The woman's last utterance was a plea for pain relief, and a low, guttural moan. Faith assumed she must have described it to her in great detail and with little sympathy.

When her mother came to collect her, she'd heard the headteacher mutter that Faith needed help. As Faith was led out, the woman eyed her now ex-pupil with a mixture of contempt and fear. She'd managed to make the word *help* sound like something very bad indeed.

And then they were at home, in the wagon, and worse than anything that had happened so far, she'd discovered that not only had her mother not forgiven her for being kicked out of school, but for all this time she'd also blamed her for what had happened to Tommy.

It was my fault, she thought, *and everyone knows it.* Standing there at the edge of the lake, Faith made a decision. *If I have the Sight,* she thought, *then I need to get rid of it.*

Seemed simple enough.

She took a pencil from her pocket and held it in her fist. Then, before she could think any more about it, she plunged the point hard into her left eye, right through the eyelid. She screamed and doubled over with the pain, fell back hard onto the shore, wrenched the pencil out, and threw it aside. The pain exploded inside her head, and she pressed on her socket with the heel of her hand, breathing hard, waiting, grinding her teeth. Macha looked up from where he was tethered, and Faith heard him whinnying, his reins flapping against the branch as he tried to break free and go to her. She called to him, "It's okay, boy. I'm okay."

But she couldn't quite make herself do the right eye. She sat for a long time with the pencil in her hand, clenching and unclenching her fist around it. She started to count down from ten.

"What the hell are you doing?"

Faith jumped at the voice. She hadn't heard anyone approaching. Still holding a hand to her injured eye, she looked at the person standing beside her, but the sun was blinding, and all she could see was an outline of a girl's head. The same age as her, or the same height, anyway.

"I'm—"

"Did you stab that into your own eye?" The girl sounded weirdly unfazed by this.

Faith said, "What do you want?"

"Are you gonna do the other one?" asked the girl. It was as if she found it fascinating.

Faith was totally thrown. "What's it to you?" There was blood dripping from her hand where it pressed into her eye. Not as much as she'd thought there might be, but it had splashed on her jeans and a bit on the ground.

"Ouch," said the girl, inspecting what she could see of Faith's face. "You want to get that seen by a doctor."

"I'm not . . . I didn't . . . can you leave me alone?" The pain and this girl's odd behavior were making her angry.

"Can I see that?" the girl asked, holding her hand out for the pencil. Faith handed it over without thinking.

She held the bloodied pencil close to her own face. "Pretty sharp. Do some damage with that, if you're not careful."

The girl drew her arm back and threw the pencil, so that it span and arced and landed with a small splash in the middle of the water.

"Enough damage done today, I reckon."

Faith said, "That was mine," but weakly, because really, who cared about the pencil?

"I'm Betsy," said the girl.

Faith looked into Betsy's eyes, expecting to see the girl's death, perhaps from accident, disease, or old age. Holding her injured eye shut, the two made eye contact, but Faith didn't see anything but eyes. Then her gaze was drawn downward to the necklace Betsy was wearing, and for a second she forgot about the pain in her eye. It was a silver chain, and a ring with a green stone: Grandma Rose's ring.

"Where did you get that?" she asked.

"Oh, this?" said Betsy, fingering the ring. "I found it under a rock."

It occurred to Faith that her granddad had let her have the necklace with the ring right before the dream happened. The ring Grandma Rose was wearing when she fell, the ring that caused Tommy and Peter to have their accident. Maybe it was the ring that had started all this.

"Take it off," she said, and Betsy took a step back.

"Whoa," said Betsy. "Calm down."

"I said, take it off. Right now. It's not yours."

"Is it yours?" Betsy unclasped the necklace and held it out.

Faith let it pool in her palm, the green stone glinting like the eye of something malevolent. Then she threw it as far as she could into the lake, where it disappeared from sight, sank to the bottom, leaving three perfect rings on the surface of the water, each inside the next, rippling out. After a couple of seconds, they were gone too.

CHAPTER

22

NOW
Betsy

AFTER THE SHIFT ends, Betsy and Faith return to the showground. Calm has descended: all the stalls are ready, the smell of cooking oil heating in the fryers. The two kiddie rides are up, the Waltzer off to the side, a little way away from everything else.

The sight of the tent with its flag flying seems to upset Faith as they climb out of the van. The white canvas shines brightly, dazzling in the evening sun, with its doors neatly laced. They will stay that way until half an hour before the show, but for now the carnival is waiting. The acts are pasting their faces with makeup, limbering up, dressing the horses, preparing the birds. Soon the lines will start to form at the twin entrances, the band will strike up its Afrobeat-inspired intro music, and the circus will begin.

Inside the wagon, Faith slumps down into a chair and immediately falls asleep. She sleeps through the show, and although she doesn't look at all comfortable in the chair, Betsy lets her. She needs the rest.

An hour or so later, Betsy notices what the time is and gently shakes her friend awake. The show will be ending soon, and the ride will need opening.

"Hey, you should get a shower. Not much time."

Faith doesn't say anything. She heaves herself up and heads past the bathroom to the bedroom, dragging her feet. She looks exhausted, as if the nap has made things worse, not better.

"Where are you going?"

She pauses but doesn't turn. She looks beaten. "I can't do it tonight. I just can't."

"But who's going to run the ride? We only have two days to get Calum's money, or else—"

"What? What do you think they will do?"

"They'll make it hard for you. Harder than it needs to be. You have to go to work, earn enough for this and the next buildup. He might even take the ride if you can't pay. Seems like that's his plan."

"Maybe I don't care if he does."

Betsy knows that isn't true. She knows what it means to Faith to stay with Harrington's, no matter what, no matter the obstacles. "You can't just give up."

"Why not? They've made it clear they don't want me here."

"All the more reason to show them you belong."

"It's too difficult, Betsy. I can't fight them anymore. Not without Mum. Last time, at least she was around to stand up for me."

"Your mum wants you to stay with the carnival, doesn't she? Even after she's gone?"

Faith took a moment to answer. "It never crossed her mind that I wouldn't. Seems like the rest of the family has other plans. Maybe they always did, but never told her. So now she's out of the picture they feel like they can get on with what they've always wanted to do and get rid of me properly. She was my body armor, and now they've got a clear shot."

"Do you really want to just hand it to him, though, without a fight?"

Faith said, "If everyone hates me, maybe it's best I simply let it go. Why fight that? What would it prove?"

"No. Don't think like that. You love the carnival. You love the Waltzer, don't you? That's what you said last week."

"Last week was different. Last week I hadn't met Joey Standish."

"That creep . . . You did nothing wrong there. The video wasn't clear—it twisted the truth."

"Yes. But that's how it is, now, isn't it? What is truth, if it's not what everyone thinks?"

"We should make another video, maybe explain what happened. Or go to the police. Maybe someone recorded what he did to you, maybe—"

"I like the agency work in the care homes, working in the laundry, helping old people. Maybe that can be my life. It's good, honest work, and if I do that I don't need any of them. I can make it on my own."

"You wouldn't be on your own," says Betsy. "You'd have me."

Faith smiles gratefully. "You're a good friend."

"But I know you don't mean it, about letting Harrington's go."

"Maybe I do."

"The circus, though. The traveling. You love this life, even if it's hard sometimes. There's got to be another way. You should try again, go back and talk to Mike again. He'll help you."

Faith says, "I get the impression he'd be happier if I just went away."

"It's not about Mike's happiness, though, is it?"

Faith pauses in the doorway, thinking. Her face is gray with fatigue. "I need to lie down."

She closes the door to the bedroom, leaving Betsy alone in the sitting area. Betsy thinks, *How dare those people make Faith feel this way? It's her name on the fucking wagons. She's the last Harrington left.*

Betsy pulls on Faith's coat and finds the money belt, clips it in place. She searches in a drawer and finds a spare eye patch, slips it on and leaves quietly, shutting the door as gently as she can. As she makes her way to where the rides are, her pace changes. She strides with confidence. Christine, prepping the hotdog stand, gives her a questioning look, but Betsy simply holds up her hand in greeting and keeps walking.

"Evening, Ricky," she says to the security guy. He nods at her, goes back to checking his phone.

A few minutes later, when the show ends, the canvas doors are pulled back to let the crowds out. Betsy is waiting on the Waltzer to take their money.

Stop. Go. Let them on, let them off. Time passes, music fills the gaps in her thoughts. She walks the boards, enjoying the motion of it, feeling the power she has to spin fast or slow, left or right, to make these kids scream with delight and go back round to queue up, again and again.

At some point it occurs to Betsy that one way of making more money would be to increase prices. There's nothing to say what they ought to charge; it's up to Faith to set the rates. The sign says, "All rides £3," but that was a sign that came with the machine, easy enough to change. She thinks about how much a ride should be, or how much it would need to be to make enough money in two days to pay those men. Agency shifts are all well and good, but the pay isn't enough to make a decent amount in such a short time. A few calculations and she comes up with a figure that would save them, just. If, for each ride, they charged the same as a decent pair of trainers, they would make the numbers they needed in the time. *Balls,* she thinks. *No one would pay that.*

The ride is full of a new batch of kids, and she's locked all the safety bars, when she catches sight of Calum making his way toward her through the crowds. With seconds to spare she manages to press the "Go" button before he can board the ride and get to her. He stands watching as the cars spin past in front of him, as she steps out on the platform, moves with the rotation of the machine.

He's trying to say something to her. Betsy cups her hand to her ear. "What?" The music is making it impossible to catch what he's saying, not that she's trying that hard. "Can't hear you," she yells, "Come back later."

He stomps off.

When the timer goes off, Betsy presses the "Stop" button at the center of the dashboard and waits for the ride to come to a standstill. When it does, she makes her way around and opens up the cars, letting the riders off. She can feel someone watching her from the shadows, so she ducks into the control booth. The feeling of being watched makes her skin prickle. She keeps her head down but spies through the tiny gaps in the metal frame of the booth, trying to see who it is. Around the back of the ride is a man, arms crossed, focused on her. He seems expectant, as if he's waiting for something.

Ricky has seen them too. He approaches the man, who is dressed in a suit and tie, far too smart for a trip to a carnival. The two men talk quietly to each other. After a minute Ricky shrugs and steps away, and the man disappears behind the hotdog stand, walking in the direction of the exit gate.

"Who was that?" asks Betsy once the man has gone.

"He wanted the girl with the eye patch."

"What did you say?"

"I said he couldn't talk to you, that you were busy."

"Did he say what he wanted?"

"He said he'd seen what she can do, that he was impressed. I'm assuming it was some sicko who saw that video. We've had a few of them tonight. I'm surprised you haven't noticed."

"A few? How many?"

Ricky shrugs. "They're just tourists thinking they'll get to see something weird. But I have to set them straight on that, and then they go away."

"I don't know what we'd do without you, Rick."

"I know what that creep did. I was there, remember? The rest of the video was . . . well, it should never have been made public."

Betsy thanks Ricky again and goes back to the ride, but her heart is beating fast. How did they know to come here? What did they want Faith for? Faith's image was on the internet; her video had gone viral. She'd said a man would die, and it was really scary—she looked like a crazy person in the video. If someone wanted to speak to her after that, it couldn't be good.

Betsy thinks she can now see, in some small way, why Mike and Christine want Faith to leave, that from their perspective it would be easier on everyone. She can see how the things Faith can do, viewed from a certain angle, might reflect badly on business. That was it, though, wasn't it—the angle? If you framed it a little differently, the things Faith could do might be the key to a better life. To better business.

It's a busy night and Betsy doesn't have much time to think for the next hour or so. When the crowds start to thin out, she feels like she's being watched again. She catches a white face in the hedges, staring at her. *Ignore him. He'll get bored and go away,* she tells herself, but she doesn't feel safe. Even with Ricky there, she feels exposed, running the ride that's been set back away from the rest of the circus community. She feels like a fish set out as bait. She gets Ricky's attention and nods to the place she saw the face, but by the time the security man has walked over, the face has gone.

It is earlier than the ride usually shuts down, but after a few more minutes she's had enough. The feeling of being watched remains. She closes and locks the booth at the center of the machine and hurries back across the ground to the wagon. It's in darkness, and as she unlocks the door and goes in, a sound behind her makes her jump.

"Excuse me, Miss," says a voice. "Can I ask you something?"

She stops, like a creature caught in headlights. She can't see where the voice is coming from. Then a man steps closer, the one from earlier, in the smart trousers, and she sees that he's holding out his hands in what ought to be a friendly gesture. He smiles. She doesn't buy it. There aren't enough streetlights reaching to this corner of the ground. The man's eyes are in shadow.

"What are you doing, you creepy fucker?" she demands.

"Hey, hey, it's okay. I just want to ask you a question."

"Come back in daylight, for fuck's sake."

"Don't be like that."

She leans closer, hisses at him, "If you don't leave right now, I'm going to start screaming. Take your chances if you like, but there are about ten lads in those wagons over there who may take the sound of me screaming as permission to run over here and give you a kicking."

He glances over at the wagons, parked up across the way. He steps back, hands up. "I don't mean you any harm. I have money. Lots of money."

"Good for you. Why should I care?"

"I was sent to find the eye patch girl. I can pay. You know. The video?"

Betsy pauses. She wonders how much "lots of money" means. "What exactly do you want her for?"

"Everyone saw that video, the way that man's death was predicted. It was brutal. Spectacular."

"And?"

"I have a client," says the man. "He's very rich. He wants to know exactly when he'll die. Just like with Joey Standish." Then he quotes a figure that would pay what Calum was asking for, four times over. It would pay Faith's mum's nursing fees for a month, if she needs them for that long.

Betsy tries to keep a poker face. "Double it, and I'll think about it."

"Fine," says the man, as if money is no object. "Whatever you ask, he's willing to pay. But you'll need to meet with him, correct? To look in his eyes, right? Or whatever it is?"

"Come back tomorrow. And consider not sneaking up on people in the dark next time."

"Hey, wait . . ."

She gets inside and slams the door shut.

The light goes on, making her squint in the sudden brightness. Faith is in the kitchenette, running water into a tall glass. "Who was that?"

"Maybe it was the answer to our prayers."

"I heard what he said. I'm not doing it. No way."

"But did you hear what he said he'd pay us?"

"I heard. It was a lot."

"Enough to pay Calum. You can stay with the carnival, and it will buy enough time to do whatever you like. All that money."

"It's not about the money."

"What are you talking about? The possibilities, Faith. Hey, you could get a carousel, and I'll run it. Maybe we could buy Mike and Christine out eventually, run the show ourselves without any of them. Imagine."

"It's not allowed, Betsy. It's literally written into the constitution. No fortune-telling, mediums, anything like that. After that video, if anyone found out I was doing it on purpose, taking money for it—"

"Don't you think that ship has sailed already? How much worse could it be for us?"

Faith sits at the table. "I've been thinking about it. Right now, I have a chance, just like I did after Tommy. I can prove to them that I'm no danger, that I can control it, and after a while, when they've calmed down, things will go back to normal. But if they found out I had an actual sideshow doing the very thing they've forbidden . . ."

"How would they know? We don't need to advertise it to anyone. If that's what people are willing to pay, we could just do one or two, and then we'd be home free. One or two—that's all we need to do."

Faith stares into her glass for a while. "My great-grandma isn't buried with everyone else. Did you know that?"

"She's not?"

"No. There's a family plot, a mausoleum, space for the next few generations. But Daisy was buried on her own, a ways away, up the hill. You can't even see her from the Harringtons' graves. They say I'm like this because of her. I'll never be able to change that. Leopard, spots, you know. I might be a Harrington born and bred, but I'm also like a half-breed to them, tainted with whatever Daisy was supposed to have had, her witchy blood. She was magic. The bad kind. And I guess that's what I am too."

"You shouldn't need to change. They shouldn't ask you to."

"They'll never accept me if I start that kind of thing at Harrington's. Under the family flag."

"But, Faith, they don't have a choice whether to accept you. Daisy was an outsider—she married in. You didn't. You're a Harrington. Your mother was a Harrington. Your granddad, your great-granddad. You go right back to David Harrington, the founder, just like Mike and Calum. Roots of the same tree. No matter what you do, you're family. They can't do anything about that."

Faith thinks about it. Then she asks, "How did we do tonight?"

Betsy hefts a sack of cash up onto the table and starts to count it out. She totals that with the amount on the card reader. They had done really well, taken in more than usual. But staring at the money in stacks and groups of tens and twenties, they both know, even if they do the same tomorrow, it isn't going to be enough. Nowhere near.

"Maybe tomorrow we'll take in a little more."

Betsy says nothing.

"Maybe I'll think of something," says Faith. She looks at Betsy. "But it won't be that."

CHAPTER

23

NOW
Faith

I SIT IN THE dark, listening to the sounds of the night. Young people squeal, music blares, laughter explodes. I let it wash over me, wondering why they are still hanging around now that the carnival is shut, the show's over. They've brought their own sound systems, portable speakers, alcohol. Don't they know there are people here needing to rest? I grow cold, my thin T-shirt no match for the damp air as the temperature drops. This motor home, despite its flashy price tag, isn't insulated very well. I should go put on two sweaters, like I usually do, but it's as if I'm glued to the seat, weighed down, stuck.

Light leaks in, orange light from the streetlights, white from the moon. Then there are occasional flashlights from phones. Outside the wagon, voices are getting closer, hushed tones, only snatches of words reaching me where I sit.

"The lights are off—she isn't in there."

"I saw her come back."

There is a knock at the door but I don't move. "She's not there," says a voice. It's Calum. He's here to collect, but it's too early. It's not even been a day. "Try again."

Knock knock knock. I remain very still. Where is Betsy? I look around, but she's not here. Her bedroom door is ajar, and I can see she's not in there. Night shift, I presume, though I can't remember what she said. Her shift patterns are a mystery to me. If she's at work now, I hope it's a sleep-in. She'll be tired after a full evening of running the ride. I feel bad about that. Grateful to her, but still bad. I owe her so much.

"Do you think she knows already?"

"Shut up, idiot."

What is it I don't know? I grab my phone: no messages, nothing from Home Farm, from Linda or the nurses, Terri or Toni. So, no change with Mum, or I'd have been told. There is a little more knocking, then the voices recede into the melee of sound, covered by the joyful, raucous noises of the scattered knots of young people on the field.

A while later and again someone is knocking. Gently this time. "Faith? You awake?" It's Amara. I want to answer her, but the effort it would take seems insurmountable. I shift very slightly and then almost cry out, my shoulder hurts so much. It's getting worse, not better. I don't know how loud a noise I make, but she hears it, or feels it; either way, she seems to sense that I'm there, that I'm just on the other side of the wagon wall.

"Faith, I just heard what happened. You can talk to me anytime. I'm right here. Okay?"

I whisper, "Okay."

I listen. I can tell she's still there; she hasn't left yet. When she speaks again, it's as if her voice is coming from inside the door itself. She must have pressed her face right up against it. "Hey, don't let what they're saying get to you. I know you didn't do anything deliberately. You're a good person. Whatever happened, it's not your fault. I really believe that. Faith?"

She must have seen the video too. I guess everyone has by now. I have a sudden longing to get up to let her in, but I don't have the strength.

"It's okay," I say. "I just need a little time."

After a few more minutes, she goes away, leaving me in this darkness. I love her for that. Perhaps I'll talk to her soon; perhaps it would help. I think of the vision of Amir, how I willingly did that for her, and I wonder: If I could go back, would I change that decision? I don't think I would, but there's no doubt it has set off a cascade of visions, the way the dream of Tommy did back when I was ten. I've been repressing my "gift" for so long, nearly twelve years. The pressure built up and now it's been released, those floodgates opened once again. I touch my eye patch, the flimsy cotton fabric of it, and think, *It's not enough anymore.* This thing I have inside me is too powerful to resist. When I saw Joey Standish drowning, it was almost unbearably painful because of the similarities to the dream of Tommy and Peter. I thought nothing could be worse. And then something was: I saw the soldier, the knife in my hand, his face so full of surprise as he bled out on the road.

The visions are as heavy as lead upon me. I feel as if I will never again be able to rise up from this bench. I may die here. Then I think, *If I die before I can kill the soldier, then the vision won't be true, will it?* My arm hurts as if a blade is being twisted inside the arm socket. Perhaps I will die from that.

I shake out three of Betsy's pills into my hand and swallow them dry. They stick there, bitter burrs halfway down my throat.

Time passes, and all the outside noises fade to nothing. I must have drifted off for a few minutes, because suddenly the circus ground is silent and I sense that Betsy's come back, that she's in the room. I can hear her trying to move stealthily so as to not disturb me. I flick the light on and she nearly jumps out of her skin.

"For fuck's sake, Faith. What are you doing?"

Then she looks at me properly, and she knows that right now she needs to be kind. She comes over to me and lets me put my head on her and weep until she's soaked in my tears, in my sadness. She tells me it's okay. She tells me she understands.

"It's so late," she says. "I thought you'd gone back to bed."

"I'm going to see Mum. Terri and Toni's night off. Linda said she'd sit in until three. Then I need to take over from her."

"She was sitting in so you could sleep, though, right? Did you?"

"I'll be fine. Don't worry about me." She doesn't dare say I ought not to go. These precious last days are too important, and she knows it. But I'll admit, I'm not looking after myself, not treating myself right. It just seems so pointless now.

"Thanks for covering for me with the ride."

"You don't have to thank me." She checks the time. "There's an hour before you need to be there. You eaten?"

I shrug. I don't know if I did or not. There was a sandwich, but I don't know anymore when that was.

"You can't go to your mum without anything in your stomach."

"It doesn't matter."

"I'll make noodles." She gets up, goes to the stove, puts on water to boil.

"I don't want anything."

"Eat them or don't, I'm making them."

My stomach growls at the smell of the flavoring when she opens the packet, but I still don't want to eat.

"Do we have any booze?" I ask.

"Vodka."

"Perfect." I pour two half tumblers and hand one to Betsy.

"To Iris," she says.

"To Mum."

I down my drink in one. Then Betsy looks at me for an uncomfortably long time. I can feel the alcohol burning in my stomach, entering my bloodstream along with the pills. My cheeks start to heat up, my head spins. Maybe I do need to eat something.

"What?" I ask.

She purses her lips. "Might not be the time."

"What is it?"

"That man, Joey whatever. He died."

"He died?" It doesn't make any sense. "Already?"

"Yeah. And it was just like you said. In the river."

"But he wasn't . . . I mean, what I saw, I didn't think it was that soon."

"It's online. People are posting about it. Here." She shows me a video, or tries to. I push her hand with the phone away.

"People are saying you're an oracle. The Oracle of Death. The eye patch girl. You're famous."

I think, *This is bad.*

"He was found in a river?"

She nods.

I am transported back to the vision I had when I looked into his eyes, on the side of the Waltzer. The weeds in his mouth, the water . . . sinking, choking, and not coming up. It's mixed with the dream of Tommy and the dream from last night, that strange mix of dreams and imaginings, and glimpses of lost treasure.

"So, he drowned?"

She places the phone on the table in front of me, presses play on a video with thirty thousand plus views, the numbers ticking up and up before our eyes, like fruits spinning on an arcade machine.

Joey has set the camera up so the river is in the frame. He sits cross-legged in front of it and starts to speak.

"So, a lot of you have seen the video where I get my future death told to me, and to be honest, it's been freaking me out a little, what with everyone's responses. I'm not going to avoid rivers for the rest of my life. I love wild swimming, so I'm making this video to prove to everyone that the prediction isn't true! Just a bit of fun. How could I drown on such a lovely day? I'm a great swimmer."

Joey stands up and rolls his arms back, clicks his neck left and then right. He takes his top off, revealing a sculpted torso, so he's just in his shorts, and then bends down to the camera.

"One of the things the eye patch girl said was that I would be alone. Well, I swim alone all the time! Face your fears, people. We can all cheat death if we try."

He salutes.

"Here I go!"

Against the glare of the sun, the river seems black and shiny as a snake. On the screen he takes a running jump and dive-bombs into the slow-flowing water with a great splash. For a moment he's gone completely, and I think, *Is that it?* But then his face appears above the water, and his eyes are full of terror. He makes no sound, his mouth opening and closing like a guppy fish. The water must have been too cold, the contrast of temperatures too great between the water and the air. Cold water shock. He's drowning, just the way I told him he would.

Joey looks at the camera in desperation, but there's nothing he can do, the process has started already, his lungs are full of the water he inhaled when he went under the first time and his reflexes made him breathe in. The video fades away, my mind returning to the vision as he sinks under the surface for the final time, so that I don't just see it, but I also feel the weak struggle he makes. I taste the weeds and the mud. I gasp, as if I'm drowning too.

"Faith, what is it?" Betsy touches my hurt shoulder, and the bright burst of pain yanks me back to her with a squeal. "Oh no, is that still troubling you?"

I wave her away. "It's not that bad. It's getting better." I can't think about my arm. I'm more worried about the video and what it means. I wonder if telling him he was going to drown made him pull this stunt, and if I hadn't said anything, then he would be alive now.

"But it wasn't going to be that soon."

Betsy's eyes widen. "You said you couldn't tell when."

"No, but I get a sense. I thought Standish would last a few months at least."

I feel shaky and unstable, on the edge of something. I don't trust myself, no longer certain of anything.

I need to quit thinking about it. The stress of Mum being so close to the end, all this shit with the ride and with Calum. This is going to make things a hundred times worse.

I wonder about the man who came to find me, who wanted to pay me to predict his rich client's death. "Do you know when it happened?" I ask Betsy.

"It was on the news. It's everywhere online. Have a look."

I swipe to open the first social media app on my home screen, and there it is, trending with #JoeyStandishDies.

I click the hashtag, and there are hundreds of hysterical threads offering opinions about what has happened to Joey and why. They all mention #eyepatchgirl and #oracleofdeath.

I am the eye patch girl. I am the Oracle of Death.

"They found him at the river near the circus ground. Where Harrington's was a couple of days ago. The day after you saw it in his eyes."

"When we were doing the pull-down, and Calum was giving me a hard time?" My body goes cold. That was the night I had the dream. By then it had already happened. We were on the ground, fighting to get the machine in the truck, and only a few hundred yards away, Joey was jumping to his watery death.

I have to sit down before I fall. The vodka, the drugs, the day I've had. And now this. It wasn't supposed to happen yet. How could he be dead already?

"Did you see in the vision that it was the river where the circus was?"

"I didn't recognize the place. I'd never been down to the river."

"Fits, though, with what you said to him."

"I don't even remember that. I thought, I thought . . ."

"You said—"

Suddenly it's too much to bear. "Can we not?"

The pan is boiling hard, and Betsy turns to drop the noodles in. She pokes them with a fork. "Chicken, okay?"

"I honestly don't care."

She looks at me. "You don't have to wear that in here, you know. Especially not now. Why do you?"

I touch my eye patch. "You know why. I see things when I take it off. That's why this whole thing happened. You know this—why are you asking?"

Betsy says, "You don't see things when you look at me."

"No, but I never looked at you without it. Not properly."

"Maybe I want you to."

I stand up, walk to the other end of the wagon. "Never."

"It helped, though, didn't it? With your mum, I mean. She said she felt free after the vision."

"She didn't have a choice but to see the positives. Come on, Betsy, you don't need to know that about yourself. Imagine if the answer was tomorrow."

"I was thinking of you, really. It would be neat if you could see a vision and not be wiped out by it. Desensitize yourself." She turns to get a bowl out of the cupboard. "Noodles are done."

"Nah. It's too risky."

I go over to the counter, where the noodles are sitting in two bowls, steam rising. I reach for a fork.

Betsy says, "You could just try it out on me. Aren't you curious? Maybe you won't see anything. Imagine. I might be immune."

"Don't," I breathe, but there are fingers in my hair, fumbling for the elastic that holds the eye patch in place.

I spin away, arms flying out.

Betsy cries out in pain. "You burned me!" The noodles have spilled on us both, the glutinous liquid sticking to Betsy's arm, sinking into the fabric of my trousers.

"Quick, get it under the tap." I pull Betsy to the sink and turn on the cold. But the water's low in the tank. I pump the pedal but it's such a slow flow now, barely a trickle. We need to get to a proper tap.

"Why did you do that?" she cries. "What's wrong with you?"

"I'm sorry, I didn't mean it. I just—"

"My arm—oh, heck. I'll have to go to the hospital. It hurts, it hurts so much!"

"Keep it under the tap."

The skin on Betsy's arm is reddening, and she's whimpering, trying to pull her arm away. The water is dripping. Then there's none left.

"It's not even coming out anymore—let me go!"

"But . . ." Betsy pulls her arm free. We both stare at it.

"It seems a little pink."

"It's burned! I need medical attention. What is it, third degree? Full thickness burns? I'll be scarred!"

There is a patch of angry red skin with a layer of white forming, wrinkles on the top. "I can't tell . . . but if you think you need to go to the hospital, I can take you."

"If I think so? What are you saying? You think it's nothing? It really hurts!"

I'm focusing on Betsy, trying to ignore the pain in my own arm, where my shoulder is injured, the pain in my leg where the hot liquid landed. I touch my thigh gingerly. The liquid has cooled off, but it still feels like my skin is burning.

"I'll just change my trousers. Then we'll go. We can take one of the vans."

Betsy is already at the door. "I can't wait. We need to go now. My arm—it hurts." Her tone is accusatory, and I feel guilty that I have caused this to happen to my friend, so I help Betsy get her shoes on. Then I unbolt the door and hurry to the key safe in the box office, ignoring the burning sensation on the skin of my leg and the dull ache deep in my shoulder.

CHAPTER

24

NOW
Faith

As we wait in the Emergency Department to be called, I keep my head down.

The patch I wear has become my identity, and while I would never go outside without it, tonight it seems to be attracting attention. Sitting there, I notice more than one or two people nudging each other and looking at me, then down at their phones, then back at me. Usually I get stares. People call me names or they ask me rude, intrusive questions, but that's not what this is. They're not intrigued by the patch per se. They recognize me from the video. I swear I hear someone whispering, "Oracle of Death."

I nudge Betsy. "Exactly how famous was that Joey guy?"

"He was ,like, four million followers famous. But it gets worse."

"What do you mean?"

"The papers have picked up the story. You're on all the news channels."

"Oh, fuck sake."

A girl walks by, pretending to look at texts, but I can tell she's photographing me.

Betsy says, "I tried to tell you."

"Do you have a hat or something? Shades?"

Right now, the patch is catastrophic, as it's so identifying. It's the main thing that people remember from the clip. The eye patch girl. When it came off, I turned into some kind of evil, ranting oracle, right in front of their eyes.

"I might take it off," I whisper to her.

"If you'd done that back in the wagon, we wouldn't even be here."

"If you hadn't tried to force me to do it, we wouldn't be here, you mean."

Betsy looks ashamed. "I'm sorry I did that. I was trying to prove a point, that it doesn't necessarily have to be bad thing. But I was wrong and I'm sorry."

I check the time: two forty-five. I'll need to tell Linda I'm going to be late, that she might need to hang on a little longer.

She sees me check the time. "You should go. I'll be fine."

"But how will you get back?"

She shrugs.

"I'll wait. How much longer can it be?"

A nurse walks past, phone in hand. She points it at me, doesn't even try to hide that she's doing it. Then she scuttles away before I can form the words to tell her how much I object to her brazenness.

Enough. I slip my patch off and put it in my pocket, pull up my hood so it nearly covers both eyes. Feels risky to go without covering my eye entirely, but I decide it can work. The people in the waiting room will lose interest eventually, I hope. As we sit there, people are called through, and new ones arrive. After a while no one looks at me at all.

My leg feels angry beneath my trousers, the rough fibers rubbing my skin raw every time I move even slightly. Betsy sees me wince but doesn't comment. She says, "What's taking them so long?"

"I don't know—I guess they're busy." My stomach rumbles. The smell of the cold noodle sauce stuck to me is making me both ravenous and nauseous. A man is wheeled past, one paramedic pushing the trolley, the other running alongside and holding an oxygen mask to his face. I look at their legs, avoiding the head area. Don't want to see any deaths today, if I can avoid it. Shortly afterward, another trolley is rushed through.

Betsy is holding a wet paper towel to her arm. She lifts it, sucking air between her teeth as she does so. The white layer has lifted at the edges, revealing raw, glistening flesh underneath. "Does it still hurt?"

"Of course it still hurts," she snaps.

When I go to the bathroom, I peel off my trousers slowly, using my good arm. I see the broken, blistered skin on my thigh. I know I need to get it clean, get a dressing on it soon, or risk infection. But I could do that by myself, back at the wagon. I don't need the hospital, not in the way that Betsy needs it. Also, I need to get to Mum's side. It's not fair to let Linda down.

Back in the waiting room I'm about to tell her I can't stay much longer when a voice calls her name, and Betsy rises to her feet slowly, holding the towel in place. I help her up, and the two of us make our way to where the nurse, a harassed-looking man in green scrubs, is propping the door open for us to go through.

In the examination room, the nurse says, "Sit there, please."

Betsy sits down, still holding her arm. The man gives us both a curious look. "So. How can we help you, this morning?"

Betsy makes a small whimpering sound and glances at me. "It was my fault," I say. "I spilled boiling hot noodle juice."

"No, it was an accident," says Betsy.

"An accident?"

"We weren't paying attention," she says. "No one's fault."

The nurse types something into his screen, then turns back to us. "Whereabouts?" He glances at the wet patch on my trousers.

"On my arm, of course," says Betsy, holding it out. "It really hurts."

He takes the wet paper off Betsy's arm and peers closer. "Did you get it under the cold tap?" he asks.

"Yes," says Betsy. "But not for long. We ran out of water."

I notice that Betsy is behaving strangely around this man. She's toned down the whining, and she's pulling her mirror face. I take another look at him. Not bad-looking, but not really my type. I can tell he works out, though. Bit of a Ken doll.

He is still holding Betsy's hand when he looks at me, points to my shoulder and says, "What about that? You're holding it strangely. Is there something wrong there?" I wasn't ready for him to look at me. His eyes meet mine, and in the air between us, fanning out all at once, full color, is his death scene. The room around me recedes. I am inside an operating theater, where this man is lying unconscious on his back, the masked faces of the surgical team above him. Tubing snakes from his throat, and most of his body is covered in green surgical sheeting except for a large incision in his abdomen. Something has gone wrong, I don't know what, but the anesthetist is panicking, the surgeon raising her voice. She is struggling to hold an artery closed, the cavity filling with blackish liquid. "Clamps," she yells, and "Someone shut off the radio," and the vision ends at the same time as his life.

When I come to, I'm lying on a hospital bed too, but still in the examination room, the nurse holding my wrist, looking at his watch.

"Oh," I say, spying the worried look on Betsy's face, the trace of relief when she sees I've come around. "Sorry. I was having a moment."

The nurse says, "You were absent for a while, there. Has this happened before?"

"Yes," both Betsy and I say together.

"A lot," says Betsy.

"Not for a while," I say, tasting this lie as it comes out. My head is full of other people's deaths, layers of it, like weeds growing around inside my mind. "I didn't pass out, did I?"

"You were unresponsive, but your eyes were open the whole time. I helped you lie down before you fell. You say it happens regularly?"

"No," I say.

"Yes," says Betsy.

"Only under certain circumstances," I say.

The nurse says, "It might be a kind of seizure. Has anyone ever done any investigations?"

"Oh, I don't think that's necessary," I say.

"I need to book you in for a scan. They'll send an appointment through, should be a week or so."

"No, it's fine. I just go blank every now and then. It's not a big deal."

I get down from the bed to return to my chair. As I do this I stumble, my knees lose all their strength and the nurse catches me before I hit the floor.

"Whoa, there. Back on the bed now. You're not going anywhere just yet."

Betsy is eyeing me. She knows what has happened, that I've seen the end of this handsome nurse, that this is what has caused me to go blank, to lose time.

As he helps me back on the bed, my shoulder jars, and I suck in air to stop from screaming.

"There is something very wrong with that joint," he says. "Also, I noticed you were limping on the way in."

"Really?" says Betsy, and my cheeks flush red as they both stare at me. "I didn't notice."

"I wasn't. Not really." I place my hands lightly over the place on my leg where it hurts. As I do so, my arm bursts with bright, stabbing pain.

He won't leave it alone. "Does it hurt here?" Before I can stop him, he touches my shoulder, and I yelp.

"How long has it been like that? Some kind of accident?"

"I bumped into someone, but it's been getting better. I'm sure it will be fine tomorrow."

"When did it happen?"

"Not long ago. Anyway, this isn't about me."

"Of course it is."

He picks up the phone next to the computer and dials a number. "Can you come over when you get a second? I think I'm going to need a hand."

A hand doing what? I wonder. I thought I would be on time to see Mum, but now it looks again as if I won't. I glance at the door and calculate what I would need to do to get out, past this man, before he could stop me. My legs are too weak for fleeing. I sag against the bed in defeat.

"That was the doctor. She won't be too long. Just lie back and relax for a minute. We can have a look at your leg while we wait."

"My leg is fine."

"If you could just pop your trousers down so I can see."

"I don't need that." I'm trying to get up again, but my head is spinning horribly.

"Oh," he says, looking at me. I avoid his eyes but the death scene is still in the air between us, faded only slightly. "Well. I can't help you if you don't consent."

"I don't."

He turns away and types into a nearby computer. "And the shoulder? I assume you don't want to stay that way forever?"

I can't remember what it's like to not be in pain. The idea is tantalizing. "How long will it take to help with my shoulder?"

"If it's what I think it is, not very long. But it's up to you. You're free to go." He smiles tightly.

In the end I don't have time to think it over. The door opens and a woman comes in. She asks me to extend my arm and I can't. Then she feels my shoulder, and it hurts more than ever.

"Dislocated," she says. "For how long?"

"A couple of days."

"Tricky," she says. "If you'd come straightaway, it would be easier. The muscles will have seized up, so it might not be a simple pop-it-back job." She turns to the nurse. "Gas and air, for now. Let's have a go, shall we?"

I suck on the mouthpiece, three big gulps of the good stuff. It's heavenly.

"Will you be able to fix it?" I ask, my teeth clamped on the plastic of the device like it's a bit.

The doctor holds my hand as if she's about to shake hello. She places the other hand on my forearm and even this small movement is agony as she lifts it. I stare at the ceiling. "I can't promise anything," she says, "but I like a challenge."

The nurse is behind me. At a signal from the doctor he takes hold of me with both hands, bracing under my armpits, one foot on the bedframe. I think it is the worst pain I will ever feel in my life. Then they pull.

The pain is immense, bursting through my shoulder and blooming into the rest of my body. I want to scream, but instead I suck again and again on the Entonox gas so that my head begins to seem as if it's not attached to my body, that it's floating just above it. I'm making a growling noise as the muscles and sinews in my shoulder fight against the doctor and the nurse, as the bones strain against their strength. There is a crunching sensation much worse than any pain, which seems to fly from my shoulder and up my neck into my forehead, making me yelp in surprise and shock. I suck again, breathing it in, thinking of flying and floating, and what it might feel like to die. Then it's over.

They let go of me and place my hand gently on my leg, the gentleness rather pointless considering what they just did, fully stretching me out with everything they had. I breathe in on the mouthpiece, but before I can suck again, it's taken from my hand.

"Done," says the doctor.

It takes me a minute to realize that the pain is very different now. My arm aches horribly, but I can move it without the stabbing sensation, the awful knowledge that something is very wrong in my body. I raise it up experimentally.

"Hey," says the nurse, grabbing my hand and easing it back down. "Take it easy for a couple of days, okay? It might be a while before your arm is completely better. Try moving it up above your head a few times a day, but don't do any handstands or anything."

I think of the handstands that until a few weeks ago I was required to do nightly, twice a day on weekends. "Okay, got it," I say. "No backflips either, I guess."

"That's right. I'm sure you'll get by."

How little you know, I think.

I feel ridiculously grateful to these people—for putting up with me, for fixing me, for not giving up. I want to hug them, tell them I love them. I stare at the side of the doctor's face, and she goes all fuzzy, like she has a halo.

"You're so beautiful," I say.

"That's the gas talking," says Betsy, and I think, *Yeah, and the rest.*

The doctor snaps off her gloves and bows out. It seems as if the nurse will do the same, when Betsy says, "Hey, what about my burn?"

"Ah yes," he says. "The noodles."

The nurse finishes examining the skin on Betsy's arm and tells her that it looks deep, that it may scar. He cleans it gently, applies a dressing, says it'll be sore for a few days but should heal fine if she keeps it clean, airs it out daily and to come back if it gets any worse. As we leave, I see another flash of his death scene and I want to say, *Don't have the operation, whatever it is.* I don't say this. It's not my place: he hasn't asked. I raise my eyes as far as his chin and say, "Thanks."

"No problem," says the nurse. "Just doing my job."

CHAPTER

25

Faith

THAT MORNING, WHILE I'm at Home Farm with Mum, Amara calls. She says I need to get back to the ground, that something's going on, that I need to be there.

"What is it?" I ask.

"I'm not sure. But they've ordered the chaps to start pulling down your machine."

"What?"

"Mike didn't stop them. I don't know who they are, some kind of officials . . ."

"I'm coming."

When I arrive at the ground, it's hard to pull into my usual spot because there are four black SUVs parked in a line just beyond the entrance, blocking it.

I leave the van where it is, half on the grass verge, and climb out, though my legs are reluctant. I want to turn that van around and drive away fast, but I know this is one of those times we'll need to pull together as a company, in the face of the common enemy, despite everything between us.

When the men come in their matching cars, in their suits and ties, to take us away or move us on or stop us or attack us or threaten us, that's when we put aside our differences, because as circus people we are more similar to each other than we are to them.

The Waltzer is being dismantled, the boarding on the outside already on the truck, the lighting panels being removed. I head over to where Calum is crouched on the upper part of the machine, wielding an electric screwdriver.

"Have we been told to move on? Some kind of problem with the license?"

Occasionally councils have had the carnival shut down, but not for years. They need a certain number of legitimate complaints to be made for that to happen, since all of our pitches are booked and paid for months in advance, years sometimes. I'd be very surprised if he says it's that: this is an old ground. We've been coming here forever, every single year, and the locals welcome us with open arms.

He carries on removing the panel, passes it down to one of the others. "I don't know. You need to ask Mike."

On the other side of the ground, Harrington's cast and crew are lined up along the outside of the tent, as if queuing for a show. They are waiting their turn to be spoken to by the men from the black SUV cars. I can see Blissi and his brother, hands thrust in pockets, head down, next to Mike as they talk together, off to one side of the tent. They aren't in the queue; perhaps they've been seen already. Beyond them is the rest of the company, or most of them, one behind the other, shifting from foot to foot. I can hear a female voice, an American accent: it's Shona, one half of a trick-roller-skating couple who joined only a few days ago, from Vegas. She and her partner filled the void left when they threw me out of the show, so I haven't had much to do with her. She's not in the depressing-looking queue yet, but voicing her frustration from somewhere among the living wagons, where at this time the cast ought to be sleeping, recovering from last night's show. The morning air is humming with uncertainty—and something uglier: fear.

I count eight men in matching jackets and hats, most of them wearing sunglasses. There are three women, also in the jackets and hats, but instead of trousers, they wear stiff-looking skirts. The uniform is cut with a kind of military precision. The men are in shiny shoes that clash badly with the baseball caps on their heads, and all are carrying iPads, with styluses poised. I spot a ninth man standing in the back of Mike's newest lorry, supervising and directing our Argentinian tumblers as they do the hard work of emptying everything out on the grass. There are all sorts of things in there: speakers, rolls of wire, mixing desks, bits of metal welded together that were part of last season's set. Also, rolls of fabric, two spare petrol generators, lamps from the lighting rig. As each item is removed and placed on the grass, the man in the back of the truck makes a note with his stylus, with the seriousness of a policeman logging a haul of illegal drugs.

Christine is standing there, arms folded, holding on to her anger and powerlessness in the face of these people. I stand by her side. I can't remember the last time we were raided, only that there was a huge sense of injustice then too.

One of the uniformed women spots me and starts to walk over to us. I ask Christine, "What's going on?"

"Debt collectors."

The woman with the iPad and the jacket is making a beeline for me, but she's still quite far away, so I think about taking off. I make to leave but Christine puts a hand on my arm.

"Don't. You need to talk to her," she says. "No point running. Things will just get worse when they catch you."

I stay put, but my feet twitch to get me away. The woman is nearly here, and her face is eerily serene with a kind of plastic calm, like a living mannequin. She stops in front of us and looks me up and down so quickly that I almost miss it. "Do you work here?" she asks, and I think about what to say.

"Yes, she does," says Christine. "This is Faith Harrington. One of the owners." I'm open-mouthed with shock that she's told them this with no hesitation. I want to slap her for her disloyalty.

"Oh yes," says the woman. "We've been waiting for you. Mr. Ward has informed us you're jointly liable for the debt."

I don't think I know what she means. It's true I'm in debt, but not to her. I'm in debt to Calum because of his extortionate build fees. Apart from that, I don't know about any debt. I wonder if this is anything to do with Mum. I'm not in debt to the nurses yet, but I will be if I don't do something very soon.

"Are you in a position to settle?" she asks. Her eyebrows rise and she smiles faintly, as if she's just asked something innocuous like if I'd like a cup of tea.

It's the weird smile that breaks me. I wasn't going to ask, to let on that I don't know. It puts me in a position of weakness. "Settle what?"

The woman looks at Christine with a questioning expression, as if she's surprised.

"As I told your colleagues earlier, we're a debt recovery agency, here on behalf of Her Majesty's Revenue and Customs. Harrington's has built up a very large value-added tax bill, that I'm sure, as one of the owners, you're aware of. You've been given several chances to pay up."

Oh, I think, my heart sinking. *The tax man.* I manage to keep from showing any particular emotion.

I say, "I haven't had any chances. I didn't know anything about it."

"Oh yes you did," the living mannequin seems to be thinking as she nods at her screen. "I have a record of the many letters delivered to you at this address." She shows me her iPad, where the address of Home Farm is indicated. The letters have all arrived in the past three months.

"I don't remember seeing any letters." I'm genuinely confused. The only post I've seen at Home Farm has been junk. If I'd noticed a serious-looking brown envelope, I would have opened it, or I would have at least passed it to Christine or Mike. Mike must have picked them up when he visited Mum. He didn't say a word to me about it.

"It's not up to me," says the debt collection officer, "or anyone at our company, to make you aware of your debts, Ms. Harrington, especially when HMRC have done everything in their power to make you aware before it got to this point. We're just here to bring it in."

"It's up to someone. I don't owe anything. I don't *know* anything. I don't even have a say in that side of the business. Christine and Mike are in charge of tax and wages, and all that stuff, aren't you? Tell them."

Christine has the look of a woman who is trying very hard to be sorry but isn't, really. "I'm the administrator for the business, Faith. But Mike and I only own half of it. The rest belongs to you."

"Not me. It belongs to Mum. Not my debt. You can't take anything from me. She's only got a few days left. Are you going to put her through this, now?"

"I'm sorry to hear about your mum, Ms. Harrington. But thankfully, it shouldn't affect her. The paperwork states that the shares your mother owned in Harrington's were passed to you quite recently."

She eyes me smugly, as if she's caught me out, but I still don't understand.

"Passed to me?"

She's getting irritated now. "Yes. So you're the shareholder named on the certificate."

I think of the stack of papers I signed when we bought the ride. I didn't read any of it. Mike just pointed where I should sign, and I did. There seemed to be endless things to sign, fifteen or twenty documents. Could it be that some of it was to do with Mum's shares in the business? And he never said a word?

"But Mum would have to sign, wouldn't she?"

The woman says, "All the relevant paperwork is in order. Your mother would have had to agree to pass the assets on to you. She's signed all the correct documents." The way she's telling me this, in a slightly bored, patronizing tone, it's as if she doesn't buy my dumb innocent act. As if she thinks I know these things, that I'm just pretending to be in the dark so they'll feel sorry for me.

"Mr. Ward has showed us the records, so we know that some of the more substantial machines here belong to you. The auction value of these is enough. We are going to seize them to cover the debt so that the business can keep the majority of the rest of its assets."

Mike appears behind the tax woman, and I stare at him, the pieces suddenly fitting together in my mind.

"You're going to let them take the ride?"

Mike says nothing. He slips his hands into his pockets, clears his throat.

"But without that ride . . . what am I supposed to do?"

He sighs. "We can sort it out, Faith. For now, there's no other option. It's that or close the whole show. There's nothing else that would make up the amount you owe."

"But . . ." But he bought the ride and put it in my name. I agreed that it would be the sum of my stake in the business, and now the tax man is simply going to take it away.

The officer cuts in. "We'll be seizing the ride and three of your trucks. They'll all be auctioned later this week. For now, everyone is free to go."

Mike tells the acts they can go back to their wagons to prepare for the afternoon show. Many of them look upset and exhausted after the ordeal, and because of that I doubt today's performances will be the best. The show will go on, though—you can count on that.

I follow Mike around like a shadow as he makes his way back to his wagon. "What does it mean, though? For me, I mean." I think I know, but he needs to spell it out. Finally, he turns to me.

"It means you don't own anything at Harrington's anymore. The ride covers your part of the debt, but all yours and your mum's shares were in that ride."

"So?"

"So, you won't owe us anything. We can all make a clean break of it."

The final piece slots into place. This is Christine and Mike's way out. They've found a way to get rid of me, to have my stake in Harrington's taken away, neat as that. I wonder if they planned this, and think they must have been planning it for months, ever since that first tax bill came, before I predicted Amir's death. It was when Mum became fully reliant on the nurses that it must have formed as a plan, when they could see she wouldn't last much longer, and they didn't want to be stuck with me, millstone that I am. What were they going to do to get me out of the ring if I hadn't handed them a reason to banish me? I guess they would have thought of something.

I am betrayed, rejected by my own. My face burns with shame and sorrow.

He closes his eyes. "If it makes any difference to you, I'm sorry. I am. I wish it could be different."

I turn away, deciding I need to take my horse and go, start over somewhere else. As if there's any choice now. Mike's apology echoes, meaningless, the last thing I hope to hear him say.

Just after I get back to my wagon, Amara comes to find me. She's heard what happened to the ride. She's sorry for everything.

"I just feel like if it wasn't for what I asked you to do with Dad, they wouldn't have started down this road."

I don't tell her that I suspect it began way before Amir collapsed, that this has been coming for years. "I would do it again," I say. "It's not your fault, not at all."

"Even so, if there's anything I can do."

I glance over to where the horses are stabled at the edge of the ground. It will break my heart to be without him, but I realize it wouldn't be fair to take him back to Home Farm if I'm always going to be looking after Mum or at work in the laundry. He's a circus horse, and he'd be better off here.

"Can you look after Macha for me?" I ask.

"Of course," says Amara. "He'll be treated like a prince—don't you worry."

"You'll take him out every day?"

She nods. "I might even brush up my trick-riding skills. He's too good not to be in the show."

"Yes. He is."

She puts her hand on my arm. "You are too, you know."

The grief of having the circus taken from me is raw. From here, I can't see a way back into the ring, where I belong. I say nothing.

Rain has begun to fall, wet lumps of it that hit the ground like tiny bombs. I hug Amara a little too tightly before she leaves.

It takes all day to pack everything down properly. In the dark I start the engine and pull off the ground. The rain is falling steadily, so by the time I'm on the motorway, the road is slick and black. It's not until I'm nearly at the next junction that I remember Betsy, that I need to tell her what's happening, and not to try to find me at the showground when her shift ends. I pull over to send a message, but when I get my phone out, I see that the screensaver isn't the one I remember. I turn it over in my hand and realize it's Betsy's phone and not mine. I'm confused, wondering if she's got my phone, and if not, where it might be. The screen is locked. but I think I remember her passcode. I try it and it works.

For some reason the video of Joey Standish and me is right there, paused on my twisted face. I flick the screen to get rid of it, and the comments section comes up. Message after message, asking if I can do the same for them. The first thought I have is that they are sick, that no one in their right mind would actually want to know when they will die. But then as I keep reading, it starts to make a little more sense. It could help people if they do it for the right reasons. And it could help me if they have the money to pay for it.

I need the Oracle of Death! Anyone know where to find the eye patch girl?

Looks to me like Harrington's circus. I went there but she's gone. No ride either?

I've heard she does private readings, but it costs a LOT.

How to get in touch? I'd love to know when I'm scheduled to shuffle off this mortal coil. Maybe I'll take my father along, for inheritance planning ha ha!

EYE PATCH GIRL! WHERE ARE YOU?

How much do you think? Thousands? Worth it, I reckon. I WOULD PAY ££££ for her to tell me when I will die!!!!

There are also comments from the other end of the spectrum, those who think it would be a kind of curse to know your own death, and a few crazies who think the whole thing is blasphemy, that I'm an abomination. What's increasingly apparent is that hardly anyone thinks it's a scam. The very public death of Joey Standish, tragic though it was, has made people believe in me. It's made them want me for the very thing that has always, until now, made people reject me.

Without thinking too much about it, I flip open the video function on the phone and set it up on the dash. I drape my face in a scarf with the eye patch on the outside and record a simple message. A few minutes later I've got a YouTube channel and a new email address. I click "Upload," and then post the link in the comments under the other video. If they can pay and they want it that bad, they can have it.

CHAPTER 26

Faith

The clock ticks another minute, red numbers crawling up, glowing in the darkness. The dashboard readout says 01:02, when I decide it's time.

"Tell them we're coming."

Betsy presses "Send" on a message she typed out an hour ago. It simply reads:

> *ten minutes*

The phone immediately lights up with a response:

> *Okay*

I can feel my pulse increase, and my instinct is that I ought to back out. I place my hand on my pocket, where the wad of cash is sitting. I can't think of a time I've been in possession of so much money. And the amount he gave me was only the first half, so there's more to come. I don't particularly want to do this thing I'm being paid to do. There's a cold sweat on me, and a feeling of wrongness in my body. But I want the money. Toni gave me the nursing invoice this morning, and it needs to be paid by the end of the week. So, it's this or nothing. My reservations about doing the prediction might be left over from the shame I always felt at being able to do this thing at all. I remind myself I'm not doing anything wrong, no matter what the family thinks. Their views are stupid, nothing but superstition. Betsy backs me up. "To the hilt, honey."

I roll out of the yard without turning on the engine, let the wagon roll as far as it will, wait until we're almost at a standstill before firing her up. As we drive away, I check the house again in my rearview. Still in darkness. I relax a little. Don't want anyone to know what I'm up to, just in case.

We drive into town and out the other side. In the suburbs, where the money people live, driveways are generous, houses far from the roadside, big old trees lining the avenues. Further out still are the houses with the huge gardens, gates obscuring the view from the road, remote-operated bollards that rise from the concrete, cameras to eye you and record every visitor.

Eventually it returns to countryside, where there are a few older detached houses, and then nothing but fields.

"Where is it?" I ask Betsy.

"Hard to see in the dark," she says, but then the lay-by where we've agreed to meet comes into view. Parked there, lit up in the wagon's headlights, is a long, sleek, shiny car, low to the ground. It's a Jaguar in gunmetal gray. The headlights pick out a figure sitting up front and the vague shadow of a person in the back seat.

I pull up behind this shark of a car, and as I do, another comes by, slowing when it reaches us, eyes peering out. I wonder if I've misjudged this meeting place. We're alone in an isolated spot, meeting men we have never met before, about whom we know hardly anything.

The name is Sir Phillip Landry. Betsy looked him up, and he's a real Sir—there was a picture and everything, so I thought it would be all right. I feel stupid to have thought that, based on a photo and a page of information. It doesn't mean this person is who he says he is. Maybe we should cut and run. I notice that the car cruising by is also a Jag, matching the one parked, and it underlines how much money is involved with this meeting. An amount that means so much to me, but that he probably spends on wine in a single evening. The second car is security. Sir Phillip, if that's who it really is, must have a fleet of these things. And if it's not Sir Phillip? We'll simply have to take our chances. Betsy suggested carrying a blade each for protection, but I couldn't explain why I was so vehemently against that idea. Every time I hold a knife, I see a flash of my hand in the vision with the soldier, the blood dripping, the shock I felt. No knives.

Betsy gives a low whistle. "Those are not cheap cars."

I might have been impressed if I had the slightest interest in cars. What I am is rattled, that we are outnumbered, that we are unarmed, vulnerable, and taking huge risks.

"Maybe you get a discount if you buy in bulk," I mutter. Whatever happens tonight, I won't die. I know I'll live to be with Mum. I know I'll live to whenever I see the soldier again. But it doesn't mean I can't be hurt badly. My shoulder tingles, and I shudder thinking about the way they pulled it straight at the hospital.

I grip the wheel to stop my hands from shaking. Betsy says, "Don't worry. Turn the engine off. And keep this in your fist, for emergencies." She hands me a small canister of pepper spray.

Having killed the engine, I sit there in the driver's seat and wait. The phone in Betsy's hand remains dark. Eventually, the driver's door on the Jag opens, and a man in a suit emerges. Intimidatingly large, the sight of him just makes things worse. He peers toward us in the dark, eyes glittering. He walks around to the other door, movements fluid, oversized muscles working beneath his too-tight suit.

"I don't think I can do it," I breathe. I squeeze the little can of pepper spray hard.

"You are going to be amazing," says Betsy. "You were born for this."

I grab the phone and type out the word:

WAIT

Silhouetted in the moonlight, the man pauses, his hand on the right-side passenger door. He's looking down at the phone in his hand. After a second, he says something to whoever is in the back, closes the door, and gets back inside the car on the driver's side. A second later, a message makes Betsy's phone glow:

?

"Why did you do that?" She's whispering.

"I'm supposed to be the Oracle of Death," I say.

I unclip myself and head into the wagon's living space. "We need to make it look proper."

I've brought some drapes and strung up washing lines to use as curtain rails. We start to hang these velvet curtains around the space, making it smaller, more intimate, screening off the modern fittings and doorways. It becomes a cave in which light is absorbed by the opaqueness of the fabric, so the mind can focus. We have a table, a pack of cards, and a lamp. Betsy lights a candle and a stick of incense. Then I settle in the corner. I place a headscarf so it covers most of my face. I'm pleased with the effect and satisfied that there are no extraneous objects on show. Objects absorb energy and disrupt thought patterns. I make a mental note to get hold of a large crystal ball for if we ever do this again. Crystals, I read, are for clarity and sight. Also, I think you'd expect an Oracle to have at least one.

Betsy pauses, sweeping her eyes over the space we've created. The stage is set.

"Too much?" I ask.

"Perfect," says Betsy. We make a few more adjustments, close a small gap in the drapes. Betsy sends another message:

You may enter.

I can hear the Jaguar's doors softly opening and closing, slow steps approaching the trailer. I concentrate on my breath, and wait.

There is a knock on the door. My stomach clenches.

"Come," I say.

I let them fumble with the door, watching as it opens and two men climb up inside the wagon. They are very different from each other: one older, who I am relieved to recognize as Sir Phillip from the photos online. The other is younger, taller, and broader, with rimless glasses. Both are dressed overly smartly for such a secretive rendezvous, if you ask me. I hope it's dark enough in here that they don't notice the joggers I've got on under the oversized shawl and headscarf. They look around and then at me. The older man smiles without showing his teeth. The younger does not. He eyes the still slightly wonky velvet curtains, the candle and pack of cards, then me, with equal forensic disdain.

"Please sit." I breathe the words, unsure what kind of voice to use and going for something I think will be mysterious, both airy and deep. With an open palm I indicate the two chairs opposite. The taller, younger man watches as Sir Phillip settles into the chair we've placed there, and then sits down himself. When they are inside the circle of light thrown by the lamp I realize that Sir Phillip is as nervous as I am. The younger man exudes a kind of teenage skepticism, staring at me hard, curling his lip. I'd judge his age at around mid-forties, and Sir Phillip as around thirty years older than his companion.

Sir Phillip leans across to the younger. "Is that definitely her?" He speaks with the undisguised rudeness of the over-privileged. He's not trying to hide the fact that he's talking about me, right in front of me.

The younger man doesn't take his eyes off me. "I don't know," he says. He opens his phone and swipes around. "This is the one from the video," he says, showing the screen.

They both look at me. I wait.

Sir Phillip says, "Well, I can't tell anything from that. Could be anyone under there." He turns to address me. "Can't you take that off?" He points, meaning the headscarf.

With a flourish I pinch the cloth in the center and reveal myself—ta-da! I give a half smile. Neither man reacts beyond a certain narrowing of the eyes.

"Yes," says the younger man, his voice slow and deliberate. "That's her. I think."

There's a beat in which the two men exchange a glance. I lean in. "I'm sorry, am I not what you were expecting?"

The younger man snorts with laughter.

"Hey," says the older man, turning in his direction. "Have some respect. This is her place."

"She's a kook," says the younger man. "It's obviously not real."

I wonder what it is he thinks isn't real. The crazy look in my eye in the video? Or the vision that I described to Joey of how he would die, which came true only hours later. The prediction, swiftly followed by the death. Brutal. Those two things took so much away from me, but they gave me the authenticity I have now. I can taste the power of it, like blood in my mouth. His words say one thing, but there's a tremor there, an edge of apprehension. I'm glad we took the time to hang the drapes, to control the space. They are in *my* lair now. My nervousness is dwindling. I'm getting into it.

"I hope you haven't come here to waste my time," I say.

I never asked these people to seek me out. They went to a lot of trouble to find me.

The younger man doesn't respond to that. He says to Sir Phillip, "I just think you'll be wasting your money."

The older man grits his teeth. "It's my money to waste, son."

The younger man is the son, then. Worried about his inheritance.

"Well, sure, but you don't want to . . ."

"If you can't keep your mouth shut," says Sir Phillip, "you can wait in the car." It's as if he's talking to a petulant child, which in a way he is. The son crosses his arms and, I assume, tries not to put his lip out.

"I'm sorry about him," says Sir Phillip to me.

I don't do anything, but simply wait, let the atmosphere settle a while. When all is quiet, I say, "I know why you've come."

The words seem to send ice into the space. Both the men visibly shiver. I bring the cards to the center of the table and cut the pack, placing the new top card up. It's the nine of spades. It means fear of the future. I shiver too, because the pack could easily be talking about me.

"I am the Oracle of Death," I say quietly, carefully pronouncing each syllable. I push the nine of spades toward Sir Philip and tap it twice, leave it there in front of him. "You want to know how you will die. But you're afraid of knowing."

"Yes," says Sir Phillip. "There are things I want to do. I need to know if I've got time to do them."

"Time can be imprecise," I say in the same quiet voice. "There are no guarantees."

I place the deck close to him, tuck the nine underneath. "Cut."

He cuts the pack, turns up the new top card. Queen of diamonds. I smile. "That's me. The truth teller."

The son snorts, earning a sharp look from Sir Phillip, who asks, "What do you mean, that time can be imprecise?"

"I will see your death play out, but I can only describe it to you. I can't say exactly when it will be."

"Sounds like a waste of time then," says the son, folding his arms.

"Shut up, will you?"

The son presses his mouth closed.

I give the cards to Sir Phillip to shuffle, then he hands them back. I cut the pack this time, turn up the top card. Two of spades.

"What's that one?" asks Sir Phillip.

I tip my head, considering. "It signifies tough decisions. Or sometimes deceit."

More huffing from his companion, and Sir Phillip flicks his eyes to his son.

"That's it," he says. "Enough. Wait in the car."

"But, Dad—"

"Just get out."

The son gets up violently, crashing out of the wagon and slamming the door behind him. I let the air settle a while, breathe in and out slowly, before placing the cards in front of Sir Phillip. He cuts the pack.

"Four of diamonds," he says.

"That's about money. Someone's about to receive some."

He seems confused. I guess he has enough money. I imagine he receives more every day, one way or another—dividends, bonuses, interest.

"It's probably for me," I say, holding out my hand, and he laughs. He reaches into his jacket and draws out a fat envelope. It matches the one I was given a few days ago by his aide when we met to discuss terms; that one sits in the pocket of my trousers, a reassuringly solid wad. I slide the second into my pocket next to the first, the stretchy fabric of my joggers bulging with cash and promise.

"Before we do this, I need you to know. There are things I can tell you about your end and things I cannot. Do you understand?"

He nods. "You'll see the death, and you can describe it?" It's interesting to me that he says *the* death and not *my* death.

"Yes," I say. "I can tell you where, and how. Those things will not change. They never do. You can rely on the vision and glean from that what you can and any clues about when it will happen."

"Then tell me. Everything you can see."

"It's not without sacrifice that I do this," I say. "There is a personal cost to me."

"I am grateful that you've agreed to it," he says. "I know from my man that you were reluctant."

I was reluctant, until a certain point. Up to a certain amount of money. After that, I don't think many people would have turned the offer down. I don't think many people would be able to live with themselves if they had. Everyone has a price, and Sir Phillip knows that better than most.

"That's true," I say. "But I stand by my word. And now let's begin."

Keeping my gaze trained on Sir Phillip, I reach up to remove my eye patch. The room disappears.

I'm inside the vision, but I strain to retain a link to myself in the present. I can hear myself narrating the scene, describing it to Sir Phillip.

"You die playing cards. You are wearing green trousers, boat shoes, and a short-sleeved shirt. There are people there, laughing, drinking, and you're surrounded by them, by your family. It's indoors, but the walls are curved, and there is water outside. Inside a boat? Yes, a luxury boat."

I hear Sir Phillip's voice. Not in the vision, but from the wagon. "How old am I? How far in the future?"

I try to concentrate on the Sir Phillip in the vision. His skin is tanned, wrinkled like a prune. "I can't tell. You're older, thinner, but not ill. You look good. A year? Perhaps more. You're opposite a woman, she has red hair and blue earrings, shaped like the tails of fish. No, not fish. Whales."

"What else?"

In the vision, the party rolls on. There is the clinking of cutlery, laughter, the sound of a live band in the next room. "The red-haired woman, she's dealing to the group. Canasta, I think? You are all being served iced cocktails by a young man in a white uniform. No one is looking directly at you; they are looking at each other, at the waiter, at their cards. When the game gets to your turn, you're gone. It is quick, silent, painless. Your eyes are closed, you look as if you are sleeping, or taking a moment. They still don't understand what's happened. When the person to your left nudges you, you slump over, and there are gasps all around."

While I remain within the vision, I hear a gasp too, from inside the wagon. Then there's a coughing sound, and I swim toward it. Sir Phillip is making the sound. He is doubled over, laughing into his knees.

"Oh my," he says. "That's hilarious. On my yacht? With my wife right there, and wearing those earrings I finally bought her."

Abruptly he stops laughing and looks thoughtful. "I've always hated canasta."

CHAPTER

27

Faith

SIR PHILLIP THANKS me again for the prediction. He seems happy with what I told him, and I wonder if he's going to tell his son or keep it to himself.

I see him out of the wagon and wait in the doorway as he drives away. I stand and breathe deeply, taking in the night air. I feel strangely calm, strangely humble. I'm not frightened by the vision I saw. I hope my own death will be as gentle as that, as whimsical. He'll die at his own party, surrounded by his friends and family. No one will be expecting it, but that means they won't be sad or glum in the moments before, the way I try not to be when I talk to Mum. Seems perfect, in a way. Perfect for Sir Phillip, certainly; perhaps less so for the people who will witness it.

I resolve to be less sad when I see Mum next, to try not to weigh her down with my own problems. Her last few days should be carefree, free of pain and worry. Betsy has promised to make sure we have enough emergency meds to see us to the end of this so that Mum can float on the lightest cloud through the gates to the other side, without a struggle, and maybe there will be some left for me and Betsy too.

After tonight Betsy might not need to risk stealing it for much longer either. With the money we made, we can buy as much of the stuff as we want. I'm not addicted, I'm pretty sure, though I'll admit that Mum might be. I tell myself I can take it or leave it, but when I make up a new solution for Mum, it's only sensible for me to test it out. A couple of sprays under the tongue to make sure the cocktail isn't too potent. I made a mistake once, when I added some ketamine I'd swiped from the vet's and didn't measure it properly. I spent half a day convinced that my face was stuck to the wall of the wagon, unable to move. Since then I've been more careful. I'll only use things prescribed for humans.

All is silent, the stars and the moon bright against the black sky. I reach out to pull the door shut, and there is a man there, his chest an inch from my face. I cry out and push him away, his body hard and unyielding, one of my fingers catching awkwardly, crunching and bending back against him as I shove. He stumbles, falls backward, and I think he's going to land flat on his back on the road, but before I can grab and slam the door, he's sprung up somehow and he's back, filling the doorway, both hands gripping the sides, and he's saying, "Wait, I just want to talk to you."

But I kick him as hard as I can, and the force of it throws me off balance. Now I'm the one flat on my back, my head hitting the leg of the table as I fall. The man makes a noise like an injured beast, a deep roar that chills me, the anger in it. He crumples, half in, half out of my wagon, his hands covering the place between his legs where my foot connected.

"Get out!" I scream. "Betsy, help me."

He drags himself half up so he's kneeling, panting in the doorway. When he turns his face toward me, I recognize him from the park. From the shadows. It's the man who's been following me, the soldier. The man I will kill. I flash into the vision for a split second, see that blood dripping, his shocked face. In the wagon I scuttle backward until I'm up against the bench. I can't get any further away.

"It's okay," he says, grinning through the pain. If he's going for nonthreatening, he's very much wide of the mark. He looms in the doorway, still bent almost double. "I'm not here to hurt you."

"Oh, you're not?"

If I hadn't already been thinking he was here to hurt me, I am now.

Betsy says, "What the hell do you think you're doing, creeping around like that in the dark?"

"I'm sorry—I didn't mean to startle you. I was waiting until they left. I didn't want to interrupt."

We chose this meeting place because it was remote. We didn't think about how exposed we would be if anything went wrong. Because of the reading, I'd put it aside, forgotten about the risk, but now I'm feeling dumb all over again for putting us in danger. Once the other two had gone off in their big expensive car we were completely alone. How did this guy even arrive without one of us noticing? I glance past the soldier and see the answer in the light from the doorway: a pushbike lying on its side not too far away, the rear wheel still moving slightly. So stupid of me.

My sense of self-preservation kicks in, and I clench my fists. "It's the middle of the night. You didn't mean to startle me?"

"I didn't know what else to do. You wouldn't talk to me. I've been trying. That time in the park, I thought—"

"You've been following me. Of course I wasn't going to talk to you."

"This guy? This is who's been stalking us?"

I glance over at Betsy and nod. "That's him."

He looks from me to Betsy and back again, his face set in an expression of bafflement. "I wasn't stalking you. I needed to get you on your own."

"Oh, sure, and that's not terrifying in the slightest, is it?" Betsy puts her hands on her hips. She's furious. "And even if you did get her on her own, why would she talk to you? You look like a total fucking psycho."

The soldier straightens up, running one hand over his shaved scalp, keeping his other hand in the door, probably afraid we'll slam it and try to get away. He's right, I will do just that if I can get the chance, hand or no hand. Don't want it slammed in a door, better move it. I'm feeling a little more relaxed. At least we outnumber him. Betsy's got my back, and I see that she's also got a small paring knife clutched in her hand. I check it in a panic, to make sure it's not the one from the vision.

"I think you better go." I say.

"I will. But can I ask you something first?"

"No, you fucking can't." I move to slam the door on his hand, but he's quicker. In one movement he's inside the van. He wrestles the knife from Betsy's hand and points it at me. I freeze.

After a second, he seems to realize what he's done, what he's doing. He stares at the knife in his hand and then opens his grip, letting the blade fall. He backs off, collapsing into a chair, his eyes downcast as if he's ashamed of himself. When he speaks, his voice is small and meek. "I just need you . . . I need you to tell me how I die." And again I flash to the vision I saw, of a different place, a different knife going in, the feel of it puncturing him, the flesh resisting as I push on it with everything I have. The way it comes out easy, like out of butter, and a spurt of red lands on the ground between us, then he steps backward, confused. How he doesn't realize what I've done until he sees the blood, how his legs give way and he falls to the ground.

The knife in the vision is much bigger than the one on the floor of the wagon, which has a blade only two inches or so. I should be afraid now. I should try to kick the knife away, but it's pointless. Even if I was holding it, it wouldn't protect us. He could strangle us both with one hand on each neck. Only he won't, will he? The danger is not to me and Betsy, but to him.

I have to get him out of here. I don't know when I will stab him, or why, but I'm not going to sleepwalk into it. I know it's futile, that there's nothing I can do to stop it happening but I can't help but try. He doesn't know how close to death he is, being close to me.

"You came here to get a reading?"

"I know you saw something in the park. Our eyes met. That's how it works, right?"

"I didn't."

"Then look now. Tell me now. I need to know. I can't bear not to."

"You think this is how you get me to help you?" I say. "Jumping out of the dark and threatening me with a knife?"

"I'm sorry I scared you. I didn't mean to, but I'm desperate. I'm about to go on tour. I want to know if I'll survive it. The last time I saw men die, one of them was my best friend. He didn't know it was coming. Maybe if he had, he could have done something about it. I could have done something. He died laughing, with a cigarette in his mouth. It could have been me."

"There's nothing he could have done even if he did know. What I see is something that will happen. The death is set, a path that can't be changed."

"But don't you see how that would make you brave? In battle, what a weapon to have. If I know I won't die on tour,

I can fight without fear of death. And if I do, even more so, because I'll know there would be no way to change the outcome. It's the uncertainty that's the killer."

What he can't know is that we are both set on a path, being washed toward a future where I will hold his life in my hands. I look at him begging for me to make him brave. I still don't know why I would do it, why I would want to kill him, what it is that pushes me over the edge.

My mind is a jumble of thoughts and feelings, but mostly I just want this man to leave.

"I can't do a reading for you."

"You have to," he says, his voice hardening somewhat, though he keeps his eyes on the table. "I mean, please will you? I don't want to force you."

"Can you pay?" asks Betsy. "You know this is a business, right?" She sounds unflappable, even in the face of the threat this man poses. I know it's an act on her part, but I'm grateful she's taking charge.

"How much is it?"

The figure she quotes is twice what the billionaire Sir Phillip paid. The soldier bursts out laughing. Then he stops. "Not a joke?"

I stare at him. "No."

His face changes. I see a flash of cruelty there. And something familiar about the set of his eyes. I think I know him, but I can't think how. "Some people are saying you're a fake, anyway."

"Good," I say. "There will be fewer people hassling me about it."

"You don't care?"

"I don't care. It doesn't affect me. There are those who know the truth, who are willing to pay for my knowledge. You're free to believe what you like. Now you need to leave."

"There's a rumor going around that Joey Standish was set up. That he only did what he did because of what you said, and if you hadn't said it, he'd still be alive. I've heard the police are launching an investigation."

"That's ridiculous. There's a video of him. He was alone."

"Yeah, but he names you in it, or as good as. They can find out who you are. They can find you liable."

"That can't be true." But I don't know if it can or not.

He leans back. "Even if it turns out you didn't break any laws, some of Joey's fans are pretty pissed about it. He had a strong following. They might decide to teach you a lesson. I've seen things online, chat groups, threads full of threats to your life."

"This is bullshit."

"You'll need protection, that's all. And I could do that. Maybe I could do that for you instead of payment. I know people, heavy people, ex-military. They'd make sure you were safe."

"We've got security, thank you."

"Oh yes, and they're doing a grand job of securing you right now, aren't they?" He gestures to himself and to us, indicating how we are alone, in the middle of the night, on a secluded country road.

There is a silence as this sinks in. Betsy says, "Oh, just fuck off, will you? This isn't for you. You'll need a lot more money if you want to have a reading. It's too much for you to pay, Private Piss-take."

"Hey," he says, annoyed. It's clear to me he's not used to being told "no" by the likes of us. "What's it to you, anyway? It won't cost you anything to have a look."

"You won't get what you want from me. Come back when you've got the money, and I'll think about it."

He takes a deep breath. Then he says, "Right, fine. I'll go." But he doesn't move. I don't know what to do. I'm thinking about asking him what the hell he's still doing in my wagon when he darts forward, rips off my eye patch and holds my head on a level with his. Our eyes connect. Then I'm gone.

I see the vision again, the night, the road, him lying there on the asphalt, looking at me with wide, shocked eyes. I hear the sound of the knife falling, clanging on the ground. I see the headlights, how I turn and run, the images like flashcards, jerking from one to the next. The soldier is dead, I killed him, but I still don't know why.

If I could see the moments before, hear what he says to me, what we say to each other, I might be able to fix it. And if not, at least I'd know what pushed me to do that to him. I try to replay it, to return to the beginning of the vision, to just before it happens, but I can't.

"Faith?" Betsy's voice cuts in from far away. I'm still trying to run, half of my brain still inside the vision, the death of the soldier, the rage I felt just before, the fear after. He must have done something for me to be angry enough to want him dead. What was it? What will it be? "Faith, wake up. He's gone now. You're safe."

My hands instinctively go up to feel my face, my naked eye, and she puts the eye patch in my palm. I'm on the floor of the wagon, a pillow under my head. My body is wrecked with exhaustion from two visions in one night. I can barely maneuver my arm to place the patch.

"How long have I been out?"

"An hour or so. You fell asleep, after. I thought you needed it."

"What did I say to him?"

She hesitates.

"Come on, Betsy, tell me. What did I tell him?"

"You were pretty vague. But it was . . . weird. I've never seen you react like that before."

I realize something then. Both Tommy's dream and Mum's vision had been, up to this point, so much worse than any of the seeings I've had for strangers, because of who they were about. This one is the worst of all, by far. I would rather see my own death than see myself become a killer.

I'm begging her. "You have to tell me exactly what I said. What words?" *I need to know what he knows.*

"I think you said there was a knife. I think you said, *"Drop the knife*, but I couldn't make it out, not really. All your words were jumbled up, and you kept screaming. But then you just stopped speaking and went completely unresponsive. I was thinking about calling an ambulance, when you seemed to relax and go to sleep."

"What else did I say?"

"You were yelling at him to get away from you, mostly. But then I was too."

"What did he do, how did he react?"

"I don't think he knew what to make of it. He just got up and left, got on his bike. Good riddance. How dare he do that to you, take your patch away like that?"

Part of me thinks, that's rich, coming from her, but mostly I feel relieved that I didn't tell him anything specific, that what I said didn't make sense. If he knew I might kill him, awful things might happen in the time between now and when the vision comes to pass. I wonder if everything we do is fixed now, since I saw the end of him.

"You should get into bed," says Betsy. "Let's drive back to Home Farm."

I get up from the floor, and together we fold the table away, take down the drapes. I collect the cards from the floor, where they have scattered.

"What did you do with the money?" I ask her.

"The what?" she says, and I freeze.

"The money. The envelope, with the rest of the money in it, that Sir Phillip gave me. I put it with the other envelope in my pocket. It's not there."

"Faith, I didn't see it. It must have fallen out."

I search the floor of the wagon, using my hands to feel the carpeting right to the edges as if it might be there but I can't see it. I pat my pockets repeatedly. I search the benches, the table, and finally I start opening the storage cupboards.

"It's not here," I say.

I open the door of the wagon and step outside, search the ground outside in the moonlight.

"He's taken it."

Without that money I can't pay the nurses. I can't fill Mum's prescriptions, let alone pay for the extra drugs I know she needs.

Now I think I know why, in the vision, I am so angry with the soldier.

CHAPTER 28

Betsy

SHE ROLLS THE laundry cart along the corridor to the room she needs and gently depresses the handle. Inside, Ethel is there, her wasted body beneath the blankets so frail, so vulnerable. Betsy feels a stab of pity.

She sits in the chair next to the bed, places her hand on the old lady's, where it lies by her side. The skin of the hand is soft, the bones delicate. It's entirely cold. She concentrates on Ethel's chest, which appears unmoving. Betsy checks for a pulse and finds one, very weak. Not quite yet, but she's fading fast.

By the bed is a clipboard with a prescription attached. Betsy often fills these at the pharmacy, when she's asked to, and delivers the drugs to the office. At most of the homes there is a strict system, a locked medication trolley only operated by the registered nurses. Here it's not quite as organized. When patients die, unused prescriptions go missing, and sometimes paper bags full of medication disappear. She hears them talking about it in the staff room sometimes, and that woman,

Celeste, often stares at Betsy accusingly. Celeste has the right culprit but the wrong idea—she thinks Betsy is giving the drugs to the patients, to send them on their way, but she would never do such a thing. All she's doing is tidying up. Once the patients have passed on, no one has a use for those expensive drugs. They go back to the pharmacy to be destroyed. Betsy and Faith have come to rely on them. For kicks, sure, but also to give to Iris. It would be cruel, now, to cut her off, to make her experience withdrawal at the end of her life. Betsy told Faith the first time she should never have started down that road, that she'd need to sustain the supply for that reason, but Faith just said, "There are ways and means. I don't have to get it from you, but I'll get it from somewhere."

"It won't be medical grade," Betsy had said.

"Ricky knows a guy," Faith replied. "Better than medical, he says. But it can cost."

She hadn't meant to do it again, after Celeste accused her. *This will be the last time,* thinks Betsy. *Things would have been different if that soldier hadn't robbed us.*

She slips the paper prescription from the clipboard and folds it, put it in her pocket. Then she places a soft kiss on Ethel's cheek.

"Thank you," she says.

In the corridor outside the room, the manager of the home, Fiona, is waiting. Betsy is confused, because it's three AM and Fiona only works days.

"My office," she says. "Now."

Betsy hangs her head. She has been shown the CCTV footage of her taking the key to the medicine cabinet, using it to take a sheet of pills from a box belonging to a recently departed resident. She has seen the footage of her slipping an entire bottle of liquid morphine into her tunic just after that. Finally, she saw herself folding the prescription and placing it in her pocket, then leaning over the body of Ethel. They've been waiting for her to come back, to commit another crime. They've planted cameras where they knew she would go. There is no defense.

Betsy's backpack is open on the desk. The morphine and the pills are there.

"You've been on a bit of a spree, haven't you?" says Fiona.

Betsy doesn't reply.

"Tell me why I shouldn't call the police."

Betsy thinks about telling Fiona about Iris, about how she's become addicted, how Faith can't quite keep up with the need for extra supplies. She wonders if Fiona would understand that they've run out of money, that they thought everything would be okay and then yesterday that man took them for everything they had.

She wonders if, should she beg, Fiona would not tell the police and also not inform the agency who employs her, because she needs to keep this job. But she looks at the manager's face and she knows it's no use.

CHAPTER

29

Faith

"SHOULD WE TELL Linda?"

"Tell her what?" I ask. "That we can't pay for Mum's care anymore or that we might run out of the illegally procured drugs she's come to rely on, because of me? Oh wait, we'd need to tell her about those first, and I don't think she'd be in favor, do you? Or maybe we should tell her we've been meeting strange men in the middle of the night and getting ourselves robbed for our trouble."

Betsy says, "No need to be like that."

"Sorry," I say. "But no, I don't think we should bring Linda into this."

Linda hadn't wanted to hire the private nurses in the first place, but I'd insisted. My aunt wanted us to have Mum placed in a public hospice, where the care would be free, but I didn't like the idea on principle. I knew Mum would hate it if she had to share a space with people she didn't know, be cared for by scores of different people. Leaving the carnival was bad enough, and if it had been possible, I would have kept her in the wagon until the end. Home Farm was the next best thing, and I'd declared I was going to pay for everything, so that was that. Linda went along with it, but only because I was so determined it should be that way. If we told her the full extent of what was happening now, she'd make me have Mum moved, I know she would. And I know Mum can't be moved, that she won't be, because I've seen her final moments. That vision is like a beacon of certainty, the light that guides me on. Everything is crazy right now, but at least I know where we'll end up.

"When does the nursing bill need paying?" Betsy asks.

"Yesterday," I say. Betsy looks surprised. "I know. I've explained that I've got a bit of a cash flow difficulty. Terri said they could hang on for a couple of days, but after that I suppose they won't."

My phone pings with another email notification, and I glance at the subject line:

ORACLE

I assume it's more of the same, someone else asking if they can have their death predicted. We've been getting scores of requests, but after what happened last time, we need to think carefully before we do it again. I'm waiting for another rich one, like Sir Phillip, but no one has yet agreed to pay the amount we need. These emails are from everyday people, some of them desperate to have a reading, but as soon as we name the price, they back out. With Sir Phillip it seemed like the perfect solution—money no object. Small fish is all we have right now. But it's not nothing.

Betsy knows what I'm thinking. "It's too risky," she says. "After last night, I don't see how we can . . ."

"I don't see how we can't."

Together we draw up a plan.

"First things first," I say. "I don't want anyone coming to Home Farm or knowing where we live. We need to take the wagon somewhere secluded."

"Not too secluded," says Betsy.

There's a site on the side of a double roundabout, near a motorway. Sometimes used by traveling communities, it's private enough for our purposes, but there are a couple of streetlights, and the town is a short drive away.

"We'll have our phones," she says. "We've got the pepper spray. We could have knives . . ."

"No," I say. "No way, no knives."

"I wish we could hire someone like Ricky to help out."

"We couldn't pay him. Next time. If it goes well. We can get a whole van load of security. But this time, we just need to make as much cash as we can, and be on our guard."

We go through the emails, only responding to the ones we can verify as real people who have social media profiles or personal websites that seem legit. Our price is set at two hundred pounds, which I think is high enough to get us out of trouble if we see enough clients, but low enough that people won't be spooked. I scour the emails twice, looking for someone with real money, but there are none that check out.

Betsy comes up with an appointment system, and we make a little sign for the door of the wagon. Then we email everyone we've chosen and ask them to send us a mobile phone number, so we can ping them the location at the last minute.

"I don't feel like there's anything else we can do," I say.

We park the wagon up and get into our places to wait for the first customer. We've tried our best to filter out anyone who seems obviously dodgy, but we keep the canisters of pepper spray close at hand just in case.

* * *

Judy is first through the door. She's young, maybe no more than a few years older than me. The second she sits down, she starts talking. "I'm just really worried about it. I can't stop thinking about it. It's not normal, is it? I mean, I obsess about it—I can't sleep. I get it, at least I think I do, that once I'm dead I won't know about it, but the idea that I won't know anything anymore, that I won't even know what my kids are doing, who they're with, whether they're happy—all of that."

"You have kids?" I ask.

"No, but when I do. I mean, I've been thinking maybe I won't have any, because can you imagine how awful it would be to bury your mother? Could I really do that to them? It's going to happen, right?"

I take a slow breath. She can't see my face beyond a vague outline, and I'm glad.

She doesn't need any encouragement to continue. She says, "My mother's still alive, and even thinking about her dying is like—oh my god. She's not even ill."

I'm getting a little tired of Judy. "I am the Oracle of Death," I intone darkly. She just keeps talking.

"I'm not even that old, am I? So it won't be soon, but I can't stop thinking about it, like I'm thinking about it more than anything else, that it will be like going under anesthesia, only forever, and my brain will be gone, just not exist anymore, it will be blackness, nothing. I can't comprehend it. Do you know what I mean?"

"Sure," I say. "Do you want me to look now?"

"I don't know if I do. I thought I did. But now I don't know. What if it's in, like, two days?"

"If you want to know how you die," I say, "you need to cross my palm with silver."

"Cross your what with what?"

"Money, Judy. I need you to pay me."

She gets out a small fold of notes and holds it, stares at it. Then she gives it to me, but she doesn't let go. "If it's soon, don't tell me."

I try to take the money, but she's still gripping it.

"No, do tell me. I need to know. I need to stop thinking about it."

I pull on the notes, and she lets go reluctantly.

"I'm going to take my face covering off now, Judy. Once my eye is uncovered, I'll see a vision of your death. I'll describe everything I see. Are you ready?"

She closes her eyes. "It's just so scary that one minute in the future I'll just be no more, and I don't even know when. I'm going mad. I need to know. Thank you for doing this—I really mean it. It's going to change things for me. Maybe I'll be able to sleep."

I wait. This is going to take longer than I thought.

"Are you ready now?" I ask.

"Yes?" she says, though it comes out sounding like a question.

I take off the scarf that covers my face, and wait for her to open her eyes. When she does, she screams and jumps up from the table. I've still got my eye patch on, so I don't know what's made her scream.

"I'm sorry," she says. "It's not you, it's me. I'm not ready. I don't know what I was thinking." She starts backing out of the wagon, turns and opens the door, goes through. She shuts the door, and I hear her drive away.

Betsy comes out from behind the screen. "Well."

"You can say that again."

"Did you get the money?"

"Yeah, but, wow. I hope the next one isn't like that. It was as if she just wanted to talk."

"Therapy would cost more," says Betsy.

"I didn't do anything. She wouldn't let me. She's not really gotten her money's worth, has she?"

"Her loss."

Betsy sends the next message, and we wait for the arrival of the couple who told us in an email that the husband had been diagnosed with cancer at the age of forty-three. They have two children in their early teens, and want to know if he will live to see much more of their lives. After not very long we can hear an engine approaching, and headlights break through into the space. We listen as the car parks in front of the wagon and the doors open. There is the sound of two doors slamming, two voices talking, a man and a woman.

Betsy and I exchange a glance. Once more, the game is on.

There is a knock at the door and Betsy says, "Come."

The door handle is pulled from the outside, and cool air rushes in. I remain very still under my head covering, watching as a well-groomed man in an open-collared shirt climbs the steps into the space. He is followed by a younger woman, who reaches out to him, looking around for a place to sit and leading him by the hand to the chair we've put out. He lets himself be led. On first glance, he doesn't look like there's anything wrong with him. He has well-pressed clothing and impeccable hair, a subtle tan. Must be early days for the cancer. I suppose we'll see, won't we.

The couple leave happy, handing me a big tip for my trouble. I was able to tell them he had at least another five years, if not ten. Time enough to grow a large beard, for his hair to fall out and come back in, completely gray. Time for those children to become adults, for one of them to be present at the death, a woman by his side, holding a tiny baby.

"Grandchildren," the wife said, and burst into tears.

The man in the vision may not even have been dying of cancer, but I'm no medic. It was a happy reading. It felt good.

The next customer is a woman in her sixties. She does not want to chat at all. She sits down, hands over the money, and says, "So how does it work?"

I don't even bother with the Oracle of Death line. I take off my eye patch and our eyes lock.

"You will be old," I say. "You die in a hospital."

"What of?" she asks.

I look closely at the vision, search for signs of the same kind of machines and equipment that Mum has at her bedside, but it's all different. "I don't know. In the vision you fade away. There are beeping machines. Seems painless."

She relaxes visibly. "Thank you," she says, and gets up to leave without another word. That was my kind of customer.

The woman who enters the wagon next eyes me in a way that makes me feel strange. When she asks me to, I take off my face covering, and she smiles triumphantly. I worry that she is a journalist, or maybe a policewoman.

"I knew it," she says. "I thought it was you in that video."

She sounds slightly unhinged. This is not how it's supposed to go. We were meant to weed out anyone with a grudge. My fingers find the pepper spray.

"You don't recognize me, do you?"

"Should I?" I look around to see where Betsy is, and catch sight of her behind the curtain.

"You were at my school. Not for long, I'll grant you. But it was memorable."

So this was one of the girls on the playground.

"What do you want?" I ask. "You don't want a reading—that much is clear."

"Oh, I had my reading already. You must remember that?"

I think of those girls, circling me like vultures, how I fought back. The deaths I saw, one in hospital, one from choking, and one in a car accident. I want to ask her which one she was.

She gets out her phone and starts recording. "When I was ten years old," she says, addressing the camera, "this woman told me I'd die in a car crash before I was twenty. Well, now I'm twenty-two."

The woman stands up. I feel threatened, like I want to slap the phone out of her hand. She thrusts it in my face. "Remember this woman. She's a fraud. Don't waste your money, guys."

"I remember now," I say. "There was another girl, who was going to die of some kind of disease."

"Cindy?"

"I don't know her name. What happened to her?"

The woman falters. "She died. She was diabetic."

"Oh," I say. "I didn't know that. Sorry to hear that." She's still pointing the camera at me. I say, "So you don't want a prediction yourself?"

"You did it already, and it wasn't true. Why would I pay you for the privilege of having you make up some other complete lie about my future? It was so scary. I was only a kid."

I decide to be professional about it. Her hysteria is tiring me out. "With respect, I didn't make anything up then, and I wouldn't now. I could check whether the vision is the same. But you'd need to pay the fee for that."

"You must be joking. You already got it wrong. You said I wouldn't be twenty."

"I just see it and try to judge the age and the timing. Doesn't mean it was wrong. Anyone ever tell you that you look young for your age?"

She looks frightened now, the phone held out between us like a shield. "Why would that matter?" But she knows why, I can tell.

"You and your friends were bullying me. I guess you don't remember that part?"

"No, I do. It was wrong, but we were kids, we didn't deserve—"

"Another girl, the one I said died of lung cancer. What's she up to? She a heavy smoker, by any chance?"

The woman doesn't have to tell me I'm right. She confirms it with her silence.

"I think you should leave," I say, opening the door for her. She lowers the phone.

"Joey Standish only jumped in that river because of what you said. It's your fault he drowned. The same thing happened to Sarah."

"Which one is Sarah?"

"She believed it. She only started smoking because she figured it wouldn't matter if she did or didn't, that after what you said, her future was set."

"How do you explain your diabetic friend?"

She gets angry instead. "You're a fraud, a manipulator. I know it. I can prove it."

"Let me look in your eyes," I whisper. "Then you'll know for sure."

She moves fast to get away from me, almost stumbles as she gets in her car.

"Drive safe," I say.

CHAPTER

30

Faith

I'M SCROLLING THROUGH the comments below the Oracle video I posted when a link pops up. I see it's a news article, and I click on it. The article just went live, and it stops my coffee halfway to my mouth.

"Betsy, have you seen this?"

She comes out of the bedroom, yawning. "What?"

I show her the headline: *Mysterious "Oracle" linked to second accidental death*

"Bloody hell," she says, and starts reading it out.

Local police are searching for an online sensation who calls herself the "Oracle of Death" after two people recently died under what are now believed to be suspicious circumstances. At the beginning of the month, the TV personality Joey Standish tragically died in a drowning incident, which police now suspect may be linked to the death of a young woman in the early hours of yesterday morning. Although originally Standish's death was ruled as accidental, the online content recently viewed by this newspaper has prompted the police to launch an investigation.

Shortly before their deaths, both of the deceased allegedly had contact with a woman who claims to be able to predict death, and has posted online to advertise the service. Police are warning that there is more to this than simple quackery and that there may be elements of hypnosis or other activity involved, which may cause people to act out of character following a meeting with the so-called "Oracle," who currently is contactable only through an anonymous email address. If you are worried about a family member who may have engaged with this person, or should you have any information you think may be useful, please call.

My phone starts pinging frantically, with people emailing the Oracle. Ping-ping-ping-ping. I turn it to silent.

"This is bad."

"Yes," says Betsy.

"She must have crashed the car on the way back from seeing me."

"Yes."

"Do you think they'll find us here?" I look out the window at the empty yard.

"Only a matter of time, I guess."

"How much money do we have?" I ask.

"Six hundred from last night."

That's nowhere near enough. It won't pay the nursing bill this week, let alone next week. We need more if we're going to be able to survive more than a couple of days.

"Should we run? Go and park somewhere they won't find us?"

"Faith, think about it. We haven't done anything wrong. That article, it's just people gossiping."

"It said they opened an investigation."

"Let them investigate. If they find us, what are they gonna do? But if we hide, we look guilty."

There's the sound of an engine, and I'm convinced it's the police. I duck down and peep around the edge of the curtain. Outside, one of the Harrington's vans pulls up to the house.

"Who's that?" asks Betsy.

I watch from the window as Calum climbs out from the driver's side and approaches the front door of the farmhouse. Before he can enter, I open up the wagon door and step down into the yard.

"Can I help you?"

He turns and shades his eyes. That's when I see that Mike is there too, climbing out of the passenger side.

"We've come to see Iris," says Mike.

"I didn't know you were coming," I say.

Mike glances at Calum before he replies. "We should have let you know. Didn't think. Sorry."

It's the first time I've seen them since they threw me out. It had to happen sooner or later—Home Farm is theirs too. "I guess it's fine. Just don't tire her out, will you?"

They go inside. After a few minutes I follow. Toni is in the kitchen, bustling about, making food for Mum that she will no doubt barely touch. Mike says hello to her. Calum hasn't said a word.

Toni glances from me to them and back again. When they've gone upstairs, she has me sit at the kitchen table and puts a mug of cocoa in front of me.

"What's going on between you and the big man?"

"Family stuff," I say.

"You want to talk about it?"

I shake my head no. "I just want to be here in the house while they are. I don't trust them."

"Oh," she says. "That kind of family stuff."

"Mum probably won't even know they're here anyway, so I don't know why they're bothering."

"Now, Faith," says Toni, "you and I both know that's not true."

"Yeah," I say.

"And they come every week, you know. Have done ever since your Mum's been bad."

I'm surprised at this. Most surprised at the fact I had no idea.

"Every week? Those two?"

She nods. "Once or twice they've come at night too. They never told you?"

"Uh-uh."

There's a short, awkward pause before Toni says, "About the bill . . ."

"I'll sort it. I will."

"I know you will, Faith. You have so far. But if you're having trouble paying us, it might be time to think about changing things up a little, going to a hospice where she can . . ."

"This is the best place for her."

Toni nods. "Yes. But if you can't afford to keep paying, there may come a time when you have to think about it. I know you're not working now."

"That's their fault." I jerk my head to the stairs, where Mike and Calum have gone up to the bedroom. I'm getting upset, angry at the situation.

Toni sits opposite. I'm frightened about what she might say to me.

"We won't leave you alone, Faith. We won't leave Iris, not now, when she's so close to the end."

"You won't?"

"No. We'll do everything we can to support you. Everything we can."

And I know that she's saying they have to eat too. They have to make a living. They do this job for love, but they can't do it for free.

"I'll find the money, Toni. You can rely on me."

"I know you will, Faith. You're a good girl."

When Mike and Calum come out of Mum's room, I follow them outside.

"Toni said you visit a lot."

"Yeah," says Calum. "She's my auntie. Of course I visit."

"Well, I just wanted to say, that's fine. I mean, it's okay. I won't stop you."

"That's big of you," says Calum with an edge to his voice.

Mike glares at him. Then he turns to me. "Is there somewhere we can talk?"

"I don't know if I want to."

"Will you just come and talk to me for a minute?" he asks. "A few minutes, Faith. It's important."

And I think maybe I should, just to clear the air, so that the Farm will be peaceful for Mum. We head over to the wagon, where I expect to see Betsy, but she's made herself scarce. On the kitchen counter my phone screen is lit up, more notifications of messages for the Oracle. They are coming thick and fast, too many to deal with.

At the table I wait patiently for whatever it is that Mike wants to say to me. Out the window I can see Calum leaning on the van in the sunshine, vaping and staring at his phone.

Mike sighs, folds his hands together on the table.

"First, I feel bad for what happened with the ride. The contract we made, it didn't work out well for you. I feel terrible about it."

I stare at him. I don't know why he thinks I'm interested in his feelings.

He sighs again. Sits back, folds his arms. "I'm trying to say I'm sorry, Faith."

"Try a bit harder, maybe."

He hangs his head, and I think I see moisture collecting in his eyes. "I'm sorry. For everything, the circus, the ride, Calum. It wasn't supposed to . . ." His voice catches. "I love you, kiddo, you know that."

He reaches for my hand, and I flinch away.

"Faith, please."

"So, you're sorry, okay. I can come back to Harrington's, then? Ride Macha in the ring?"

He clears his throat, looks at his fingernails. "Maybe that would have been possible before."

"Before what?"

"The thing is, I've been hearing stories about your new business."

My phone is buzzing. I didn't think to turn off the vibrations. "Ah."

"Yeah, this Oracle of Death. Not exactly a secret, is it? I believe they call it 'trending.'"

Starting the Oracle was one of those moments, I realize now. A fork in the road. A choice I made that I can't take back, no matter how much I wish I hadn't had to choose it, that Mike and Calum hadn't made me. "Well, that's good. That's what I wanted," I say, what's left of my pride talking. "I'm making more money now anyway." I don't tell him that I made and lost more money in a single night than I made in a season with the circus. I don't tell him I have less now than I did when they pushed me out of Harrington's, or that even if I'd not been robbed, I would still rather be back in the ring. I miss the circus—almost everything about it. I miss Macha, riding him, practicing every day. I miss the other acts, the talent and spectacle, the lights and the smell of it, the thrill, the hard work. I even miss the Waltzer, that second chance it gave me.

"I'm better off without you, really. I don't think I'd come back anyway."

He pauses like he has something to say but is finding it hard. "I care about you. I want to help. If you ever need anything."

"Like what? If you can't make it okay for me to come back, what else is there?"

He pauses again. "Do you need me to spell it out?"

"Spell out what?"

"I think . . . I've been thinking for a while now. That there's something wrong with you," he says.

"Oh," I say. I thought he might be about to talk about the news article, if anything. "Well, there isn't."

"But you know, sometimes you do things that don't make sense. Not just the visions, but . . . you say things, strange things. Sometimes I worry about you, Faith. That you'll end up in a bad place."

"A worse place than you put me in right now? What does that look like, Mike?"

"No, I mean . . . it's hard to say what I mean."

I shrug. "Well, if you ever work it out, you know where I am."

"But you're . . . I think you need some help, that's all."

"I don't need your pity. I'm doing just fine, thank you very much." My phone is still going off, buzzing away on the side. "Hear that noise? That's the sound of people willing to pay thousands just to have me do the thing you all think is so evil. What does that tell you?"

"You should be careful, Faith. Those people aren't like us."

"Nobody's like me, though, are they?"

He's silent for a while, his eyes downcast. "After Tommy, when we saw that you were the same as Daisy, I promised your granddad I'd look after you, always. I promised it would be different for you than it was for her, that we'd find a way to manage it within the family. But since I took over the big job, well, I can see I've let you all down."

He's not wrong about that, but I don't have time to think about his feelings on the subject. They have nothing to do with me.

He looks at Calum, still waiting, clouds of vapor rising from the fist at his mouth.

Mike says, "He's a strong personality, your cousin. I felt for him too, when he came back. You're my niece, he's my nephew. You know his mother gave up all claim on the business when they left? Well, Calum felt cheated. He wanted a piece of the pie too."

It makes sense to me now. Mike's not in charge anymore. Calum is.

"He wanted Mum's piece."

"I never planned it."

"You hung me out to dry, tricked us. Me and Mum."

"That wasn't my idea," says Mike.

I get up from the table, go out of the door and across to Calum. He seems amused at the pissed-off look on my face.

"Mike says all this was your doing."

"What was?"

"Pushing me out of the business. Using the ride to pay the debts. That dodgy contract me and Mum signed. All of it."

Calum laughs.

Mike says, "Calum, don't . . ."

My cousin plants his feet, folds his arms like a bouncer. "Yeah, seemed like a neat solution. Business decision, at the end of the day. Anyway, it's not like you have no way to make money, is it? Every cloud, and all that. No hard feelings?"

He puts out his hand, as if I would shake it. As if I might forgive him just like that.

I don't know why I do what I do next. I'm overcome with anger, for his betrayal, for his plotting, for the fact that he should be on my side and is not. For the sheer arrogance of him in this moment. I pull him in toward me and yank up my eye patch.

* * *

We are no longer in the yard. I'm taken to the carnival, onto the Waltzer, and Calum is there, wearing a Harrington's shirt, what looks like my money belt wrapped around his waist. The ride is almost at full speed, every car stuffed with excited kids, faces blurred as they spin by. Only Calum is almost still, standing where I once stood at the booth in the center of the ride. He steps out and is immediately swept along, walking the boards, the music swirling and thumping like a huge heartbeat beneath his feet. He spins the cars in turn, working his way around to everyone.

One of the cars has stopped spinning. The kids inside are chanting, "Spin it, spin it, spin it!" and he reaches out to grab the back of the car, but as he sets it off, there is a creaking noise, a metallic snap, and the car comes away, spinning from the boards, out of control. There are gasps and screams, the thud of it hitting the ground. The machine carries on turning, the music blaring out. No one is there to press the "Stop" button, and the people in the other cars are screaming too, not with excitement now, but with real fear when they see what's happened, when they are taken past the carnage again and again, round and round. The broken car has landed on the grass; the people inside are sprawled, groaning in pain, one of them unmoving. Calum's legs are trapped underneath it. There is dark blood coming from his mouth.

Ricky rushes over, he doesn't know what to do. He says, "Calum? You okay?"

But there is no answer.

"Someone stop that fucking thing!" he yells.

Someone, I don't see who, gets into the booth at the center of the Waltzer and presses the "Stop" button so that the music fades, the ride slows to an eventual halt. Everything goes quiet for a second, and then all hell breaks loose. People rush to the aid of the riders; circus people appear and together they lift the car from Calum's torso, revealing his twisted legs. He doesn't react. More than one person is on the phone to the emergency services, but it's too late for him. Calum's eyes glaze over, and he's gone.

* * *

"Faith?"

I come to, the vision receding like clouds parting. I'm sitting on the doorstep, with the nurse's arm around me, comforting me. Mike's voice, murmuring nearby, and Calum's, high and agitated. Feet shuffle on the rough stone of the yard.

"They've still got the ride," I say.

Toni says, "What's that?"

I check my patch is in place, then I look up. Mike has turned from where he is talking to Calum. He's got one hand on Calum's arm, as if to restrain him.

"You've still got the Waltzer," I say.

"Yes," says Mike. "I would have told you, but . . ."

"But how? The tax people took it to pay the debts. I was there."

He hesitates. "They took it, yes. But then we bought it back. At the auction."

"You did?"

"Calum did."

"When?"

He mumbles something. I make him say it again. "The same day."

I turn my gaze to Calum, trying to take in this fresh betrayal. He stares back at me. "What did you see just now, Faith?"

I stand up, but my legs aren't ready for it. Toni says, "Whoa, there, Faith. You need to sit. Let's get you inside."

"What did you see?" he's almost yelling at me.

"You don't want to know," I say.

"Well, why did you look then?" He's upset, his voice unsteady. He doesn't want to get too close to me.

"I guess I wanted to see how much longer I'll have to deal with your shit," I say.

"How long?" He's desperate now. "How long have I got?"

I feel the power shifting between us. "That's for me to know," I say, "and you to find out."

As Toni helps me back across the yard to the wagon, I hear Mike murmuring to Calum, trying to calm him down. After a minute they get in the van and drive away.

Inside the wagon, Betsy takes over from Toni. She makes me get into bed, where sleep tugs at me instantly. The buzzing of the phone follows me into my dreams, until I hear a single beep as the battery dies.

CHAPTER

31

Faith

I WAKE TOO EARLY with a bad feeling in my stomach, thinking about the soldier. Every time I try to replay the vision of his death, my mind won't let me see it all, the part I need to see most of all, the why of it. I see the knife, I feel the fear, but I still can't see what happens in the moments just before I stab him.

In the dark, I feel my way to the shower, let the hot water drill into the top of my head until it runs out. I dry myself without looking in the mirror. My eye patch is in the pocket of my dressing gown, where I left it, and when I've tied back my hair, I put the patch on. Once I have it on, I flip the light switch, my uncovered eye taking a minute to adjust to the brightness. From the bedroom I hear my phone, not the soft ping of a notification, but the terrible ringtone I've never seen fit to change, since nobody rings me unless it's bad news. I slam the door of the bathroom back so hard and fast, to get to my phone, that I dent the wall.

Linda is in the house with Mum. She says, "You need to come. Now."

I run across the yard, in through the door of the house. Terri is in the kitchen, boiling the kettle.

"Linda called me," I say.

Terri nods. "I think it's time."

I go up the stairs to Mum's room. When I get there, I'm ready to rush inside, but then I hear someone with a deep voice is in there talking to Linda. There is the rustle of a person moving around. This throws me. I find myself knocking gently to announce my presence.

Linda opens the door, her face drawn, her eyes haunted. She clearly hasn't slept; she stoops as if gravity is too much for her body to cope with.

"Is she gone?" I can't have missed it—it's not possible. But I'm scared anyway.

"No," says Linda, "but I think she's close."

My eyes settle on Mum, on her chest, which seems eerily still to me. I can't move forward until I can tell she is still breathing. Then I see it, the tiniest of shifts in the sheet, an expansion, and I rush to her, take her hand in mine.

"I'm here, Mum."

She doesn't move at all except for the smallest rise and fall of her chest, the movement coming once, maybe twice a minute. I squeeze her hand and she doesn't squeeze back, but I feel like she knows I'm there. I knew she wouldn't leave this world without me by her side. She's been waiting for me.

Off to the side, silently pulling focus in the room like an insect buzzing at my consciousness, is my great-uncle. I grit my teeth, try to make my voice calm. "Are you staying, Mike? Because I would rather you left."

No one moves. His betrayal sits between us like a hunched creature, an evil little elephant.

Mum makes a small noise, just a gentle murmur in the back of her throat. Her hand twitches a little, and I stroke it. My problem with Mike is not Mum's problem. Mum loves him despite everything; Mike was twelve when Mum was born, and they pretty much raised each other in the way of circus kids. It's a strong bond, one I should have had myself with my own cousins, that I did have until Calum and his siblings were taken away when Uncle John William and Auntie June left. Those family ties that I thought were unbreakable. Seems as if they've been severed all along.

Mike gets to his feet. In the small room his huge, shadowy presence dwarfs Linda and me. With him standing next to it, the chair he's just vacated seems like it could be made for a child. He takes a shy shuffle in the direction of the door. "I'll be on my way, then. Call me if . . . you need to."

I ignore him. I don't really care what he does, one way or another; I just want him out.

Mum makes another small sound, a low moan, as if she's in distress. She was always really attuned to me, to anything that stressed me out. She'll be able to feel this, even if she's not fully aware of anything else. Mike being here is generating bad vibes, when I wanted this place to be calm and quiet and perfect, especially now, when time is so limited. I'm so angry with Mike for what he's done and for what he allowed to happen. But that can wait.

Finally, he goes. His heavy footsteps take him out of the house, to his van, where I hear the engine start before he drives away.

I move up as close as I can get, lay my head on the sheet next to her. "It's okay, Mum," I say. "I won't leave you again."

She makes a sudden breath in, a rasping sound that whistles on the exhale.

"Did she say anything to you tonight? Before you called?" I ask.

Linda shakes her head. "Not really. She was confused," she replies. "But she was aware of Mike for a few seconds. They said hello. And a kind of goodbye."

"Is that all?" I'm grasping at anything meaningful, a word or two. I want to remember everything if this is to be the last thing ever.

"After that, she closed her eyes and started making these weird noises. That was when I rang. Terri said it was a sign. Since then she's just been like that. Sleep, then gasping, whistling. She's not long now."

Sitting there at Mum's bedside, I feel like I'm slotting into my own vision. My hair now has those dyed pink tips—Betsy and I had them done in purple, but over the weeks mine have faded to the exact pink I was trying to avoid. The tattoo is showing too, a mermaid sleeve in green and red that I had done, despite knowing that I got the idea from seeing it in the vision, because I loved it so much.

Linda picks up a pot from the dresser, unscrews the top, smooths lotion on Mum's arms where the skin is paper-dry. A sweet smell fills the room.

I look at Mum's face then and nearly jump out of the chair. She's been asleep for days, hardly aware of anything, but now her eyes are fully open, focused and staring at something I can't see. I dig in my bag for the opioid spray, a quarter-bottle I've been saving just in case she shows signs of being in pain and needs a little extra. I hold it to her nostril, but with a huge effort she pushes my hand away.

"Tommy's here." The words are quiet but precise. She grips my hand, her bony fingers suddenly strong.

"That's right, Mum. Don't be scared. Your dad will be waiting for you, and Grandma Rose and Great-Grandma Daisy and . . ."

"Yes," says Mum, a smile blooming on her face. "Dad's there, and Billy, and . . . Mummy? Is that you?" She starts crying, sounding the way she might have then, the cries of a little child, no more than six years old when her mother passed over. I hold her until the tears stop. Then she looks right in my eyes and says, "Where's Daisy?"

"She'll be there, Mum. In her rocker, just like before."

"No," she says. "Daisy's gone."

"She's gone? She'll be along soon, I'm sure."

"No, she's gone. She's . . . I can see a light. There's a light, baby . . . it's so beautiful . . ."

Her voice trails away, her eyes become unfocused again. I gently lay her back on the pillows, and she closes her eyes.

Her lips are dry and cracked. "Are you thirsty, Mum? Have you drunk anything tonight?" The cup on her bedside table is still full, the straw sticking up. I look at Linda for an answer and she shakes her head no. Then I freeze.

"What is it?" asks Linda, following my eyes to where she's just tossed the cocoa butter back on the dresser. The formation is exact. All the tubs and bottles have been knocked into place. The vision is now. I stare at Linda, wide-eyed, and her eyes fill with understanding.

We both see that Mum's eyes are open and staring at the ceiling, for what I know will be the final time. I want her to look at me just once more. But I know she doesn't do that.

"I love you, Mum," I say, and I hope she can hear me, wherever she is. And then her eyes go dull, and all the air falls out of her mouth in a rush. We wait, but the in-breath doesn't come. Her mouth is open like a little bird's, and she's gone.

We wait. Both my hands are holding one of Mum's, and I don't want to let go, even when I start getting pins and needles. Her eyes are empty, and I'm grateful when Linda moves to close them, with two fingers, like they do in the movies, like she did in the vision. I experience the strongest feeling of déjà vu. Although I'm right here, I'm also outside myself, looking on. The vision has come true, but at the same time it feels completely new to me, completely shocking and unexpected. Not how I thought it would feel at all.

The silence in the room grows. Where there were three people, now there are two and one empty shell. I think I will feel her presence as her soul leaves her body, but I don't. All I feel is her absence. I rub the back of her hand. I know she won't move again, or speak or think anything. But in my deepest heart, I can't admit to myself that she's not coming back.

We are at the end of the vision, the beginning of the unknown. What happens next? I feel like I'm freefalling.

"Travel safe, Iris." Linda places her cheek on her sister's. "God bless you, darling."

We sit in silence for a long time. The ticking clock, which I've never noticed before, is obtrusively loud. Mum looks asleep. But she's not. I stand up, almost knocking the chair over. I need air.

"I'm sorry, I can't . . ."

"It's fine. Go. I'll stay with her."

I pull on the door handle, throw it open, and I'm gone.

CHAPTER

32

Faith

S*HE IS DEAD, she is dead, she is dead.* I've known it was coming. I've seen it, talked about it, warned her about it. I lived with it in my head for twelve years. Why do I feel like I didn't? The shock of it. The world without her. I am numb and burning. I feel nothing and everything. I am hungry and sick, light and heavy.

I'm sitting in the yard on the bench when Mike's van appears. He climbs out and goes into the house, the sun shining off his bald head.

After a short while he comes out and sits next to me.

"Is Linda okay? I ask.

He nods. "She asked if you wanted to be there."

"Now?"

"Yes. She said she would pick out the funeral clothes."

"Already?"

He nods.

"I should be there," I say. "She'll go for the wrong ones."

"Yes."

I don't move. Everything feels so final. I know it's important to spend time with Mum because this is my very last chance, but I also don't want to because I'm scared it might replace my memories of her as a person. I want to remember her as she was alive. Her limbs will be stiffening now, her soul gone from that vessel. Nothing affects her anymore, so why should it affect me? We've said goodbye already.

It's not about me, though, or Mum. It's about Linda up there alone. I should get up now and go to my aunt, to help prepare my mother for the next world. Pick out her final showgirl outfit, make sure she has the lipstick she needs.

I stay where I am.

He says, "We were wondering about what her memorial will be."

In the days after one of the company dies, the show incorporates some kind of memorial into its fabric, a symbolic act, a nod to who that person was when they were with the circus. When Grandma Rose died, they didn't replace her. For the rest of the season there was no trapeze act: When it came to the moment in the show when she used to perform, they lit the apparatus with a spot and raised up a bouquet in her honor while the band played a ballad. For Billy, who was the ringmaster for years, until he couldn't get about fast enough, his walking stick was placed on a podium that sat at the side of the ring for an entire season. Granddad's tribute was woven into Mum's act: she made a silks routine to his favorite waltz, wore a waistcoat of his when she performed. I still have it.

"I wasn't sure we still did that," I say.

He knows what I'm talking about. "It was different for Tommy."

"Why? He was as much a part of the show as Mum was."

"The truth is, we didn't honor him because Iris wasn't there. You weren't there. It seemed wrong. Everyone was hurting too much."

"He never got the tribute he deserved because me and Mum had been banished? How is that fair?"

"I know, Faith. I thought we'd do it the year after, but everyone wanted to make a fresh start."

"To forget about him, you mean."

"It wasn't him they wanted to forget. They didn't want to remind people of why . . . of what . . ."

I cut him off. "I'm not there now either. So why are you discussing it with me?"

"Amara's been learning the backflip trick. With Macha and one of the other horses. It was your mum's specialty. We thought we'd go with that."

"It should be me."

"Yes."

"But it can't be, can it?"

"I'm sorry, Faith."

"Fuck's sake, Mike. Stop saying that." There is a pause. I say, "Don't you need to be getting back?"

Even when people die, the show doesn't stop. They've never stopped, not since it was set in motion all those years ago by my great-great-grandfather. The show is life and death, and everything in between: the ring contains it all.

"I set them up this morning. The show runs itself, really. Any problems, Christine will be taking care of it."

"Who's going to be ringmaster, if not you?" I think I know, though I'm still surprised when he replies,

"I told Calum he could cover for me."

I laugh, not kindly. "Calum? He's not exactly a showman, though, is he?"

"He's good. And he's keen."

"Keen to take over, you mean. You want to watch that nephew of yours. He's got a foot in the door now; he'll want to stay in the ring."

"I can see why he wants to be a part of it. He'd no claim on what he thought was rightfully his by birth. Felt like he'd been robbed."

"I know exactly how he feels, in that case." I think of what Calum has in store, the accident on the Waltzer, and I'm ashamed to say that I don't feel sad at all, and I ought to. But I'm still too angry. "I'd like to see him all done up in the outfit. Need to take the trousers up a bit, won't he?" I don't intend to sound sarcastic, but it definitely comes out like that.

"Don't," he says. Then he mumbles something I don't quite catch.

"What?"

"I said, he's had his own suit made up. He's been doing every other night since you left."

"Who runs the Waltzer then?"

And his answer is almost too quiet to make out. "I do."

"Huh." The circle of betrayal seems to come together neatly in my mind, with me on the outside. I'm suddenly desperate to talk to someone who understands me. Mum. I want my Mum. But she's gone.

"Are you going to go up, then, to help?" he asks.

I think about what Linda's doing, her final task, a little bit of love for her sister. Truth is, I don't know if I can. Don't know if I want to.

"Not sure I'd be much help."

"You'll regret it."

"Maybe."

"Linda says the undertakers will be here in an hour."

"She called them already?"

"I did."

"What will happen to her now?"

"She'll go to the chapel of rest at Bill's, where she won't be disturbed."

Bill Gamble and his family know us because we used to be them, once upon a time. They've buried every member of the Ward and Harrington family ever since our great-great-grandfather sold them the business back in 1903.

Silence covers us for a while. Then Mike says, "Then next week we'll take her up to be with Tommy. If that's what you want?"

Tommy lies with the rest of the family in a sunken stone crypt in the cemetery up on the hill. You can read the names on a stone slab at the entrance to the crypt: David Harrington, born in 1873, who founded the circus, is buried there. He rests among several generations, undertakers, and their wives who went before. You can trace tragedy in the dates, in the unnatural order of burial: there's a Harrington baby, born and died the same year, a great-great aunt of mine. David Harrington's wife's dates show she died a few years after her husband, but the next death in the family should never have been Grandma Rose, married to the founder's grandson; a young mother, gone at twenty-five. Great-Granddad followed close behind, as if he knew it should have been him, if anyone, to die that day and was trying to put things back in the right order. Tommy's next in the list, the worst of them all to me. Then Billy, when he passed the show onto Mike. Finally, only a couple of years ago, the crypt was opened up once more for Granddad. He got to be with Rose in the end. Everyone's there—the Wards too—all except Great-Grandma Daisy, who lies nearby.

Mum's words in my head then: *"Daisy's gone."* Perhaps that's what she meant. Daisy was separate from the family and still is, even in death.

I turn my head in Mike's direction. "That's where she ought to be, don't you think? Or are we not good enough to be buried with Harringtons either?"

"No, Faith, I wasn't saying that."

"So why is it even a question that you're asking?"

"I was just talking. Of course that's where she should go. Of course."

I'm forcing words through the tears. "It wasn't her, you know. She never did anything wrong. It was me—I'm the one with the 'curse.' Bury me wherever, in an unmarked grave in a field—I don't care. But Mum deserves to be treated right."

"She does. She should be with Tommy and the others. No question at all. That plot belongs to her. Iris is one of us. You are too, Faith." He turns to me. "I never wanted to push you out. I wanted to find a way to keep you."

"That's not true."

"I just couldn't fight it anymore, with prices going up, with acts leaving, rent, fees. Christine and Calum were both on my case. They said if anyone else dropped out because of you, then we'd be ruined. I had to do something to save the circus. It was hard for me too."

"Hard for you?" I can't believe what he's saying or that he's choosing right now to say it.

"Yes, hard for me. I'm under a lot of pressure. It's just business."

"It's not just business—it's our family. It's our life. How can you say that?"

"Maybe there could be a way to have you back, eventually. Just let things cool off, and then next season, you could come back and run the ride again."

"Calum's ride?"

He seems flustered, "Yes, well, another ride then. Or you could be in charge of the admin team—you could do an accountancy course maybe."

"This is bullshit, Mike. You know I'd want to be in the ring."

"Everyone retires from performing at some point," he says. "What were you planning to do then?"

"I hadn't thought that far." I wasn't planning to retire for twenty years or more. Macha wasn't going to last that long, but I would get another horse, train it, come back stronger every year. "Alan and Elaine still perform, don't they?"

"That's different," he says.

Alan and Elaine are a knife-throwing act that have been going since the eighties. As youngsters they did several shows with Harrington's, including the year after Tommy died, when Linda joined them for a season. Their age is their unique selling point now. They don't like roughing it with traveling outfits these days, so they mostly take contracts for cruise ships. Last time I saw them, the act was truly terrifying, added to by the great show that Alan made of squinting through his glasses as Elaine rotated serenely on a large bull's-eye ten yards in front, wearing the same spangly black leotard she was wearing in 1993. He flings those knives with a wavering hand, but he hasn't skewered her yet. However, we all know it's a matter of time.

A black van pulls up, discreet lettering with the words "Private Ambulance." From the driver's seat, Bill Gamble Junior raises a solemn hand.

Mike and I stand up, follow the van as he parks with the back of the van positioned facing the front door.

"Let me pay for the funeral," says Mike.

"Absolutely not." I say.

"Please," he says. "It's the least I can do."

"No. Don't ask me again." I'm not taking any money from Mike. I don't trust him as far as I could throw his huge, solid frame. A few weeks ago I would have worried about where I was going to find the money to pay for this, but now I think I'll be okay. If I can find one or two more customers for the Oracle, it will be easy.

CHAPTER

33

Faith

A SCRAPING SOUND IN the room. I startle awake, glad to be pulled from the dream I was having, in which my head was wedged between two branches of a tree and I couldn't get it out. My neck protests as I straighten up, and the dream makes sense: I slept with my head at a bad angle, with the chair pushed into the corner of the room so I had something to lean against. My arm hangs down, temporarily numb, at my side. I have to rub it to get it back to life. I yawn and stretch. I won't be sorry to leave this place. The chapel of rest has been mine and Mum's home these past three days, but that was the last night I'll sleep here, in this chair by her coffin. If you can call it sleeping. I don't want to leave Mum, but it's time now, to lay her to rest. It's time to start living without her. But first, we need to say a proper goodbye.

Linda is standing in the doorway, dressed all in black, her Harrington's funeral kit looking as good on her as it ever did. I marvel again that she could just let it go, that life, walk away and never regret it for a second. I want to be Linda.

"Faith, honey, you get any sleep?" she asks.

"Not really."

I get to my feet slowly, feeling like I've been in a fight, my limbs bruised in places where I've knocked them, and I don't know how or when. Being tired makes me clumsy. My eyes feel gritty and raw because I've been crying, because I haven't rested properly. Linda puts her arm around me, and we both stand and look down at Mum. I think about how much she doesn't look like herself, but like a model of Mum made from wax. Doing her makeup had been surreal. I'm glad I pulled myself together and insisted I do it rather than either of the Bills, even though they are experts in natural makeup for the recently departed. Mum's makeup was never natural, even off-stage. She always had winged eyeliner like nothing they would have seen before, like Audrey Hepburn or Adele. I talked to her the whole time. When I was doing her lipstick, I kept expecting her to blot her lips together, the way she always did. She lies peacefully, beautiful and young looking, her cheeks filled out with cotton wool and no trace of the illness that killed her. She has a wig that mimics her hair from ten years ago. It's like a tribute to her, this display. Not really her at all.

"I feel like I want to take a photo," I say. "She looks so perfect, doesn't she?"

Linda touches my arm and pulls me into a hug. She holds me at arm's length, looks at my face. "Don't take a photo," She says. "Let it be a memory. Let it fade."

After the makeup, we dressed her in her bespoke, wine-red Harrington's uniform jacket and placed her feathered riding cap under her arm. Underneath her jacket is the classic leotard that all the front-of-house women wear when they're on duty. Even when she was in her thirties, Mum used to say it was too high cut for a woman of her age, but she wore it anyway, and she always looked fabulous. She has on two pairs of tights, the shiny ones and the fishnets. Black patent T-bar high heels, just like the ones Linda's got on. All ready for the finale, the cancan line, where in her prime she could kick up as high as anyone, higher than I ever could.

Bill Senior enters, his movements strangely smooth, like he's not walking but gliding across the floor on castors. He's the model of a perfect undertaker, if that's a thing. Never puts a word wrong and is never less than respectful, solemn, and gracious. He knows when to take charge and when to back off. I wonder how old he is, his hair almost white, his skin draping softly from the bones. When his eyes land on me, there's a fondness that makes me feel like he cares. I hope he does, and it's not just a performance for my sake. He touches my arm then, and I know it's real.

"I'm going to place the lid very soon," he says, and then he pauses, letting the finality of that sink in. This will be the last time we can look at her. My desire to take a photograph of her body has passed, and I don't feel sad about that because I have hundreds of photos of her. She's alive in those photos and alive in my mind. This vessel is important, but it's just a body now. Something symbolic for us to bury. The image of her lying dead in the box may fade, like Linda says, but it will never be erased from my mind, not until I take my turn on the coffin board the way all of us must.

When I'm dressed in the clothes Linda has brought for me, we stand side by side in front of the mirror. Matching costumes, of course. Exactly like Mum's but black. She's the only one allowed to wear colors today. We make our way up to the glass doors at the front of the building, shoes clicking, echoing on the stairs, while Mum is brought up in the lift by the undertakers.

The day outside is wind whipped, sunny and cold. Mike is standing there in his funeral costume with black shirt, top hat and tails. It's very similar to the undertaker's outfit, only Mike's jacket is embellished with black embroidery at the edges, and his hat has a single black feather.

"Where's Christine?" asks Linda.

Mike says that his wife is meeting us at the crem.

"Oh, okay. I thought she said she'd pick us up, is all."

We stare at the shiny black funeral car, a Mercedes, something I don't remember requesting. The funeral director opens the rear passenger door and retreats, suggesting that we ought to get in.

I'd seen the prices for the cars when we were going through the arrangements. I told them we couldn't afford it, that we would make our own way. That was when Christine offered the lift.

"There must be some mistake," I say to the undertaker, "We never said—"

"I'm taking care of the transport," says Mike. "Me and Christine. Don't worry about it."

I roll my eyes. If he wants me to be grateful for that, then he'll be waiting a long time.

Behind us, the glass doors of the funeral parlor open, and Mum's coffin is wheeled out to the loading area. The two suited and booted men who have brought her out stand to the side, hands clasped, eyes down.

The way the undertakers are standing makes me nervous. "Where's the hearse?" I whisper to Linda. "We definitely ordered one of those."

Mike hears me and nods toward the road.

I hear the hooves before I see it. A few moments later it rounds the corner, and there in the road is a horse-drawn gun carriage, pulled by four black horses. They have black feathers on their heads, and the driver is dressed like one of us, top hat and tails.

I look again and see that one of the horses isn't black, but chestnut, and smaller than the others. It's Macha, my beloved.

"Oh, Mike," I say, tears coming quick. I can't get out another word.

It's an echo of my brother's funeral. Tommy had a carriage too, only it was draped in white. White for purity, because he was only a kid when he died. Fifteen. Nearly a man, but not quite, the chance to grow up properly snatched away from him at the last second. I wonder what he'd look like now. I know that if he were here, I'd still be performing. We both would.

Macha is happy to see me. I throw my arms around his neck as the coffin is loaded onto the wagon, and cry like a baby.

Mike might have paid for the great posh car, but the only people who get in it are the undertakers and Mike himself. When Mum is secured on the carriage, Linda climbs up with the driver. I tuck in with the coffin, my legs dangling down over the back end. The smell of roses fills up my whole head and takes me back to Tommy's funeral. All these circles, round and round again, like the Waltzer, up and down, always the same. At Tommy's funeral I walked behind the carriage with Mum, holding her hand, breathing this same scent, filling me up in the exact same way.

We travel slowly through the streets, horses trotting at a brisk walking pace. We are a spectacle to be stared at, a carnival without sound or color, only black, and the trotting of the hooves: a carnival of death. People stop and bow their heads as we go by. Children point, their mouths open with wonder, their faces showing a tinge of horror when they realize we're not there for entertainment, that we're a funeral caravan. Traffic crawls along behind us, and for once no one is impatient enough to try to overtake the horses. We turn off the main road and start traveling up the hill to the cemetery, and although I want the journey to last forever, I know it can't. I know it's the last journey I'll take with my mum, and I suddenly wish we'd done something a little less traditional, maybe taken her up in a convertible, driven with scant regard for the rules of the road, leaning on the horn at drivers with the gall to get in our way. The way she drove, rather than this solemn, dreary trudge toward her final resting place. It's this thought that sets me off, and I lean my forehead on the wood of her casket as I cry. So many of the other family funerals have been like this. We all make this journey up this hill. Harringtons spend their life on the road, but we end up in the same place. What if Mum hadn't wanted that? She never said.

Up on the hill I count seventeen of the Harrington's crew around the graveside, dressed in their finery, heads bowed in respect. Andre the strongman is there. Fyodor and Yoki, the contortionists. The Fantastics: Amir, Amara, Stacey. The tumbler troupe: Aron, Rico, Thomson, Dodi and Steven, as well as Dodi's wife, Thomson's mother and two teenage apprentices called Robert and Huel. There're a few circus people from other shows there too, people we've known all our lives. I feel proud when I see them, all dressed up in black velvet, black tights, dark eyeliner. They are milling about in front of the crematorium, but when we come into view, they stop talking to each other and watch us approach. Then, as the carriage comes round and I hop off, I don't even care that most of the crew won't look directly at me. They start to applaud, slowly at first, and as Mum is taken off the back of the cart and into the building, they don't stop. They are whooping and whistling and clapping for all they are worth. This is it, her final curtain call. I love them all so much for this, and I remember how much I love this life. My longing for it is bittersweet. I know they don't want me.

We file inside for the service, every performer not quite comfortable on the chairs, their bodies designed to be up front rather than in the audience. Linda reads something from Nell Gifford's autobiography, beautiful words about how the best circus ought to make you cry, how it ought to seem as if it's on the brink of something, right at the edge of falling apart, and by the end of it we are all crying. We raise our voices to sing.

As the curtains are pulled around her coffin, the band starts to play "Entry of the Gladiators" from the back of the room. They play it slowly, as if it's a funeral march and not the soundtrack to every clown show since the last century. It's so completely absurd that I start to laugh, and soon everyone in the room is laughing too, even the clarinetist, who is supposed to be playing the tune. The music dies before the end, before its natural, proper end, and it seems completely right to finish that way, cut off in mid-stride.

Outside the crematorium, they all shake my hand, but not a single one will look at my face. They line up, respectful but guarded. Sorry for your loss, they say. Iris was a one-off, they agree. She'll be missed.

Mike doesn't say anything. He takes my hand and squeezes.

Calum is there, the last one in the line. He doesn't offer his hand, just stares at me until I turn away and find Amara there behind me, ready with a hug that I need more than anything.

At the wake there is vodka and wine, and I suck something dissolvable from Betsy, which makes my body as light as air. Things are blurry for a while. I'm in a car, then I'm back in the wagon.

Betsy is there.

"If you don't want to do it, that's fine."

I don't know what she's talking about, and I say so.

"It's someone who knows Sir Phillip. He says he can pay twice what Sir Phillip paid. I think he's genuine, Faith, not another one of those trolls."

She says it's not until tomorrow. There is so much in my head—the funeral, Calum's accident, my family's betrayal—all of it piled up on itself, a chaotic layer cake iced with the thing I won't let myself think too hard about, what I might do to the soldier. I know we need money, though, and badly. We still have to pay for the nurses' last couple of weeks, and now the funeral. The small-fish system won't work for that, in the time we have.

"Faith? What shall I say?"

I vaguely say it might be okay. And then I sleep.

CHAPTER 34

Betsy

FAITH IS STILL asleep, so Betsy starts to set up the space for when they drive out to meet the customer. She checks the email again. No reply since she responded with the short message: ***Wednesday. Will send a location and time within 30 mins of meet.***

She takes the velvet drapes out and hangs them up, neatly enclosing the place where the Oracle will sit. She screens off the entrance to the bedroom area with the gauze. At one point during the morning, Linda knocks gently on the wagon door, and Betsy ignores it. She goes very still and pretends she isn't there.

"Faith?" calls Linda. After a minute of knocking, she goes away again.

Betsy isn't bothered anymore that Linda doesn't talk to her, despite the fact she's been in Faith's life since they were both children. There was a time she thought Linda might be a friend to her eventually, but she's long since accepted that it isn't going to happen.

Betsy boils water for tea. By the time the bags are in the cups, Faith is there.

"It was a beautiful funeral," says Betsy. "Your mum on the horse-drawn carriage. Macha was handsome, wasn't he? All done up in his feathers."

"Yeah," says Faith. "It was beautiful. Shame my family had to be there."

"They loved her too," says Betsy. "I guess that counts for something."

"I don't think I care whether they did or not. They've showed their true colors. I still can't believe Calum bought my ride for himself. When do you think they were going to tell me? Never, probably."

Betsy hesitates for a little too long.

"What is it?"

"I was going to tell you. I saw them with it last week. The night I got sacked."

"You knew about this?"

She nods. "I went past the ground on my way to work. I saw they'd got the Waltzer up and running again."

"And you didn't tell me because . . .?"

"Honestly? I didn't think it would help you to know. It's just more proof of what they've already shown you, that they don't care about you."

"But if I can't trust you to tell me the truth, Betsy . . ."

"I'm sorry. I was trying to protect you."

Faith looks into her lap. "There's something I never told you too. About that night the soldier came, when he stole our money."

Betsy takes out a pack of cards and hands it to Faith to shuffle. When it's done, Betsy takes a card from the top of the pack, places it face up on the table. Without looking up she says,

"I've been learning how to tell fortunes."

"Funny."

"No, I'm serious. I watched what you did with Sir Phillip. I went online and learned loads."

She puts the pack in front of Faith.

"Cut."

Faith cuts the pack. Betsy puts it back together, then deals out all of the cards in neat lines so that the table is completely covered.

"I need to talk to you about what I saw," says Faith. "Don't you want to hear it?"

Betsy puts a finger to her lips and looks at Faith. "Which card are you drawn to?"

Faith's eyes wander over the set of cards on the table. She places her finger on the three of hearts. Betsy counts along three, and down four. The jack of spades.

"That's him," she says. "The soldier."

Then she counts from the soldier, three across, four down. The queen of hearts. "And that's you."

Faith puts her hand on the table, covering the queen of hearts. "Stop now," she says. "I need to talk to you."

"You are talking to me."

"Yes, but I need you to hear me. There are things—"

"I know what you're going to say."

"You really don't."

"The cards do, though." Betsy's staring at the cards, counting up and down, left and right. "I see it here. There was . . . something in the vision that you've never seen before."

"Yes. I pretty much told you that already."

"Something that frightened you."

"Yes."

She looks at the cards again. Counts along, and down. The seven of diamonds. "It's a murder, isn't it?"

"How did you—"

"Wait. No, that's not right. Can't be." She counts again, goes back, counts once more. Then she looks at Faith again, her mouth open in shock. "You kill him?"

"That's what I was going to tell you."

"*You* kill *him?* The soldier?"

Faith nods. "I saw it in the vision."

"But why would you do that?"

Faith's voice comes out shrill. "I don't know, Betsy. I don't know."

The two of them ride in silence into the countryside. Faith parks the wagon up in the place they agreed, and Betsy thinks about when they met Sir Phillip, the dark spot they chose, miles from anywhere. At least this place has lighting, and the motorway is right there. She remembers the two Jaguars, the security men he brought along with his son, how unnerving that was. But then it wasn't Sir Phillip they needed to be frightened of that night.

"I wonder if he really will come alone."

A car drives by but doesn't slow. The minutes tick along, and the time of the meeting comes and goes.

After more than half an hour, Betsy checks the email again. Something has gone wrong; she can feel it.

"Maybe we should go," she says, and just as Faith looks at her as if she's about to agree, there is a noise outside.

"Did you hear a car?"

Betsy shakes her head no. There have been no engine sounds. But there are footsteps. Someone knocks on the door.

"Who is it?" Faith asks. But Betsy thinks she knows the answer, and she can't believe they've been so stupid.

There is no reply. The air seems claggy, thickened with her racing heartbeat as she strains to listen for any small noises within the silence. And then something heavy hits the door from the other side.

Faith screams.

A dent appears on inside of the wagon door. Silence for a second and then the thing hits the door again, and this time the aluminum frame bends, the wood-effect laminate splits, the fiberglass splinters.

Faith runs to the driver's seat, to start the engine, to escape.

"Where's the fucking key, Betsy?"

"It's not there?"

It was supposed to be in the ignition—she knows she left it there. They decided to do that for just this reason, so that if they needed to, they could just drive the damn wagon away. They stare at the window of the cab, opened just a crack at the top, and the door is unlocked where Betsy most definitely locked it. Whoever is outside must have reached in and taken the key. Silently, without them realizing.

Faith and Betsy back off, going as fast as possible into the bedroom and shutting the door, but Betsy can feel how flimsy that door is, how insubstantial the lock as she turns it. They crouch in the corner, as far from the thing outside as they can get, the person with the battering ram, the hammer, or the ax.

Another loud bang, a crash, and they know the door has given way. There are heavy footsteps, and a voice calls her name.

Faith doesn't answer. She whispers, "Who do you think it is?" to Betsy, but Betsy doesn't want to say who she thinks it is, in case saying it makes it come true. They both know it's no golfing buddy of Sir Phillip. They stare at each other in the semidarkness, nothing but the moonlight illuminating their terrified faces.

More heavy steps. He is outside the bedroom door.

"Are you going to let me in?" says the voice, and she knows that it is the soldier.

And his voice, without his face, ignites something in her, something she has buried deep.

There is a loud bang. The door holds. A squeak as what has now become clear is indeed an ax is wrenched free, drawn back. One more and it will give way.

"Stop," Faith calls out. "What do you want?"

"I just want to talk to you."

The silence stretches out as she stares desperately at Betsy in the dark. "Okay."

He is impatient. "Are you coming out?"

She struggles to form words. "Yes, I will, but—"

"I can break the door."

The idea of the door being smashed in is too much. "No," says Betsy, "she'll come out."

Faith is angry that Betsy has spoken. They both know it's better if he thinks she's alone. She indicates to Betsy to stay where she is, creeps up to the door and turns the lock, pulls the handle. But it won't open.

"You've bent it. I can't . . ."

He kicks the door without warning and she lets out a little shriek.

"Sorry," he says. "I'm sorry," the pathetic sound of this in stark contrast to the violence he had used on the door.

She stands with half of her body in the doorway and looks at him, at his chest, then his chin. It's him, it's the soldier. And she knows now, knows why he's familiar.

"Samuel," she says, and the sound of her speaking his name stops him dead.

He smiles, the faltering, shy smile of a little boy. "You do know me."

CHAPTER

35

Faith

I THINK I'M AS surprised as Samuel that I've remembered him. The man in front of me bears almost no resemblance to the small, freckled kid who caused my brother and his own to fall through the ice that day. He is more than that boy now. He is also the man who robbed us and the man I am destined to murder. Alarmingly, I realize he is dressed now the way he was in my vision of his death. So, it will be tonight. The shirt he has on will be blooming with his blood from a wound I have made.

No. *I can stop it from happening—I can!*

"I know your name," I say, "but I don't know you. I don't think I ever did."

"Well, I look a little different now. I was fat, with long hair and—"

"You were ten."

He pauses, says, "You look good, Faith. You haven't changed. Except for the . . ." He gestures at my face, at my eye patch.

I need to be calm, try to keep control. I can't think about the money he stole or anything else beyond getting out, getting away from here, distracting him so me and Betsy can escape.

"Why didn't you say so when I saw you before?"

"I thought you knew who I was. I thought you were playing some kind of game, the way you used to."

"I had no idea. You were following me, and I was frightened."

"Frightened?"

I glance down at the ax he's holding. "Yes."

"Well," he says, "maybe that's what I wanted."

I try to make my voice confident, commanding. "You better go now, Samuel. We're expecting someone to arrive any minute for a reading."

"Some rich guy. I know. I sent the email."

He's vibrating with anxiety and adrenaline from beating down the door. His hand dangles, still holding the weapon, the blade of which grazes his joggers, scratching a hole at the thigh as it rubs back and forth. I try to keep my voice steady and reasonable.

"You sent it? Why did you do that?"

"I didn't think you'd meet up with me again if I said who I was. And I needed to see you, Faith. I've been watching the carnival this week. I thought it was you working the Waltzer."

"It used to be. We went our separate ways."

"So this is . . . all you do now?" He gestures around the wagon, at the card table, at the drapes hanging askew.

I nod.

"Oh well," he says. "That's a shame." For a moment he seems as if he's really sad about this, but then he shrugs.

"You should have been honest," I say. "I would have met you."

Samuel laughs loudly, like a dog barking. His eyes are crazed, darting from side to side. "You would never have responded. Just like you would never have opened the door just now if I hadn't said I'd smash it."

"What are you even doing here? You're supposed to be on tour, aren't you?" I ask, in a voice so quiet it is almost a whisper.

"I'm going tonight," says Samuel. "I just wanted to clear a few things up with you first."

"Like what?"

"Last time we met. Did you see my death?"

I nod slowly while my mind is frantically weighing up the right thing to say. "I did." I won't tell him that I lied before, that it wasn't the first time, that I also saw it in the park, and most nights since then, in my dreams.

"So tell me, do I die on this tour? Is it a bomb, an IED, a sniper? You said something about a knife. Do I get stabbed, ambushed? You didn't make any sense that night."

"Why should I tell you when you stole from us?"

He reaches into his pocket and pulls out an envelope. "You can have it back if that's all you're interested in. Here. I don't need it."

That money is badly needed right now. I wonder if I can grab it from him and make a dash for the door before he can swing at me with the blade.

"Why did you take it, then?"

He shifts the ax under one arm, then picks up the two chairs that are sprawled in the wreck of the wagon and places them facing each other. "Here," he says. "Come sit." He's holding out the money like bait.

I sit down carefully, wondering what Betsy is doing, whether Samuel is even aware of her. I hope not. She'll have a chance of getting us out of here if she can stay out of sight.

He hands me the envelope, and I take it, place it on the floor by my feet. When I straighten up, he's staring at me intensely, something twitching in his jaw.

"I never thought I'd see you again," he says. "It's weird. I didn't know what I'd feel like. All these years, I wanted revenge. I took the money to hurt you, but it felt . . . empty."

I stare at the ax, wondering if he will ever put it down.

"Revenge for what?" I find myself asking.

I see myself in the vision, stabbing him, the knife going in. The harsh twist before I pull it out. His shocked, whitening face.

He reaches into his pocket again and pulls out a silver chain with a ring attached.

"Where did you get that?" Grandma Rose's ring. From the dream, from the lake. Maybe it's the ring that's bad luck. It was there when Rose fell from the trapeze, and again when Tommy died. It's here now, a cursed object.

He dangles it from a finger. Exactly like he did the day Tommy died.

"I saw you throw it in the lake," he says.

The day I met Betsy. The day I hurt myself, my eye. "You couldn't have."

"I was at the lake a lot that year. Used to come back, even after we moved, after everyone in the estate turned against us." He narrows his eyes at me, blaming me for that too. "Being there made me feel closer to Peter." He spins the ring on its chain so that it makes a silvery circle in the air. "Funny thing is, I used to search for this fucking thing all the time. I dived all over that lake bed, all through the spring. Only it wasn't there, was it?"

The ring stops spinning, and he holds it close to my face. I see it then, the way it must have happened. He was dangling it, like he's dangling it now. I went to grab the necklace, and he snatched his hand away so quickly. Ice had been clinging to his clothes, to his gloves. Ice flew from his hand, arcing through the air, the glaring winter sun behind it. Nothing but ice, though it could have been silver. He thought it was silver; we all did. The necklace fell out of sight, landing at my feet. It wasn't ever on the frozen lake. It wasn't in the water at all until I threw it.

Tommy went out on the ice for nothing.

I splutter. "The necklace isn't the point. It was your brother Peter's fault. He should never have followed Tommy out. If he hadn't done that—"

"No," he yells. "It was you. And now you *owe me*. When you looked in my eyes, Faith. What did you see?"

In the vision I was running. He was chasing. It won't happen here in the wagon. I will run, and Samuel will chase, into the darkness. There's nothing either of us can do about it. Maybe I should tell him. What difference would it make to the outcome? None.

CHAPTER

36

Faith

"YOU ALWAYS WANTED people to think you were magic or something. Well, you got your wish."

"I don't need to make myself look like anything. I just am."

"From here you look like a pretty nasty piece of work. But then, you always did. Remember that winter before Tommy and Peter died? You were always stirring things up then too."

I don't remember much from that winter, from before the dream, before the accident, and I tell him as much. What I don't tell him is that what little I do remember amounts to the fact that Tommy didn't really like either of the brothers, that they kept on trying to play with us anyway. Hanging around, teasing me. Peter was always trying to fight Tommy, who wouldn't fight. We were trapped there for months. When you're on the road, it's easier to shake people off. Things can get weird when you're in the same place for too long.

"That's convenient," he says.

The dream comes back to me then, all mixed up in my mind with what actually happened. It has a sepia quality. In the dream I stand on the banks of the frozen lake. The image crackles, and now it's the memory. I'm standing there, and Samuel is standing next to me. The necklace has flown, has landed far out on the ice. Or that's what we think has happened.

Something different, then.

I ask Peter to get it for me, tell him he has to because his stupid brother has ruined everything. He wants me to think he's fearless, so he starts to go, but Samuel begs him not to.

Because of Samuel, Peter won't go, so Tommy is on the ice, where he never should have been. He is too far from the shore to make it back safely. He is looking down at the ice between his feet.

"You're a coward, Peter," I taunt, watching his face become determined to prove me wrong.

I look down, and I see the necklace there, and when I look up, Peter has run out toward Tommy.

Then, in the dream, I hear the creaking. In the memory, I hear it too. The creaking sound becomes a ping-ping-ping, and his face has just enough time to show absolute terror before the surface of the lake cracks. Both boys fall through. In the dream, I stand there, I do nothing. What did I do in real life? Even in the dream I feel the guilt of powerlessness. Why can't I move or speak or rescue them?

I had the dream, the nightmare, and I woke up and went about my business, believing it was nothing but a dream. I didn't warn anyone. That's what the guilt I've carried has been about all this time. I didn't do anything; I didn't mean to harm anyone. But I told Peter to go out—I did that—and refused to remember that detail. I hoped he might fall through. I never had the guts to admit that to myself.

"I knew it would happen. I dreamed it."

"You planned it."

"No."

He leans closer. I can smell his breath, sweet with alcohol. "You knew the ice was too thin. You sent my brother out there because you knew he wouldn't say no to you. You did it out of spite. You didn't even care that your own brother would go down with him. That's the kind of person you are."

"That's not what happened." He's too close to me now. He's holding the ax in both hands so that it dangles between his knees.

"You can't see death, Faith. You're a fraud. And a murderer. You're just making things up, aren't you?"

I look at my hands. *Murderer.* The word seems deliciously tempting, terrifying, real and unreal all at once. Me, a killer? I make a dash for the wagon door. I have to get away.

"Hey," he shouts, but I've darted past, down the steps and away. I'm sprinting as fast as I can into the night, into the dark, my eyes only just able to make out the road as I run. I can hear him running up behind me, and I take a left into some trees, stumble in a ditch, fall to my knees. I push up and keep on, crashing through the woods, barely missing tree trunks, getting stuck in bushes. I see a large thicket and dive in deep, and then I stop, go quiet, some animal instinct causing me to freeze, crouching, to wait until it's safe to run again.

"Faith?" His voice is close by. I can hear a swishing, chopping sound. He is swiping at the undergrowth with his ax, breaking through creepers, slicing through twigs. "Where are you?"

My heart is beating so hard I can hear it rushing in my ears. I stay as still as I can, but I fear he can hear me breathing. The footsteps get closer, then further away, I can hear him chopping at branches, cursing, stumbling in the dark. Then, nothing.

I start to count elephants in my head. When I haven't heard anything for a full minute, I uncurl, straighten up, take a look around. Nothing but darkness. An owl hoots.

Then headlights sweep the trees, lighting me up where I stand. The road is just there, a few feet away. I don't have time to duck, but I turn and I see him coming toward me.

"Stop," he yells, and I push through hedges of brambles to get to the road, thorns like razors scraping ragged tracks along my shins. I fall, I get up, I keep running.

But he is faster. He gains on me as my legs start to fail, I feel his hand on my shoulder and I trip. We both fall.

"Get away from me," I shout, using my elbows to commando-crawl away, but he grabs me by the legs, then I feel his fingers at my waistband and at the back of my neck. I try to kick him, but he turns me on my back and pins me to the ground, both my wrists held above my head with one of his hands. Gravel from the road presses into my skin. He centers himself right on top of me, and I close my mouth so I don't have to inhale the air coming out of his.

Then he stops, as if now that he's got me, he's not sure what he's going to do. I see his eyes change—a spark goes out, and there is nothing but black. His knee pushes up between mine. He's so much bigger, so much stronger than me. I go limp.

"I have a knife," says a voice close by. It's Betsy. Where has she been? "Get the fuck off of her or I'll stab you."

He looks confused for a moment, and his grip loosens, releasing my hands. I push a thumbnail into his eye socket, and he roars with the pain, giving me enough time to wriggle out and away, and I'm on my knees and then I'm up, and I think I've escaped but he gets me by the ankle and I turn, and that's when she strikes, two-handed, with every bit of her strength, with the accuracy of a person who knows they won't get a second chance.

The knife goes in, just under his ribs. She gives it a twist and then pulls it out.

Samuel falls on his backside. He can't believe it. He puts a hand to his wound, and it comes away bloody. In the dimness I can see the blood pulsing out, pooling on the road. He tries to get up, his shocked face draining white, and it's just like what I saw.

Only there is a difference. I didn't stab him. It was Betsy.

Betsy's hand opens, and the knife clangs on the road. There are headlights and sirens, blue lights flashing.

"We need to go," she says, and she turns me by the shoulders and gives me a little shove to set me off. The two of us run straight into the woods. By the time the police cars find him, we're too far away for them to catch us.

CHAPTER

37

Faith

WE WALK THROUGH the woods in the dark, occasionally having to stop and change course because of a particularly tricky bit of undergrowth. Eventually we reach a road, and I recognize it. We're just outside of town.

"Do you think he'll be okay?" asks Betsy. "Samuel, I mean."

I think about the amount of blood that was pumping out of him. The way his eyes dimmed and glazed over.

"I saw the vision of his death," I say. "I think that's all we need to know."

"You said in that vision you killed him, though. And that was different from what happened."

"Yeah." My brain is numb. I wish Mum were here. Not even here as in with me, but here in the world. That comfort is gone. She is nowhere.

"What do you mean, 'yeah'?" says Betsy. "Don't you see what it means?"

"I don't . . ."

She stops, turns so we are facing each other. She looks straight at me, straight into my eye. The eye patch itches. I reach up and touch it, make sure it stays put.

"Faith. You always thought that what you saw in those visions was set in stone. What if it isn't?"

"But Mum . . ."

"Yes, your mum died the way you saw it. But she never tried to change it, did she?"

"No, but there was no point, because—"

"Maybe there was. Maybe you, or she, could have changed one small thing. Not save her from dying, not that, but what if something was different? If that's possible, it would mean things don't have to be the way you see them. It would mean that just seeing it, just knowing about it makes it happen or makes it not happen, depending on what the person does with the information."

"Betsy, I can't think straight. What are you saying?" I feel a pain in the center of my chest as I think of my brother. "Do you think I could have saved Tommy?"

She goes quiet. Then she says, "No. I don't think you could have."

I'm assailed by images of Peter, of me shouting at him by the lake. Samuel, the boy he was, begging me to stop, begging Peter not to go. What did I do? Tommy is there. He's alive. *Stay on the shore, Tommy. You were never supposed to go out onto the ice.* My fault. I did it.

"Joey Standish died the way you said, or close enough. But maybe those people online had a point, maybe he died because you said he would. Because he heard you say it and went and tried to prove you wrong."

"And the girl from school, the car crash?"

"She crashed after seeing you, didn't she? She was all over the place."

"But I can see the future, Betsy. I have seen it, I believe it, I do. Don't you believe in me?"

"I think you can see it too, but it's only true at the time you see it. What you see is a possible future as it will play out if nothing is done about it. What if someone decides it's going to be different? Then it will be."

I keep walking. "That's mad."

She follows me. "It's not fixed. The vision isn't fixed. None of them are. Don't you see?"

"What? What don't I see?"

"I stabbed Samuel, not you. It can change."

"Not much. He still got stabbed."

"Maybe you can save Calum. Maybe he doesn't need to die the way you said he would."

I think about the accident on the Waltzer, the way the car will come away. I realize I know why it will do that. Someone must have forgotten, or will forget, to put in part of the structure, one of the big bolts, when they were building it up. Or someone deliberately took a piece out. Someone is planning to sabotage the machine. Someone who knows enough or has seen enough to work out exactly what to do. They've already done it.

I pick up the pace. We can get there and warn him. If we're not too late already. No one has to get hurt. The vision isn't fixed. I see that now.

C H A P T E R

38

Betsy

FAITH AND BETSY arrive at the carnival, where the first thing they see is the giant Big Wheel, rotating slowly, dwarfing the tent.

"They've bought another ride," says Faith. Betsy can see Christine in the booth, selling tickets. Crowds of people jostle for room in the queue for the new ride, as well as the one for the Waltzer. The people in the queues are mixed in with those on their way to buy hotdogs and others simply milling around, swigging from soft-drink bottles. The music is deafeningly loud. The circus has transformed into a funfair now the sun's gone down, like a lurid shape-shifter, a carnival vampire, sucking all the revenue from the crowds, feeding on those who signed up to see a show but when they came out, got more than they bargained for. Not that it looks as if anyone's complaining.

Faith and Betsy push through the throng, too roughly, too quickly, to get to the Waltzer, where they can see Calum walking the boards. The machine is playing the same piece of music it was pumping out in the vision. It's nearly at full speed.

"This is it," says Faith. "This is how it starts."

"You need to tell him to stop," says Betsy.

Faith climbs up onto the machine and waves at him frantically. At first, he doesn't see her, the cars flying by and the boards swinging up and down, Calum riding it like waves on the ocean. But then his head swivels and his face darkens. He clocks her, but he doesn't stop.

"Calum!" she yells. "You have to stop the ride. It's going to break."

He can't hear her, or he chooses not to. He grabs the back of a car, sets it spinning; the kids inside scream their heads off.

"You'll have to go and stop it," says Betsy.

There's a metallic creaking sound from one of the cars as it spins by.

"Did you hear that?" she asks, and Faith nods.

There's no time left to think, only to act. Faith jumps onto the machine and almost falls, but she's up again, light on her feet like a cat. Calum is on the other side of the machine, and he sees her, turns, and shouts, "Hey, what the hell?" He starts toward Faith. The kids in the car that creaked begin chanting, "Spin it, spin it, spin it," and she sees him with his hand on the back of it, ready to pull. He turns his head, as if in slow motion, and Betsy can see him thinking he may as well, he's right there, it will only take a second.

Faith is at the booth now. She yanks the emergency stop lever.

In that same second Calum pulls on the back of the car, there is a mighty screech and snap, and the car comes away.

The machine slows abruptly. The car with the kids in it slides from the side of the Waltzer and lands on its side with a thump.

But it's not the same as Faith's vision. Betsy sees that no one is badly hurt. Calum is not under the car, but on his feet, rubbing his knee where he was thrown clear when it slid off the machine. All the kids have been tipped out on the grass and are checking themselves for injuries, finding none.

Faith is shocked, then smiling, then grinning from ear to ear. "It's different, Betsy. I changed it. He's not dead."

Calum sees Faith and seems to understand something.

"You knew that would happen?" he says.

She nods. "I saw it in your vision."

"You saved me," he says, his face full of disbelief and gratitude.

"Well," says Faith, "we're family, aren't we?"

Behind them, the Big Wheel continues to rotate slowly, and beyond the ground Betsy can hear police sirens getting closer.

CHAPTER

39

Afterward

THEY SAY THIS place is not a prison, but the doors are locked at night, I'm not allowed outside alone, and every woman in here has been accused of a crime.

Linda brings the photos from the wagon when she comes. I set them up on the bedside table. There's a color one of Tommy, and one of Mum, Linda, and Granddad together that I adore because of the way Granddad and Mum are looking at each other, laughing, their eyes full of love. There are the two black-and-white ones, one of Grandma Rose in front of the tent and the other of Great-Grandma Daisy with a tiny Granddad on her knee.

"Where's the glass?" All of the frames are without anything to protect the prints.

"They made me take it out when I came in."

They say this place is not a prison, but Linda has her bags checked for contraband at the desk.

In the photo of Daisy, I see for the first time that she's wearing on her finger a ring that looks very much like the one

Rose had when she fell, then one that Samuel ended up with. I mention it to Linda, and she nods.

"That's the one. With the green stone. Why do you ask?"

I lean in and whisper. "I think it's cursed."

"Oh, Faith," says Linda, "I don't believe in curses. It's just a coincidence."

There's no such thing as a coincidence. I like the idea that everything happens for a reason. If the ring is the cause of my troubles, then I need to get rid of it. I won't try throwing it in a lake again. I'll have to think of something more permanent to stop it from coming back. It killed Rose and Tommy, and it nearly killed Samuel.

"Do you know where it is now?"

"I've got it," she says. "There was some stuff of yours from the police that they confiscated for the investigation. What they didn't keep for evidence they gave back to me in a clear plastic bag. The ring was in there."

"Did you get it out?"

"No, I didn't open the bag," she says. "It's your stuff. I thought it could wait until you came home."

I've been here for several months, but they say I'm doing well, that I can be discharged in a few weeks if Linda is willing to be responsible for me. They arrested me and Betsy at the scene, but there were no criminal charges they could make stick, so for a long time I was confused about why I wasn't allowed to go home. Linda says they thought it was me who sabotaged the ride, but I know it must have been Samuel. There was no conclusive evidence either way.

The stabbing was another matter. When Samuel was interviewed by the police after being treated for his wound, he said I did it. I wasn't going to drop my best friend in it, so I just said I didn't and left it at that. My lawyers got together with Linda, and there was some kind of assessment, and I don't know what happened but they said that even though they did think it was me, they wouldn't be pressing charges as they didn't think I was "criminally responsible" because of my mental health problems. That's how I ended up here instead of in prison. And I don't have a date for release. I just have to be well enough, whatever that means.

"Have you heard from Betsy?" I ask Linda. She doesn't answer. The nurse arrives then, as it's time for my therapy session.

* * *

Roxanne is waiting for me in the therapy room. I like her, she's nice. I know she's my ticket out of here too, so it's a good idea to keep her on my side, try to go along with what I think she wants me to say.

"How are you feeling?" she asks.

"Classic opener," I reply, and we both chuckle. Then she doesn't say anything else, just waits for me to answer. She's really good at waiting for me to answer. Also at noticing when I'm being avoidant. "I feel good," I say.

"That's great, Faith, really great. Because you know we are thinking of discharging you soon, right?"

My heart gives a little leap at the idea of being allowed to leave. Am I supposed to show how much I want it? How much I need to be set free, that I can't bear to be in here any longer now that they've dangled it as a possibility. "The doctor mentioned it to me, yes."

"And how do you feel about that?"

"Fine."

"Just fine?"

"Better than fine. Amazing." I study Roxanne's face, but her smile is so hard to read. It seems genuine, but is it? Did I answer correctly?

"That's good," she says. "So, you'll be released to the care of your aunt, correct?"

"Correct," I say, though I have no plans to stay in the house with Linda. I need to be in my wagon. I might go up country for a while, after so long being stuck here. It's not allowed, but I don't care.

Roxanne says, "We just need to go over a few things before I can recommend you for discharge."

"Oh?" I say it like I don't know what she's talking about, but I do. They say this place is not a prison, but I'm here to prove I'm not a danger to society anymore.

Not long after we were arrested, the man from the police spoke to me about the Oracle of Death investigation. He said they couldn't prove I'd been involved in the death of either Joey Standish or Henrietta White, the woman who bullied me at school and died crashing her car, but that what he'd seen amounted to a whole lot of circumstantial evidence. He said that they'd be keeping an eye on me in future. I asked him if conducting that kind of business was illegal and he said technically, no, but he wouldn't ever recommend I do anything out of the back of a wagon in the dead of night, all alone, for my own safety if nothing else.

"But I wasn't alone. I was with Betsy," I replied, and he nodded and patted my hand, then exchanged a look with the healthcare assistant.

"Well. Dangerous business, as you found out to your detriment."

I have spoken to Roxanne about all of this before in our weekly sessions. I've told her about my visions, when they started, how many I've had, and who they were about. I'm surprised, then, when she asks me to tell her again about my ability to see death.

"I'm allowed to believe anything I like, aren't I?"

"Of course."

"You're not judging me?"

"I'm assessing you."

"What's the difference?"

She smiles. "I'm trying to help you, Faith. I'm not trying to catch you out. Your caseworker has asked me to assess if you are fit to be discharged."

"So, what do you want me to tell you about?"

"Let's go back to that first session we had. Tell me what you meant by what you said, that you can 'see death.'"

"I meant I can see people's deaths. If I look in their eyes. I get a vision. Exactly how it will look." Feels good to say it out loud. Always does. But she knows all this already—we've been over it.

"You predict people's future deaths."

"I don't know if it's a prediction exactly. I see it. I know it. Then, when the time comes, it happens in exactly the way I saw. Or that's what I used to believe."

"You don't believe that anymore?"

"No. I don't believe it."

She scribbles something down in her notes. I think I've answered correctly.

"That's good, Faith. Tell me a little but more about that. When did you start to realize you were thinking differently about those beliefs?"

"I realized it wasn't fixed. That it didn't have to happen the way it did in the visions. I wasn't seeing the future, only a possibility of a future. What happened with Calum proved it completely."

She's stopped writing to stare at me. "Explain?"

"In the vision I saw him die. But then I stopped the machine before it happened. I saved his life. He was supposed to die, and I changed it. So."

"I see, I see. And what about Betsy?"

"What about her?"

"Do you think any differently regarding Betsy? Or is your thinking surrounding her the same now as it was when you came in?"

"I don't know what you mean."

She pauses, takes a breath, then another, slower one. "Interesting." She tips her head slightly to the left, then leaves a gap in the conversation I feel no pressure whatsoever to fill. The clock ticks loudly for almost a full minute. "Is there anything else you want to tell me about that?"

"About Betsy?"

"Yes. Or about anything."

"Only that she's my friend, and I miss her. I wish she'd come to visit me. I haven't seen her since I've been in here."

Roxanne writes something down. Then she looks at me. "Amara is your friend, yes? She's been to visit more than once. I can see from your notes."

"Yes." Amara's been great throughout all of this. I really look forward to those visits. I did ask her if she could bring Betsy with her maybe one time, but she never has, probably because I couldn't tell her where to look for her. I just hope Betsy's okay, really. Once I'm out, I'll find her, and everything will be better. She doesn't like hospitals—I know that much. That must be all it is. She'd never abandon me. We're a team.

She sits back, considering. "I just want to be clear about this, Faith. Betsy is your friend—you really believe that?"

I stare at her. Maybe they don't want me to be with Betsy. Maybe they think she'd be bad for my recovery, or whatever.

"I don't know." I say. This seems the safest thing to say, though it feels like a betrayal.

"When they arrested you, do you remember what happened?"

"Yes. They put us in a cell for hours and hours. It was awful."

"At the police station, they put you and Betsy in a cell with just one cup of tea between you."

"I know. It should be illegal to do that."

She looks at her notes, and then up at me. She takes a long sip of water.

"Those are single cells, Faith. Designed for one person."

"That's right. I complained at the time. We both did."

Then something flips in my brain. Things that have happened, they are suddenly different. I remember them in two ways, in split-screen. Betsy is not me. But we are one.

I am inside the wagon, and Betsy is there, talking to me. But when Linda comes in, she's gone. In the bedroom, I thought, but no, she isn't there. She comes back when Linda is gone. *"Who are you talking to?"* Linda asks me. I say, *"Betsy,"* and she laughs.

I am with Amara. Betsy doesn't like her, or that's what I think. She avoids speaking to her, to any of the circus people. She's only my friend. She doesn't need to speak to them, and they ignore her anyway. She doesn't mind.

They don't ignore her—they never did: they can't see her.

I am with Betsy, and Samuel is there. I'm talking to myself. He looks baffled because it sounds weird, my speaking her words, me looking at Betsy when, for him, Betsy isn't there.

"She's real," I say. "She exists." But even as I say it, I know that to say this out loud is to question reality. But she *is* real—to me she is.

"When you were in hospital with your dislocated shoulder," says Roxanne.

"Yes," I exclaim, grasping at this fact. "Betsy was there. She had a burn on her arm because of me. The notes will say . . ." I trail off because I see the look on her face. "She was treated by the nurse . . ."

I roll up my sleeve, and there is a scar there. *It was my burn, my arm.*

"The nurse noted that you talked about yourself in the third person."

"That was Betsy. She was being bossy. She wouldn't shut up."

"He noted you as a callback, tried to get you in for an appointment, but you gave a false address."

"She works," I say. "She earns money, or she did."

"At the care homes? Didn't the police talk to you about that?"

"No," I say. "They talked to Betsy about it. Because she stole some drugs and gave them to me and to my mum. I asked her to do that; it wasn't all her idea."

"But if you haven't seen her since you came in, how do you know the police spoke to her?"

Because they didn't. They spoke to me.

I am in the laundry. I am washing sheets. I went there instead of sleeping. Can it be true? I stole those drugs. It was me.

No. Not me. Betsy is real. She's real, and she loves me. The first time we met, twelve years ago, on the side of the lake, she was wearing the necklace. Wasn't she? She took it off and gave it to me.

My hand goes to my throat. I remember wearing it. Images are strobing in my mind: the necklace, on my neck, then on hers. She's there, in front of me; I'm alone.

But I was never alone after that. Betsy kept me safe.

Roxanne says, "You said she doesn't drive."

"No, but that doesn't mean—"

"Does she have her own phone?"

"I . . ."

Betsy's phone is my phone. Betsy's hands are my hands.

The knife was in my hands.

I stabbed him.

It was me.

CHAPTER

40

THE AIDE ESCORTS me back to my room after the therapy session.

"You sure you're okay?" she asks, as she unlocks the door. Locks in this unit are used to 'keep people safe' rather than to keep people in, or out. I don't buy that, but I go along with it. I've seen what happens in here if you try to fight the system. It's not the fastest route to freedom, that's for sure.

"I'm good," I say, smiling vaguely. "It was an intense session, that's all. Lots to think about."

She squeezes my arm. "Call me if you need anything, won't you?"

She shuts the door behind me, locks it again.

Betsy is sitting on the bed, grinning like a little kid. "How was it?"

I drop down into the chair opposite. "Don't talk to me, Betsy. I know what you are."

"Oh, don't be silly."

Maybe if I ignore her, she'll go away. After a long few minutes of hard ignoring, I hear her sigh, and then she's gone.

Thank goodness, I think. Hopefully that's the end of that. Now I know the truth, I'll be able to control it. She's a figment. An invention. A coping mechanism.

I'm suddenly overcome with fatigue. I lie on the bed and close my eyes.

I dream of the stabbing, again. In the dream the knife is in my hand, as it must have been all along. I can see it from both angles: from outside myself, and from within. Betsy is there, and then she's not there. Then, she's there again. She grabs the knife and lunges.

I lunge, and stab, and Samuel screams.

I jolt awake.

In the dark, Betsy is lying with her face close to mine, moonlight playing on her skin.

"Hi, babe."

I'm not going to respond to that. I slip my hand under the pillow to grab my patch but then I hesitate. I set my eyes on hers, preparing myself for the slam of it, the vision that will crash into my brain, her future death. Our eyes meet, my breathing quickens. Nothing happens.

I just see eyes.

I reach out to touch her cheek, but she moves away. I look at my hands. I grab for her again as she scrambles off the bed and my fingers go right through her, as if she's made of light. As if she's made, indeed, of darkness.

"All this time," I say to her. "You made it look as if you were the same as everyone else, when you were nothing but a figment of my imagination. A fucking *symptom*."

I rub my arm where it bears the scars that I thought were Betsy's. She'd tried to force me to look in her eyes just before that happened, said *you don't see things when you look at me.* I didn't want to look. I didn't want to know. *Maybe you won't see anything.* She knew. She was trying to tell me.

I think about the times we were alone together. She never drank a whole cup of tea. Well, of course, she never actually drank any tea at all.

She'd be there, talking to me, and then if anyone else came in she would be gone, just like that, click your fingers. Why didn't I twig that I'd been talking to myself?

"Because you weren't talking to yourself," says Betsy. I turn over and face the wall. I've decided not to engage with her from now on.

I used to lock up at night, and she would be in the wagon first thing, even so. She didn't have a key. It should have been obvious.

"You knew it all along," she says. "You just didn't want it to be true."

"Stop reading my fucking mind, Betsy."

"Thought you'd stopped talking to me."

"I have to stop talking to you, if they're ever going to let me out of here."

"Fine. Don't talk to me. I can wait."

It explains why she always avoided Amara. They were literally never in the same room together—I'd thought Betsy was jealous. Or Amara was. *Tell yourself a story, make it come true. It's like magic, as elusive and powerful as that.*

"Very wise," says Betsy, and I close my eyes tight.

Roxanne says I need to accept that Betsy isn't real, but she didn't say what she thinks Betsy actually is, only that she was created in a moment of trauma. An imaginary friend, I suppose. However, to me, she was a real friend. I needed her. I still do. I open my eyes and roll over so I can look at her, sitting cross legged on the chair, implike. I glance away and then back, and the chair is empty. I hear her laughter echoing, like she's somewhere close by and yet far away.

"It's not funny," I say, and then I hear footsteps in the corridor and worry that one of the nurses is listening.

When she offered to move into the wagon was when things really started to go downhill. Roxanne says that was when I allowed the fantasy to take over my life, from a combination of sleep deprivation and stress, from Mum dying and me being forced out of the show. It was when I started taking risks, doing more shifts, relying on drugs to get me through when all they did was make everything worse. That was when I began talking to Betsy in front of people, in front of Mike and Calum, who probably thought I was losing my mind.

I remember one time when she put her finger to my lips. I must have known it was my own finger, but my brain wanted to believe she was there. There were moments when she seemed to know what I was thinking—but of course she knew. She lived inside my head.

"I lived outside of it too," says Betsy, back in the chair.

Something occurs to me then. "Sometimes I would wake up, and I'd feel like I hadn't been asleep at all."

"You were asleep, in a sense," says Betsy. "Not lying in bed though. You needed help to carry on. I did that for you."

"You were walking around in my body, pretending to be me. Didn't anyone ever notice?"

"I don't see why they would."

"And you saw things, when you did that. You knew things sometimes, that I didn't."

"I was trying to protect you."

"You stole drugs."

She raises an eyebrow. "Was that me, though? Really?"

I yell, "Well, it couldn't have been, could it? You're not a real person, Betsy."

The chair is empty again. "What's real anyway?" she says, from inside my head.

I curl up and press a pillow to my ear, though it's useless trying to drown her out. "Shut it, will you?" I shout. "I'm trying to sleep."

There is a banging from the woman in the next-door cell. She's yelling, *shut the fuck up, it's the middle of the night, you mad bitch.*

"She's one to talk," says Betsy.

CHAPTER

41

Faith

I GO THROUGH WHAT seems like a hundred locked doors, with Katy, the nursing assistant, unlocking them with her big keys as we go, locking them behind us. My rubber clogs squeak on the concrete floor.

"We'll get there eventually," she says, smiling kindly at me.

A couple of doors later, and I'm outside the building, squinting into the light.

"You go well now, won't you? You've got your meds?"

I rattle the bag I'm holding, which sounds like a maraca.

"Is anyone coming to pick you up?" she asks.

I scan the cars, see Linda climbing out of a little blue car and waving.

"That's my aunt."

Katy rubs my arm, and I wonder if she's going to go in for a hug. "They'll send you an appointment in the post, in the next week. Be sure to go along, won't you?"

I look at the ground, but I nod, sure I will.

"Well, then. Good luck, Faith."

The door clunks shut, the heavy sound of a well-turned bolt.

Linda drops me at the corner. "Just ring me if you need anything. I'll come and get you."

"Thanks," I say. I know that really, according to the conditions of my release, she's not supposed to let me out of her sight. But she knows me. She knows that I need to be alone, to walk through the world for a couple of hours, experience some blessed movement after the months of being stuck in one place.

After she drives away, I start to walk toward the town, stretching my legs, not in any hurry. I want to make the most of the sunshine before I go back to the wagon, still parked, I am assured, outside the house at Home Farm.

Something is digging into my backside. Linda dropped these jeans off last week, but before today I can't remember the last time I wore them. I put my hand in my pocket and come out with a screwed-up Harrington's flyer, dated a year ago, from before I got locked up. I flatten it out on a nearby wall and stare at it, think about throwing it in a bin. Then I fold it carefully and put it back in my pocket.

* * *

A few days later, Linda knocks on the wagon door and wakes me up. These drugs they've got me on are powerful, and I swim up, through layers of shadows, into my consciousness.

"You've got a visitor," she says, leaning in the bedroom door.

In the yard is one of the Harrington's vans. Mike and Calum are there, and Amara too, but I look straight past them at the horse box they've been towing. I run so fast out of the wagon that I almost trip. Macha is here. He's come back to me.

"Oh, thank you, thank you!" I say to Mike.

“You’re sure you’re okay to look after him? If it gets too much, he can come back to us. The grooms will keep him happy with the rest of the horses.”

I believe him. He’s healthy and strong-looking, though he moves slowly now, and Mike explains that the vet says he might have advanced arthritis in his knees. “So, you can’t ride him.”

“I don’t care about that,” I say, pressing my face into his neck, scratching him where I know he likes it. I lead him down the ramp and over to the field, where I open the gate and he goes trotting across to a large tuft of grass.

Before they head off, Mike says that he and Calum have been thinking, and that if I wanted to, they might be able to arrange it so I could come back.

“Back to the show?” I ask.

“Potentially,” says Mike.

I look at Calum. “You’re okay with this?”

He says, “I want to make things right. I’m grateful to you for what you did. If it hadn’t been for you, I mean . . .”

In my head I see the first vision, of Calum dying at the side of the ride. I nod slowly. Mike says he wants to make things fair, that he’s asked a lawyer to see what he can do about me being a partner in the business again.

It’s new, this feeling of being wanted. “I’ll think about it.” I say.

* * *

At the cemetery I go to see Tommy first. I run my hand over the letters in his name, chiseled there in the list of Harringtons, below Grandma Rose and above Uncle Billy, above Granddad. Underneath Granddad is Mum, her inscription paler than the rest, not quite weathered in. Underneath Mum is a smooth expanse of stone, enough space for another three generations of circus family.

I think, *My name will be there one day.* But not just yet.

I take the short walk over the hill to where my great-grandma lies, feel the familiar tug of injustice that even in death she is a pariah. She has no epitaph but her name and date, the birth date nothing more than an educated guess based on the age she was when she joined the circus.

When I was little, I used to make Mum tell me the story over and over.

Once upon a time, there was a coffin maker, and his name was David Harrington. David was young and ambitious. He was due to inherit the undertaker business, but he wanted something a little different: he felt the call of the road, the traveling life. His father decided it would be a good idea to teach him that being a traveling showman was a sure route to failure, so he made him a deal. If he could make a success of the show within a year, he could carry it on. His father was sure that David would be back within months, his tail between his legs, but it wasn't to be. After the First World War, people needed entertainment more than ever. Harrington's show may have been mostly dancers, rope girls, a couple of horse acts, and Rumbelow the elephant, but it was a runaway success from the start. David's father sold the undertakers, and Harrington and Sons (as it was then) used the money to make the show even better.

Years went by, and David's son Cyril became the ringmaster. Lucky enough to be freshly returned from World War II, he was still young and single, leading a company about twice the size of what we have now. One summer, traveling between towns, the circus stopped for the night on a mountain road in Cumbria. There was nothing around for miles, but in the morning she was there, knocking on wagons, selling bunches of daisies, dressed in a headscarf threaded with silver and wearing a ragged skirt. Great-Granddad Cyril bought five bunches, even though the moors were dotted with white as far as the eye could see. He looked around for the wagon she must have traveled in, but there was nothing. "Where are your people?" he asked her.

"I've no people," she replied. "It's just me."

"You could join us," he said, an offer that, up until then, he had extended to precisely no one except when he was looking for acts and building a show, and the bill was plenty full. Since the war, so many women had fawned over Cyril, both house dwellers and circus girls. His father often despaired of him ever getting on with it. Cyril was in no hurry. He was biding his time, taking his pick. Waiting for her. "But you'd need to do something."

Daisy set her big eyes on him. "I can do anything."

"Well," he said, "we always need someone who can do that."

And that was that, so the story goes. The way Mum told it, anyway. Stories are shape-shifters, different every time; they change with the teller, if they are spoken. If the words are written down, they only hold half of the meaning: the other half is in the reader.

If I actually had the same gifts Great-Grandma had, like Mum thought I did, I probably could ask her what really went on, what her story is, why she had no people. I'd light some candles, burn some incense, close my eyes, and she'd be here in the room, visible only to me. Mum used to tell other stories about Great-Grandma's seances, before they put a stop to it after Grandma Rose fell. I don't know how she knew about the sideshow in any detail, as Mum was just a baby then, Linda a little girl. So young to lose their mother. But stories travel down the generations, regifted like treasure.

Daisy only spoke directly to Mum about the Sight once or twice, after she was banished to Home Farm. According to Mum, she spent the rest of her life wishing she could have seen Rose's death so she could have warned everyone, but she always said the Sight wasn't like that. You could ask questions, but you might not get the answers you wanted. Her gift was flighty and unreliable, and interpreting it was never an easy task. The truth had to be picked out of it, like grass seed from a pelt. When it came to seeing the future, Daisy said it was like looking at shifting sands on a beach, between tides. One day it looked a certain way, but there were powerful forces beyond anyone's control that could change it into something unexpected.

Harrington's reeled with shock after Rose fell. Great-Uncle Billy declared that rules needed making, that all the family should sign: *We do solemnly declare that the family and other associates traveling with Harrington's may make money any way they choose, employing entertainment of all kinds except the following: no fortune-telling, palm reading, or tea leaves.* No magic, no contact with the Other Side. Try any of that, and you'll be out on your ear. Or words to that effect. From then on, when she wasn't watching Mum and Linda, or serving food to spectators from behind her black veil, Great-Grandma Daisy sat in her rocker, her hands folded serenely in her lap, only speaking when spoken to.

Her gravestone is small but dignified. I wonder if, when I die, they really will bury me with the Harringtons, or whether they'll put me up here with my great-grandma, just out of sight, a bad secret they want to keep hidden. I kneel down and tuck the necklace with the ring attached into the earth near the stone.

Here lies
Daisy Elizabeth "Betsy" Harrington
1922–2002

When I straighten up, I catch sight of a man standing at a grave a few rows away, and my stomach lurches. That's where Peter is buried, the boy who died with Tommy. The man standing there is Samuel.

My caseworker told me Samuel was never charged for what he did to sabotage the ride, or for stealing our money, or even for stalking me. He was treated as the victim in all this. In fact, I was nearly charged with money laundering when the police found the large amount of cash in the envelope in the wagon. They only dropped that when they got in touch with Sir Phillip and had him corroborate my version of events.

There was no real evidence to suggest it was Samuel who sabotaged the ride, even though he basically admitted it in a roundabout way that night when he mentioned that he'd thought I was still working the ride, and it was a shame I wasn't. It was my word against his. My word was tainted by the "not-fit-to-stand-trial" stuff, of course. His life was hardly affected by what happened. The last I heard, he'd recovered completely from the stabbing and returned to the army.

When his eyes meet mine, I want to run away, but I don't. I realize that I've forgiven him for what happened with Tommy and Peter, that it wasn't his fault or mine. Neither of us knew what would happen, neither of us wanted anyone to die. I understand why he wanted to hurt me when he found me again, because I wanted to hurt him too, once. I hope he's forgiven me too.

He holds my gaze for a long moment. Then he turns and walks away.

"Don't you want to keep that?"

Betsy is standing next to me, looking down at the necklace I've just pressed into the earth.

I shake my head. "I think it's bad luck. It can't do any more harm if I leave it here."

"That's dumb," says Betsy, which annoys me. She goes on, "I mean, it's just a lump of metal."

"A lump of metal that was there when Grandma Rose died, that made Tommy and Peter have that accident. And then Samuel had it when . . . the stabbing happened."

"Just coincidence. Nothing more."

"No such thing as coincidence. You of all people should know that."

She doesn't say anything, and I leave the ring and chain where it is.

"Daisy's gone," I say. "That's what Mum said, when she was dying. She couldn't see her grandmother, in the place she was going. She couldn't see you. Because you weren't there."

Betsy is silent. When I turn to her and look at her, really look in her eyes, I see what I could have seen all along, because her eyes are the same as the ones I knew as a little child, when she sat in the rocker in the wagon. When she said she could see me, see all of us, no matter where we were.

"Why are you still here?" I ask her.

"Because you need me right now," says Betsy. "I haven't forgotten about Iris. But I've got all the time in the world with her, now."

I feel tears coming. "How is she?" I wish it was her standing next to me. What I would give for one more day with Mum.

"You don't have to worry about her anymore."

And I want to demand to know why it isn't Mum here with me, how it all works, what the place she's gone to is like and so many other questions but I know Betsy won't answer me. I know that those are questions for which, in time, I need to learn the answers myself.

We stand there for the longest time until my body starts to ache at the joints. I need to move again.

"You coming?" I ask.

I know she won't leave me, now or ever. She was always there, whether I could see her or not. Family is everything.

Together we make our way out of the cemetery, to begin the walk back home.

AUTHOR'S NOTE

I LOVE THE IDEA that story is cyclical, that folklore, myths, and legends resonate because they exist, in a very real way, in our contemporary lives. I am attracted to the idea that belief and faith in the unseen can make it concrete. That's where I always begin, with the question: What would the world look like if this were true?

Faith's abilities were inspired by a particular thread of myth and folklore. I became fascinated by the ability to predict death, which is seen in stories across cultures in different forms. For example, the Morrigan of Irish mythology predicts the death of soldiers, and the Bean-Nighe of Scottish myth is seen washing the bloodied clothes of those about to die. In both of these stories the female, banshee-related figure inspires horror in those that encounter her, but I found myself asking: What would it be like to be her, to have this ability? How would it affect your outlook on life? What would your family think? In humanizing the prediction of death, I hoped to pose other questions in the minds of readers, such as: What would life be like if you knew the future? If you knew the end, the time and place, and manner?

Gifford's Circus, which has its "Home Farm" walking distance from where I live, was founded in 2000 by Nell Gifford, who died in 2019 at the age of forty-six. Her bravery and stoicism in the face of death was more than admirable, more than inspiring. It was legendary. In a documentary made shortly before she died, Nell talked about how the art of performing in a circus is about being fully in the moment, in every moment, allowing audiences to escape from reality by entering the present, the fantastical, almost impossible reality of the magic it creates. It's hard to put into words, but when I go to Gifford's Circus (we have attended every show, without fail, since we discovered it ten years ago), I feel alive in a rare, fleeting, intangible way. The daring of the performers as they defy death with their highly skilled acrobatics while making it look easy. Now that Nell herself has died, having lived a life that burned so brightly, the feeling is more powerful than ever.

Nell's circus has lived on, and I hope it will keep going forever, in tribute to her. I often think of her last show, where she rode out into the ring on a white horse and sat proudly as we applauded. She died a few months later. Her books about circus life are fascinating, and informed so much of Faith's world. I never got the chance to meet Nell, but maybe there's a place where such a meeting could happen. Depends what you believe about life and death and all of that.

Bertram Mills was another inspiration for this book, and his story informed the origin story of the Harrington Family and how the carnival first began. Mills was a trailblazer in the circus world, but like Nell, he didn't begin his life in a circus family. Born into a coach-building family, Mills had a love of horses and a fascination with the circus, having witnessed Barnum and Bailey's show when it came to England in the late nineteenth century. Like the fictional David

Harrington, his father was an undertaker, and he also began his circus, which became one of the most successful outfits in the United Kingdom, as the result of a wager. Though it was taken on by his sons after his untimely death, Mill's circus was forced to close in the 1960s because of rising costs. My fictional carnival managed to keep going, though it remained small. Harringtons are hardy types. They, like Bertram Mills and like Nell Gifford, believe that anything is possible, despite all the obstacles they face, because the dream they are holding tight to is worth the sacrifice. I believe this too: that if you have enough faith in yourself, you can shape the way stories are told, which after all is the way the world itself is changed.

ACKNOWLEDGMENTS

A BOOK IS MADE by many hands, many pairs of eyes, many dedicated professionals. I would like to thank the following people, without whom there would be no book at all, only a whisper of an idea living in my terrible brain and maybe later in a drawer, and only then if I could get my printer to work for long enough.

My most humble and heartfelt thanks to my first reader, my mother, Mary Reddaway.

My thanks also goes to the literary agent dream team, Rachel Yeoh and Madeleine Milburn, and everyone at the amazing MM agency.

Thanks, too, to the fantastic team at Crooked Lane: Matthew Martz, publisher; Madeline Rathle, marketing; Dulce Botello, marketing; Thai Fantauzzi Perez, intern; Sara J. Henry, developmental editor; Holly Ingraham, acquiring editor; Rebecca Nelson, editorial and production associate; and Doug White, behind the scenes management/printing/money stuff; Stephanie Manova, subrights manager

I'm grateful also for other publishing professionals: Jill Pellarin, copyeditor; Westchester Publishing Services, formatters; and Heather VenHuizen, cover designer

Special thanks to Jen Usher, for speed-reading and feeding back when I needed it most.

Finally, thanks to Jonathan, who thankfully is content to live with a person who constantly has one foot in another world. And to my children, Wilfred and Elspeth, neither of whom I could have dreamed up on my own.